Titles by Ken McClure

WILDCARD

Ken McClure

Polygon

First published in Great Britain by Simon & Schuster UK Ltd, 2002
This edition first published by Polygon, an imprint of Birlinn Ltd, 2010
West Newington House
10 Newington Road
Edinburgh
EH9 1QS
www.birlinn.co.uk

9 8 7 6 5 4 3 2 1

A CIP catalogue record for this book is available from
the British Library

ISBN 978 1 84697 163 1

Typeset by Palimpsest Book Production Limited,
Falkirk, Stirlingshire
Printed and bound in Great Britain by
Clays Ltd, St Ives plc

'You can be in an African village where people may be dying like flies. And twenty-four hours later you're in downtown Los Angeles and coming down with Ebola or Lassa fever, and you don't even know you have it.'

Joshua Lederberg, Nobel laureate and
Professor of the Rockefeller University
New York

Discover magazine, December 1990

'People don't realise until their house is on fire that the town hasn't bought enough fire trucks. We'll be seeing more Ebola. Population is increasing in Africa; so are incursions into the virus's habitat. Sooner or later somebody's going to haul it back out of the jungle.'

Anthony Sanchez, Ebola virus researcher at the
Center for Disease Control, Atlanta

Discover magazine, January 1996

'The eradication of smallpox is an excellent example of international co-operation, but there are many other examples of "unfinished business" such as the fight against polio, tuberculosis and malaria. All infectious diseases are a common threat, especially at a time when people all over the world are being brought closer together by international travel and trade. Infectious diseases respect no frontiers. We must work together globally to control them.'

Hiroshi Nakajima, Director-General,
World Health Organisation
April 1997

PROLOGUE

Edinburgh, Scotland

Paul Grossart, Managing Director of Lehman Genomics UK, was nervous. The head of the American parent company was coming to see him, rather than have him fly out to Boston, and this made him uneasy. His section leaders were ready to make presentations, outlining their groups' research efforts with well-prepared slides and diagrams. Technical staff had made sure that the labs were free of clutter and would appear hives of industry should the visiting party care to call, and secretarial staff were making the company office smell like the cosmetics counter at Boots. Upstairs in the accounts department, the books were open and ready for inspection; their authors ready with optimistic and glowing projections for the future. The order of the day for everyone was to smile at anything that moved.

Despite all this, Grossart found that his palms were sweating as he stood at the window of his office, hands behind his back, waiting for his visitors to arrive. On the face of it, he had nothing to worry about. All UK biotech companies had been going through a hard time in the face of a business community which believed that they had been promising more than they had delivered, but Lehman had weathered the storm of disappearing venture capital better than most. They had done so because of their success in marketing several new diagnostic kits in the past two years, and their field trials of two new chemotherapeutic agents had been going well. Target dates for licences were beginning to look realistic to those in the know. But, in spite of this, Grossart still suspected that something was wrong; he felt it in his bones. The

American visit had been advertised as routine but he just knew that there was more to it.

A black, S-class Mercedes saloon slid into the car park and Grossart walked over to his desk to press the intercom button. 'Jean, they're here. Give us five minutes, then bring in coffee and biscuits. See that the others know they've arrived.'

'Will do.'

Straightening his tie, Grossart ran down the steps from his first-floor office to the entrance hall and smiled at the tall, gaunt man who entered first. 'Good to see you, Hiram,' he said, holding out his hand, which he'd dried on a handful of tissues in his pocket. 'Long time no see.'

'Good to see you too, Paul,' replied Hiram Vance, executive vice-president of Lehman International. He gestured at the man behind him and said, 'This is Dr Jerry Klein from our Boston lab; he's chief of molecular medicine.'

Grossart shook hands with a small, black-bearded man who, in loose-fitting dark clothes, looked distinctly rabbinical. Grossart got the impression that Klein was almost as nervous as he was himself.

The three went upstairs to where coats were hung in the hall and they walked through to Grossart's office, where the talk was initially about the weather and the vagaries of flying across the Atlantic in November. Grossart's secretary brought in coffee and was introduced to the visitors, to whom she said welcome and smiled deferentially. 'Anything else I can get you gentlemen?' she asked.

'That's fine for the moment, Jean,' said Grossart. 'So where would you chaps like to start this morning?' he asked as the door closed. 'I thought maybe a tour of the labs, followed by short presentations from the research staff, then a look at the production suite and then maybe the offices?'

Vance looked at the door and asked, 'Is there any way she can hear what we're saying?'

'I trust Jean implicitly,' said Grossart, taken aback.

'That's not what I asked,' said Vance.

Grossart responded by disconnecting the intercom. 'No, there isn't.'

Vance, a painfully thin man with a sallow complexion and dark hollows round his coal-black eyes, nodded. 'We've got big trouble,' he said.

'Then this isn't a routine visit?'

Vance shook his head. 'The Snowball project's just melted. We're going to have to pull the plug on it.'

'What?' exclaimed Grossart. 'But everything's been going so well! And what about the arrangement?'

'I know, I know.' Vance nodded. 'But Jerry here has come up with a real showstopper. Show him, Doctor.'

Klein opened his briefcase and withdrew a thin blue-covered file, which he handed to Grossart without making eye contact. Grossart flipped it open and started to read. When he finished he had to swallow before saying hoarsely to Klein, 'You're absolutely sure about this?'

Klein nodded and said in an accent that sounded like New York Jewish, 'I'm afraid so. The sequence appears to be part of the host genome, but it's not. Just look at the homology.'

'Jesus Christ,' murmured Grossart. 'I should have known it was too good to be true. It's too late to put out a recall. Where the hell do we go from here?'

'All production will have to be stopped immediately,' said Vance. 'But . . .'

'But what?' said Grossart, still looking at Klein's papers and feeling dazed.

'Maybe that's as far as it should go,' said Vance, watching closely for Grossart's reaction.

Grossart looked up from the file, his eyes unsure and questioning. 'Are you saying that we should say nothing?' he asked tentatively.

'I'm suggesting that we be practical,' said Vance. 'It's too late to do anything about the material that's been used. If we start confessing all we'll be crucified, the company will go down the toilet and we'll go with it. The lawyers will see to that. I take it you have . . . commitments, Paul?'

Grossart was having difficulty in coming to terms with the situation. He forced himself to concentrate on the question. Of course he had commitments. He had a mortgage on the wrong side of a hundred and fifty thousand, two children at public school and a wife who enjoyed the good things in life, but . . .

'This company will do far more good for humankind if it stays in business,' said Vance. 'Think about it, Paul.'

Grossart clasped his hands under his chin and rocked slightly in his chair as he wondered what to do. He could actually feel his bowels start to loosen. He'd had such faith in the Snowball project that he'd sunk all the cash he could get his hands on in taking up company share options. Okay, so he'd been cutting every corner he could to speed things along, but that was business: he was in a race. It wasn't really dishonest; it was just . . . business. But now it had all gone belly-up. Suddenly and without warning he was in *this* position and he was scared.

'Christ, I don't know!' he exclaimed. 'I feel I want to throw my hands up and apologise . . . but like you say . . . it won't do any good in the long run if it's already too damned late.'

'Believe me, we've all had these thoughts, too,' said Vance soothingly. 'If there was anything we could do to turn back the clock we would be in there winding, but there isn't, Paul, there just isn't.'

'Who knows about this?' asked Grossart.

'Just the three of us. Jerry came to me first with his findings and we decided we'd sit on it until we had talked to you. The UK's the only place where we've "been on line", so to speak.'

Grossart tapped his fingertips together rapidly while his mind raced, but he couldn't think straight; there was just too much to take in. Rather than appear weak and indecisive, he decided that the other two had had time to think things through so they must have reached the right conclusion. He'd go along with them. 'All right,' he said. 'I agree. We keep quiet.'

'Good man,' said Vance. 'Company loyalty like that won't go unrewarded come annual bonus time.'

Grossart suddenly felt dirty. He looked at Vance, feeling sick inside, despising himself, but there was now no turning back. He swallowed and looked away. 'So that's it, then,' he said.

Vance cleared his throat unnecessarily and said, 'Not quite, I'm afraid. There is one other problem.'

Grossart felt as if he were already on overload. He badly needed to go to the lavatory. 'What other problem?' he croaked.

'The routine blood samples you sent in from the people working on the Snowball project . . .'

'What about them?'

'Jerry here re-tested them for our little problem as soon as he knew about it. Two came back positive.'

'You're telling me that two of my people are at risk from this damned thing?'

'It's a possibility,' said Klein.

'So what the hell do we do?'

'We can't risk them falling ill here and people putting two and two together,' said Vance. 'With your co-operation, we'll transfer them immediately – just as a precaution, you understand. They'll have the best of care, should they need it. I promise.'

'And what do they tell their families?' asked Grossart.

'Simply that their project demands that they carry out some work at one of our field stations, say the one in North Wales. We'll invent something for them to do in order to keep them there, out of the way, until we know they're in the clear. We'll sweeten the deal with money – double their British salary for the duration, if you like. That's the least we could do.'

'The very least,' said Grossart. 'Who are these people?'

Klein looked at his notes. 'Amy Patterson and Peter Doig.'

'Know them?' asked Vance.

'Of course I know them,' snapped Grossart, his nerves getting the better of his natural deference. 'Patterson's been a post-doc with us for the best part of three years. Doig's a medical technician who joined us from one of the local hospital labs about nine months ago. Both are good people.' He got up. 'If you'll excuse me, I really must . . .'

ONE

British Airways Flight, Ndanga–London Heathrow

Humphrey James Barclay had not been feeling well for the past few days, and it was making him irritable. Not even the fact that he was flying home, after what had seemed an interminable working visit to Central Africa, could compensate for it.

'Ye gods!' he muttered under his breath as the stewardess discovered that she had run out of tonic and mouthed her request with exaggerated lip movement to a colleague further down the aisle, followed by the standard British Airways smile. 'Won't be a moment, sir. Ice and a slice?'

Barclay nodded, biting his tongue as he seethed inwardly that she could run out of the stuff after serving only three rows.

Half a dozen small tins of tonic were duly delivered by a colleague, and the stewardess handed Barclay his drink. He took it without acknowledgement and hurriedly snapped open the tonic to splash a little into the gin. He downed it in two large gulps and put his head back on the seat to close his eyes for a moment. The burning sensation of the alcohol in his throat was helping, but he still felt unpleasantly hot and ached all over. The muscles in his arm hurt when he reached up to increase the airflow from the overhead vent, causing him to grimace and beads of sweat to break out on his forehead. He tugged angrily at his shirt collar and found that the button defied his attempt to undo it. This brought on another wave of frustration and he yanked at it so hard that the button shot off and hit the back of the seat in front before spinning off somewhere. But he had achieved his objective, and he didn't bother looking for the button before putting his

7

head back on the rest. The smartly dressed woman in the seat next to him concentrated unseeingly on her magazine and studiously pretended that she hadn't noticed anything amiss.

Don't make it flu, Barclay prayed silently as he closed his eyes again. Please don't make it flu. If I don't have my report on Sir Bruce bloody Collins's desk by tomorrow teatime I can kiss my bloody career goodbye. From Foreign Office to dole office in the blink of an eye; now you see him, now you don't. Sweet Jesus, Marion will just love that, her and her poxy stuck-up family.

Barclay rolled his head from side to side, fighting against growing nausea and dizziness. 'Christ, give me a break,' he murmured, as he persistently failed to find a comfortable position. Just a couple of days, dammit, and then I can take to my bed for a week – a bloody month, if necessary. He tried concentrating on what he was going to say in his report, mind over matter. Don't bloody go, he concluded bitterly. No one in their right mind should go to that bloody hellhole called Ndanga. The whole damned country is run by a bunch of two-bit crooks who are more interested in opening Swiss bank accounts than in doing anything to help the people they pretend to represent. Foreign aid would turn into Mercedes cars and Armani suits before you could say Abracadabra.

That was what Barclay wanted to say, but of course he wouldn't. It wasn't the job of a junior official at the Foreign Office to formulate policy. That had already been decided for Ndanga. HM Government was extending the hand of friendship and good fellowship. It was offering aid, not for the usual reason that Ndanga had oil or vital minerals that we wanted but because it had an airstrip and associated facilities in a strategically important position. The Ministry of Defence had decided that HM forces might find that very useful if things were to get out of hand in countries to the south, as they seemed destined to in the not too distant future. A generous financial package had been agreed, and the Foreign Secretary himself would be going there in the next few weeks to give the new regime the UK seal of approval. Barclay had been sent out to Ndanga to smooth the way and make sure that the arrangements for the visit were progressing satisfactorily. Mustn't have the Foreign Secretary running out of toilet paper in darkest Africa.

Barclay tugged open another button on his shirt as he felt a trickle of sweat run down his cheek.

'Are you feeling all right?' came the quiet, solicitous enquiry from the woman next to him.

Barclay turned his head to look at her but had difficulty focusing. She seemed to be framed in a halo of brightly coloured lights. 'A bit of flu coming on, I think,' he replied stoically.

'Bad luck,' said the woman, returning to her magazine, but almost visibly shrinking away from him, and putting her hand to her mouth, more as a psychological barrier than any practical one. 'Perhaps you should ask the stewardess for an aspirin.'

Barclay nodded. 'Maybe I will.' He gave a symbolic glance over his shoulder and added tersely, 'When she's ready.'

Still struggling against the odds, he opened his briefcase with great effort and took out a sheaf of papers. He felt he had to jot down some points he wanted to stress in his report. 'Security at Ndanga's main airport is poor,' he wrote. 'Recommend that—' He stopped writing as a large drop of blood fell from his nose and spread on the page. He was mesmerised by the sight of scarlet on white for a moment, before murmuring under his breath, 'Shit, what bloody next?'

He brought out a tissue from his pocket and held it to his nose in time to catch the next drop. He kept the tissue there as he put his head back again on the rest. God, he felt ill. Pressure was building up inside his head and making his eyeballs hurt and now another sensation . . . dampness . . . He felt wet; his trousers were wet. He put his hand slowly between his legs and got confirmation. Oh my God, the humiliation of it all. Oh my God, not that – anything but that. The flush that came to his cheeks did nothing to help lower his already climbing temperature. But how could he have wet himself without knowing it? He pondered this through a haze of discomfort. He contracted his sphincter muscles and found that he still seemed to have power over them, so how could he have done? God! He was never going to live this down. He started making plans to limit his embarrassment. When they landed he would stay in his seat until all the other passengers had disembarked . . . Yes, that was what he'd do. With a bit of luck the cabin crew would not even remember who had been sitting in that seat.

His jumbled train of thought was again interrupted as the pain in his head became almost unbearable, but through it something registered about the wet feeling between his legs. It wasn't just wet, it was . . . sticky. He withdrew his hand and half opened one eye to look at it. It was covered in blood.

The sight of Barclay's bloody hand spurred the woman next to him into action. She gasped and her hand shot to the call button above her head: she pushed it repeatedly until two stewardesses came running.

'His hand . . . It's covered in blood,' stammered the woman, trying to keep at as much distance as she could. 'He said he's getting flu, but look at him!'

Barclay was now unaware of what was going on around him. His soaring temperature had induced a delirium in which successive waves of pain and nausea swept in to torment him.

'Can you hear me, sir?' One of the stewardesses, Judy Mills, was bending over him. 'Can you tell us what's wrong?'

Barclay's eyes rolled open in response to the voice in his ear. He opened his mouth but no words came out. Instead he voided the contents of his stomach in a projectile vomit over Judy, who recoiled in disgust, her professionalism deserting her momentarily as revulsion and anger vied for its place.

'Can't you move him somewhere?' asked the woman in the inside seat.

'The flight's full, madam,' replied the second stewardess, Carol Bain.

'You'll have to do something, for God's sake. He's covered in blood.'

The woman had a point. Barclay's untended nosebleed had covered his lower face and shirt front.

'See if you can stop the bleeding,' said Judy, who had done her best to sponge the mess off the front of her uniform and had returned. Carol put Barclay's head back on the headrest, carefully avoiding putting herself in the firing line. She held a wad of tissues over Barclay's nose and made eye contact with Judy. 'What now?' she whispered.

'Just keep him like that. I'll see if there's a doctor on board.'

Judy made her way to the front of the aircraft and shortly afterwards the captain asked that any doctor on board should make himself known to the cabin crew. Carol, still holding the tissues to Barclay's face, relaxed as she heard the call bell ring at the back, and relief flooded through her. To hide this fact from the passengers, she looked down at the unconscious Barclay's lap. Her smile faded as she saw that his trousers were soaked in blood. She knew instinctively that this hadn't come from a nosebleed.

Judy walked down the aisle to meet a short, bald man being ushered from the rear of the aircraft by one of the other cabin crew. They all paused at the junction between front and rear cabins, where they had a little more privacy.

'You're a doctor?'

'I'm Dr Geoffrey Palmer. What's the problem?'

'One of the passengers at the front has passed out. He has a nosebleed and he . . . was sick.' She couldn't avoid looking down at her skirt.

'Joys of the job.' Palmer smiled, guessing what had happened. 'Probably just airsickness followed by fainting at the sight of his own blood. I'll take a look at him, if you like.'

'We'd be very grateful.'

Judy led the way up to the front of the aircraft, but her feeling that things might be returning to normal deserted her when she saw Carol's face: she was close to panic.

'What's up?' Judy whispered.

'He's bleeding heavily . . . down below.' She emphasised the point with a downward nod.

'Let's have a look, then,' said Palmer, who hadn't heard the exchange and seemed keen to take command of the situation.

Both stewardesses moved a little way up the aisle to allow Palmer access to the unconscious man.

'Gosh, you *are* in a mess, aren't you, old son,' said Palmer, taking in the state of Barclay's shirt. 'That's the trouble with blood, it gets everywhere.'

He felt for a pulse and then pushed up one of Barclay's eyelids with his thumb. His demeanour changed in an instant. His self-assurance evaporated as he straightened up and unconsciously wiped his hand on the lapel of his jacket.

'Doctor, he's bleeding down below somewhere,' whispered Carol. 'Look at his trousers.'

Palmer looked down at the dark spreading stain on the thankfully dark material. 'Oh my God,' he murmured, taking a step backwards.

This from a doctor did little to promote confidence in the stewardesses, who exchanged anxious glances.

'What do you think, Doctor?' asked Judy, more in trepidation than in anticipation.

'We must wash,' replied Palmer, his wide eyes fixed on Barclay.

Barclay's head lolled to face the inside and the woman passenger gasped. 'His eyes,' she stammered. 'Look at them! They're bleeding! For God's sake, do something.'

'Christ, it's the real thing,' said Palmer, sounding like an automaton. 'We must wash.'

Judy signalled to Carol with her eyes to stay with Barclay. She herself led Palmer away to the galley area at the front, and closed the curtain.

'Just what is it, Doctor?' she hissed. 'What's wrong with him?'

'I think it's haemorrhagic fever,' replied Palmer, clearly shaken.

She looked at him. 'That doesn't mean anything. Can you be more specific?'

'There are a number of them. It could be Ebola.'

'Ebola? Oh my God.'

'We have to wash ourselves and keep well away from him.'

'But you're a doctor. Aren't you going to help him?'

'I'm a radiologist, for Christ's sake. What the hell do I know about Ebola? Apart from that, there's nothing anyone can do,' snapped Palmer. 'Ask the captain to radio ahead. Tell him to report that we have a possible case of viral HF on board. I'm going to wash. I suggest you and your colleague do the same.'

Palmer disappeared into the lavatory, leaving Judy looking after him in bemusement. 'Well, thanks a bundle,' she muttered, before rejoining Carol at Barclay's seat.

'What's going on?' demanded one of the passengers in the row behind.

'We have a sick passenger,' replied Judy. 'There's no cause for alarm, sir.'

'No kidding,' came the acid reply. 'Just what the hell's wrong with him?'

'That's impossible to say at the moment, sir. But the doctor thinks it could be . . . malaria.'

'Poor bugger,' said the passenger. 'That can be nasty.'

'Is it infectious?' asked his wife in a loud whisper.

'No, love, it ain't,' came the reply. 'At least, I don't think so . . . Maybe we should ask the doctor.'

Palmer emerged from the lavatory and started down the aisle, still looking shaken. Judy seized the initiative and said, 'Doctor, I was just saying to a concerned passenger here that you think our sick passenger may have malaria.' The look in her eyes drilled home the message.

'Malaria's not infectious, is it, Doctor?' asked the passenger.

'No,' replied Palmer a little uncertainly and then, more decisively, 'No, it's not.'

He squeezed past the stewardesses, keeping them between himself and Barclay as he made to return to his seat. The surrounding passengers seemed surprised.

'Isn't there something you can do for the poor guy?' asked the one who had done all the talking.

'No, er, nothing,' replied Palmer. 'They'll be ready for him when we land.' He continued down the aisle.

'Whatever happened to mopping the fevered brow?' said the passenger.

'Changed days,' said a woman.

'I have to talk to the captain,' Judy told Carol. 'Are you still okay?'

Carol nodded and gave a wan smile. She still held a wad of tissues to Barclay's face. The red stains on it reached up to her flimsy plastic gloves.

'Are your gloves okay?'

'I think so. Why?'

The look that passed between them explained all. 'Keep checking them. I'll be as quick as I can.'

'Hi, Judy. How's our casualty?' asked the captain as the flight-deck door closed behind Judy.

She got down on her haunches between the two seats and said, 'Our "doctor"' – she endowed the word with distaste – 'thinks it may be Ebola. He's not an expert, he's a radiologist, but he seemed pretty sure it was one of the "viral HFs", he called them. He asks that you radio ahead and warn London.'

'Shit, that's all we need,' said the captain, all trace of humour disappearing from his face. 'They're highly infectious from all accounts, aren't they?'

'Actually, no,' interjected the first officer. 'Everyone thinks they are, but in reality they're not as bad as some less exotic diseases. They're spread through contact with bodily fluids.'

'Good to know, John. How come you know this?'

'I went to a seminar on the spread of disease through air travel a couple of months ago. It scared me shitless, but I do remember them saying that about Ebola.'

'You haven't been exchanging bodily fluids with chummy, have you, Judy?' asked the captain, his sense of humour returning.

'He was sick all over me.'

'Shit! Have you washed?'

14

'Not properly.'

'Do it now. A complete change of clothes. Put everything you've got on into a plastic bag and seal it.'

'Will do.'

'Is our doctor looking after him?'

'No, Carol is. He's bleeding heavily from his nose and eyes and somewhere down below.'

'So what's the doctor doing?'

'Shitting himself.'

'Like that, is it? Look, if Carol got soiled in any way, get her to change, too. When you're both done, cover up chummy with plastic bags and blankets.'

'He's running a high temperature,' said Judy. 'He'll cook.'

'Can't be helped. Your priority must be to contain all bodily fluids. Understood?'

Judy nodded.

'Go on, get washed. I'll tell Heathrow the good news.'

'ETA?' asked Judy.

'Seventy-five minutes.'

Judy left the flight deck and locked herself in the lavatory with a change of uniform and a plastic sack to put her soiled clothes in. When she came out she put on a new apron and a pair of fresh plastic gloves, which she inspected carefully for holes or cuts. Satisfied that they were undamaged, she took a deep breath, put on her smile and opened the curtain. She beamed at Carol, and rejoined her at Barclay's seat. They spoke in guarded whispers.

'How is he?'

'Sleeping or unconscious, I'm not sure which.'

'Go and change your uniform. Put all your old stuff in a plastic sack and seal it. What have you done with the used tissues?'

Carol looked down at her feet, where she had a plastic disposal sack. 'In there, but we're running out of tissues and I think he's running out of blood. Can't we stop the bleeding?'

Judy shook her head. 'Not in the circumstances. We'll just have to contain it. Okay?'

Carol nodded. She let Judy take over holding the wad of tissues to Barclay's face, picked up the sack at her feet and went up front. Left with Barclay, Judy watched the tide of red spread up through the tissue to where her fingers hid behind a thin layer of clear plastic. The thought that the Ebola fever virus might be coming with it induced a shiver of panic inside her. Her concern for the passenger was momentarily replaced by the wish that he would just die and stop bleeding. When Barclay moved his head her pulse rate soared over 150. Please God, don't let him come round and start moving about, she prayed. Barclay's seat companion showed similar signs of concern. She caught Judy's eye and each knew what the other was thinking, although the passenger's concern was for aesthetic reasons – she simply didn't want to have a sick, blood-covered man rolling about beside her. Judy was concerned for her own and everyone else's life.

Barclay was not going to recover consciousness; he was far too ill for that. But somewhere inside his head some automatic warning, instilled in him since childhood, said that he needed the toilet. His head moved from side to side and he made an effort to get up from his seat. Judy restrained him as best she could with one hand while the other held the tissues to his face. Barclay became more and more agitated, and Judy more and more alarmed. She looked anxiously for Carol's return but as yet there was no sign.

The passenger behind Barclay noticed her discomfort and said, 'Maybe you should fasten his belt?'

It was such an obvious solution that Judy had to smile at her of all people not thinking of it. She tried to fasten Barclay's seat-belt with one hand but he kept moving restlessly at the wrong moment. The woman in the seat next to him leaned over to help. After all, she had a vested interest in Barclay staying put.

'Thanks,' said Judy as she pressed down on Barclay's shoulder to keep him still. The woman fastened the buckle, then took up the slack with a sharp tug. She looked at the backs of her hands and saw that they were red from blood soaked up by the blanket in Barclay's lap. Judy looked at her wide-eyed and then recovered her composure. There was no room for the woman to get out without unbuckling Barclay and trying to move him. She would have to stay put. 'I'll get you some tissues, madam,' she said calmly.

Carol returned from her clean-up, and Judy said, 'Would you get some wet tissues for this lady, Carol, and a bottle of mineral water? Quick as you can.'

Carol returned with the items and a plastic sack. She handed them to the passenger, and Judy said, 'Please rinse your hands thoroughly, madam, and put everything in the sack.'

'But malaria's not infectious, is it?'

'No, madam, it's just a precaution.'

'A precaution?' repeated the passenger anxiously. Then she understood. 'Oh, the blood. My God, you mean he might have AIDS?'

'AIDS? Who's got AIDS?' came an angry enquiry from the seats behind. 'I thought he had malaria.'

'No one has AIDS, sir. Please calm down. It's a misunder-standing.'

Barclay chose this moment to abandon his semi-conscious struggle to go to the toilet, and relaxed his bowels. The smell brought rumbles of protest from the nearby passengers and pushed Judy and Carol to their limits of coping.

'Please, everyone, I know this is all most unpleasant,' announced Judy, 'but we'll be at Heathrow in less than forty minutes. We have a very sick passenger to deal with, so please bear with us and remain calm. There but for the grace of God and all that? Open your air vents and Carol will hand out scented tissues. Hold them to your face.'

Carol looked puzzled, and Judy said, 'Use the duty-free perfume.'

TWO

'Ladies and gentlemen, this is your captain speaking. As some of you will already be aware, we have a sick passenger on board and unfortunately for this reason none of us will be disembarking immediately. I know it's inconvenient, but we have been asked to taxi to a position some distance from the terminal building and await further instructions. I will keep you informed. In the meantime, please be patient and bear with us.'

Judy felt as if a firework had just been lit and she was waiting for the explosion. It came soon enough. A general rumble of discontent was followed by an angry assertion of 'I thought you said it was malaria' from the man in the seat behind Barclay. 'You were lying, weren't you?' he accused. 'Just what the hell is going on? What's wrong with him?'

'We do have a very sick passenger, sir. More than that I can't say right now, but please be patient.'

'Patient be damned. There's something going on here and we deserve to be told. Just what are you keeping from us? Tell us what's wrong with him.'

'I'm not a doctor, sir—'

'But *he* is,' said the man angrily, gesturing down the aisle with his thumb. 'What did *he* say it was?'

'Look, I'm sorry, I can't really discuss—'

'It all makes sense now,' interrupted the man. 'He wanted nothing to do with him, did he? He buggered off to his own seat pretty smartish, as I recall. Just what the hell's wrong with this guy? Bugger this – I'm going to go back there and ask him myself.'

He started to undo his seatbelt but Judy was spared an argument to stop him by an exclamation from his wife, whose eye had been caught by flashing blue lights outside the window. 'Oh my God, Frank,' she exclaimed, 'there are spacemen out there!'

The hubbub died as passengers looked out of the windows and saw that the plane had been surrounded by emergency vehicles, their lights blinking into the night sky. In front were a number of men standing on the tarmac: they wore orange suits, which covered them from head to foot. The flashing lights reflected off their visors.

'Hello, everyone, this is the captain again,' said the calm, friendly voice on the cabin intercom. 'I understand that when the airport buses arrive we will all be taken to a reception centre, where we'll be given more information about the situation and the opportunity to make contact with friends and family. Thank you for your patience. I hope it won't be too long before we can all be with them. Please remain seated until the cabin crew instruct you otherwise.'

The captain's voice was replaced by Vivaldi's *Four Seasons*.

The sight of what was on the tarmac outside seemed to have a sobering effect on the passengers. The general air of belligerence was replaced by anxiety and an acceptance of the situation. Angry protests and muttered threats of compensation claims were supplanted by real fear of the unknown.

Barclay was the first to be taken from the aircraft. He was enveloped in a plastic bubble by two orange-suited men and carried down the steps to the tarmac, where he was loaded into a waiting ambulance. The passengers immediately behind Barclay for four rows and those in the rows in front were next to leave. They were directed down the front steps to an airport bus driven by another orange-suited man. The smell of disinfectant was everywhere; the floor of the bus was awash with it. There was a short hiatus while a decontamination crew boarded the aircraft and sealed off the newly evacuated area with plastic sheeting before spraying it all down thoroughly. The remaining passengers were then evacuated through the rear door on to more waiting buses. The flight crew were the last to leave the aircraft. They were ushered on to a separate bus to follow the others to the emergency reception centre. They looked back as the bus moved off, and saw that their aircraft was being sprayed down both outside and in.

'Wonder what happens now?' said the captain quietly.

'The word "quarantine" springs to mind,' said the first officer.

'Shit.'

'Can't be too careful.'

'Suppose not.'

'Any idea how long?' asked Judy.

The first officer shook his head. 'Maybe they won't keep everyone, just those who were closest to chummy or had contact with him.'

'A comfort,' said Judy ruefully.

'Come on, Jude, won't be so bad. Think of all that daytime television.' The first officer smiled.

'I think I'd rather have the disease,' retorted Judy.

'You two did well, handling that situation,' the captain told Judy and Carol. 'Couldn't have been easy.'

'I'd like to say it was nothing really,' said Judy. 'But I think it was one of the worst experiences of my life. He seemed to be bleeding everywhere.'

'Ditto,' said Carol. 'I once considered nursing as a career and now I'm awfully glad I didn't. Trolley-dollying isn't all it's cracked up to be, but having to deal with that sort of thing day in, day out? No thank you.'

Passengers who had had no contact with Barclay before or during the flight were allowed to leave the reception centre after giving their home addresses and being instructed to contact their GP should they feel at all unwell. Passengers sitting closer to Barclay were subjected to hospital quarantine as what the authorities called 'a sensible precaution'. To this group were added the two stewardesses and Dr Geoffrey Palmer, twenty-six people in all.

Humphrey Barclay died four days later. His fever did not abate, so he was never conscious of the plastic-bubble world he inhabited in the special unit of the hospital or of the nurses in spacesuits who did their best to make him comfortable through his last hours on earth. He did not see his wife, his two daughters, his parents or his dreaded in-laws before he died, due to the strict no-visitors rule in the special unit. He never got the chance to file his report on Ndanga to his superiors at the Foreign Office, but his death spoke volumes.

Senior Stewardess Judith Mills died eight days after Barclay, one day before Mrs Sally Morton, the passenger who had been sitting next to Barclay, and two days before Dr Geoffrey Palmer. There was a scare over Carol Bain when she became unwell after five days, but it proved to be just a cold. Geoffrey Palmer was the last of the people from the aircraft to die, but he was not the last to succumb to the virus. One of the nurses looking after Barclay became infected, despite the protective clothing, and she also died.

'African Killer Virus Contained' announced *The Times*. No further cases had been reported or were expected, according to health officials, it said; the situation was under control. The papers had kept up a daily assault on their readers, some of the tabloids initially predicting a plague that would sweep through the capital just as the bubonic plague had done in the seventeenth century. The more thoughtful articles concentrated on just how easy it was these days for viruses lurking in the heart of the African jungle one day to be transported to the West the next, courtesy of high-speed air travel.

The relatively low death toll and the quick containment of the virus left the papers that had predicted a more extreme scenario looking rather silly, although one of them expertly diverted attention by going on the offensive and demanding to know exactly what the virus was. Its readers, it maintained, had 'the right to know'. It was a line of attack that the others had missed because it was in fact true that there had been no official statement about the identity of the virus. It was also true that there had been no clamour to know. The 'new African diseases', as many of the papers had called them, were generally thought to be just that, and therefore of no real great concern to readers in Chingford or Surbiton.

The Foreign and Commonwealth Office, London

'They're right, you know,' said Sir Bruce Collins, putting down the paper. 'We still don't know the identity of the virus that did for poor old Barclay and the others.'

'I thought they were pretty sure it was Ebola fever, sir,' said one of the other eight people seated round the table.

'That was and is an assumption,' said Collins. 'It's probably the correct one, I grant you, considering all the symptoms, but we don't have the official lab report yet.'

'They're taking their time, aren't they?'

'Apparently the scientists can only work on such viruses under what they call BL4 conditions. All the samples had to be taken to the government defence establishment at Porton Down for analysis. Anyway, what we have to decide now is whether or not the Foreign Secretary's trip to Ndanga can go ahead.'

'I don't see how it can in the circumstances,' said one man, and there was a general murmur of agreement.

'I must remind you that this trip is important to us and to Ndanga, gentlemen. They need the respectability it will afford them and we in turn need access to their airstrip in the south and what goes with it. If we call off the visit, they just might renege on the whole agreement.'

'But surely they'll understand that such a visit doesn't make sense during an outbreak?'

'And there's the rub,' said Collins. 'According to them, there *is* no outbreak. The authorities in Ndanga maintain that there has been no case of Ebola or any other haemorrhagic fever in the country in the past two years.'

'But there must have been, otherwise how could poor old

Barclay have picked it up? You have to get it from an already infected person, don't you?'

'Or an infected monkey, I understand.'

'I can't see Barclay consorting with chimps during his visit, can you?'

'So that leaves us with a bit of an impasse,' said Collins.

'The Ndangan authorities must be lying.'

'I have to admit that that thought did occur,' said Collins. 'So I made some discreet enquiries of the World Health Organisation. They have no record of any case of haemorrhagic fever in Ndanga in the past year.'

'Did Barclay perhaps travel around a bit while he was in Africa?' suggested someone.

'I considered that, too,' said Collins, 'but I've seen his diary. He didn't have any time to play the tourist. Apart from that, there has been no Ebola in any of the countries bordering Ndanga during the last six months.'

'How about contact with a carrier?'

'As I understand it, the medical profession is a bit vague about carrier status where these diseases are concerned. Some don't think a true carrier state exists,' said Collins, 'but there is agreement about transfer of the virus through body fluids from a person who is recovering from the disease.'

'So if old Humphrey had slept with a lady of the night who'd recently had the disease, that could have been it?'

'Barclay was more a *National Geographic* and mug-of-Horlicks man, in my estimation,' said Collins. 'But even if what you suggest were true, what happened to her other customers? They should all be dead by now.'

'Well, even if that *was* how Barclay picked it up, I don't see anything there to prevent the Foreign Secretary's visit going ahead.'

'No,' agreed Collins. 'Just as long as we're satisfied that there really is no outbreak in Ndanga.'

'If I might make a suggestion, sir?'

'Go ahead,' said Collins.

'You could have a word with the Sci-Med people in the Home Office. They're sort of medical detectives, aren't they?'

'They are indeed,' said Collins, 'and that is a very good idea. I'll have Jane make me an appointment to see the head of that outfit . . . What's his name?'

'Macmillan, sir. John Macmillan.'

The Sci-Med Inspectorate was a small independent body operating from within the Home Office under the directorship of John Macmillan. It comprised a number of investigators, well qualified in either science or medicine, whose job it was to take a look at problems, with or without possible criminal involvement, occurring in the hi-tech areas of modern life, areas where the police had little or no expertise.

This was no reflection on the police. They could not be expected to notice when, for instance, the surgical success record of one hospital fell well below others carrying out almost identical procedures, nor were they in a position to investigate the possible causes even if they did. Likewise, they were unlikely to notice that certain chemicals being ordered by the staff of a university chemistry department were in fact being used to manufacture hallucinogenic drugs. Both of these scenarios had been encountered in the past by Sci-Med and resolved, through enforced resignation of an ageing surgeon in the first case and criminal prosecution of a number of lab technicians in the other.

After Sir Bruce Collins's visit, Macmillan asked his secretary to call in Dr Steven Dunbar. Dunbar had been a Sci-Med investigator for something over five years, and was currently on leave after his last assignment.

'He's only had a week of his leave,' said Rose Roberts.

'I'm aware of that, thank you,' snapped Macmillan, 'and of the tough time he had with his last job. But this won't take him more than a couple of days, so please just make the call.'

Steven Dunbar took the call as he was packing. 'I was just about to head north to see my daughter,' he told Miss Roberts.

'I'm sorry. I did point out that you'd only had a week and post-operational leave is always a month, but he asked for you anyway. If it's any help, he said it wouldn't take long.'

'All right.' Steven grinned. 'See you at three.'

Steven had a lot of respect for John Macmillan, not least because of his unswerving loyalty to his staff and his constant battle to preserve Sci-Med's independence and freedom of action. It had been his brainchild from the outset and had shown its worth many times over, uncovering crimes that otherwise might never have come to light. Sci-Med might be small but it was an object lesson in how a government department should be run. Against the modern trend, its administration had been kept to a minimum and existed first and foremost to serve front-line staff and smooth the way for them, rather than the other way round as was sadly the case in modern Britain. According to some of Steven's medical friends, NHS staff now spent more time filling in forms and undergoing audits, assessments and appraisals than they did treating the sick.

No one came directly to Sci-Med. It was one of its great strengths that its investigators, when appointed, brought with them a wide range of abilities and experience. Dunbar, as a medical investigator, was of course medically qualified, but he had chosen not to pursue a conventional career in medicine. After two hospital residencies following medical school, he had found that he simply did not have the heart for it. A strong, athletic young man, brought up amid the mountains of Cumbria, he had felt the need for more of a physical challenge.

After some heart-searching he had joined the army at the end of his clinical year and had been assigned to the Parachute Regiment, where he had found all the physical challenge he could ever have hoped for, and more besides. He had thrived in this environment and had been trained as an expert in field medicine, an expertise he had been called upon to use on several occasions during his subsequent secondment to Special Forces. He had served all over the world and had been called upon to use not only his medical skills but often his powers of innovation and initiative. He would have liked nothing better than to stay with the SAS, but the nature of the job dictated that it be the province of young men and the time inevitably came when he had to step down, an 'old' man at the age of thirty-three.

Luckily, the position at Sci-Med had arisen at exactly the right time. The job had seemed perfect in that, although he'd still require his medical qualifications, he was not going to end up in some bleak surgery, freezing warts off feet and dishing out anti-depressant pills. Instead, he would be involved in Sci-Med's day-to-day investigations. He would be given assignments judged suitable to his expertise and allowed to pursue them in his own way. Sci-Med would provide all the back-up he needed, ranging from expert advice to weapons if need be.

From the Inspectorate's point of view, Steven had appeared from the outset to be well suited to their requirements. He was a doctor with proven ability to survive and succeed in extremely demanding situations. Real situations, a far cry from the 'How would you cross this imaginary river?' problems of office team-building exercises. And so it had proved to be. Steven had progressed over the years to become a much-valued member of the Sci-Med team, and the admiration was mutual.

Steven left his fifth-floor apartment in Docklands and took a taxi to the Home Office. He wore a dark-blue suit, light-blue shirt and Parachute Regiment tie, and cut an imposing figure as he entered the building and showed his ID. No less imposing was John Macmillan, who in many ways could have been an older version of Steven, tall, slim and erect but with swept-back silver hair instead of Steven's dark mane.

'Good to see you, Dunbar. Take a seat.'

Steven sat and listened to Macmillan's apology for bringing him back early from leave. 'Jamieson and Dewar are both out on assignment right now so I was faced with asking one of the scientific chaps to take this on or recalling you. I decided on you.'

'I'm flattered,' said Steven with only the merest suggestion of a smile.

Macmillan looked at him for a moment, searching for signs of sarcasm, but didn't find any. 'Anyway, you must be aware of this Ebola thing on the African flight?'

'I read about it in the papers,' replied Steven. 'Nasty.'

'It could have been much worse but the emergency procedures for just such an eventuality worked well, and the problem was contained with only five dead – not that that's much comfort to them or their families.'

'So what concerns us?' asked Steven.

'The aircraft had come from Ndanga and the passenger who fell ill and infected the others was a Foreign Office official. He had been in Africa, making arrangements for a visit by the Foreign Secretary. The Foreign Office is worried.'

'It would be crazy to go ahead with the visit until any outbreak is over,' said Steven.

'The Ndangan authorities say there *is* no outbreak.'

'So how did our man get the disease?'

'Precisely.'

'God, you're not going to send me to Ndanga, are you?' exclaimed Steven.

'Nothing like that.' Macmillan smiled. 'The Foreign Office would simply like to be assured that the relevant authorities aren't lying. I've already been on to the WHO in Geneva. They've heard nothing about an outbreak, but I thought you might get in touch with some of your friends and acquaintances in the medical charities and see what you can come up with?'

'Will do,' said Steven. 'Are they sure it's Ebola?'

'There's been nothing back from Porton yet, but from all accounts it has to be one of the haemorrhagic fevers.'

'But it could be something other than Ebola, like Lassa or Marburg disease. Not that it makes much difference: there's not a damned thing anyone can do about any of them, anyway.'

Macmillan nodded and said, 'I understand that there's going to be a briefing for officials tonight at the Foreign Office. Maybe they'll have some news. I think you should go along.'

Steven agreed.

'Miss Roberts will give you details.'

Steven spent the remainder of the afternoon telephoning friends and colleagues to find out which medical missions and charities were currently operating in Ndanga. He established that three were, including the large French organisation, Médecins sans Frontières. He had a friend who worked as a co-ordinator at their Paris office. He called her.

'Simone? It's Steven Dunbar in London.'

'Steven! How nice. It's been ages. How are you?'

After an exchange of pleasantries Steven asked about haemorrhagic fever in Ndanga.

'No, I don't think so,' replied Simone. 'Give me a moment . . .'

Steven looked out of the window of his apartment while he waited. It was sunny but there were black clouds coming in from the west.

Simone came back on the line. 'No, no reports at all of haemorrhagic fever in Ndanga or the countries surrounding it at the moment.'

Steven liked hearing the word 'haemorrhagic' spoken with a French accent. It made him smile. 'Thanks, Simone,' he said. 'I'm obliged.'

'So when will we see you in Paris?'

'Soon, I hope. We'll have dinner.'

THREE

Steven arrived for the 7.30 p.m. briefing at the Foreign Office at 7.20 and found more than fifty people already there. Some he knew, many he didn't. One of those he did was Fred Cummings; a consultant microbiologist attached to the London Public Health Service. Fred tended to stand out in a crowd because of his sparse but bright-red hair and a liking for loud sports jackets.

'Big turn-out,' said Steven, coming up at his elbow.

'Porton wanted to speak to everyone concerned at the same time, rather than have a series of meetings with health chiefs and local authorities,' said Cummings.

'So they've identified it?'

'Let's hope so,' said Cummings. 'They've taken long enough about it. A fiver says it's Ebola.'

'Ebola fever in the Old Kent Road – now there's a thought to conjure with,' said Steven, ignoring the bet.

'Tell me about it.' Cummings smiled. 'I haven't needed All Bran since that bloody plane landed.'

A distinguished-looking man, whom Steven took to be a Foreign Office official, appealed for quiet and the hubbub died down. Four people mounted the platform and were introduced jointly as the investigating team from Porton Down. Their leader, Dr Clive Phelps, a tall, gangly man with bushy grey hair and a straggly beard, took the Foreign Office man's place at the microphone and tapped it twice unnecessarily before speaking. Steven wondered idly how he would get his beard inside a surgical mask.

'Good evening,' said Phelps. 'I understand that everyone here – apart from Foreign Office personnel, who have their own reasons for requiring information – is a health professional so I won't beat about the bush. It's a filovirus.'

'Surprise, surprise,' muttered Cummings. 'The *Daily Mail*'s been telling us that for weeks.'

'But, contrary to popular reports and rumour, it isn't Ebola,' continued Phelps.

'So it has to be Marburg,' whispered Cummings. 'There only are two filoviruses.'

'And it isn't Marburg disease either.'

'Bloody hell,' breathed Cummings. He felt like the straight man in a comedy double act. 'Then how can you call it a filovirus?' he asked out loud, as hubbub again filled the room.

'Under the electron microscope the virus appears filamentous, forming branched filaments of up to fourteen thousand nanometres in length. In other words, it looks like a filovirus and, of course, it causes a haemorrhagic fever very similar to Ebola, if not identical. The victims suffer high temperature, stomach cramps and nausea, and bleed profusely from just about everywhere.'

'So why do you say it isn't Ebola?'

'The four subtypes of Ebola that we know about and have characterised in the past all have a uniform diameter of eighty nanometres. This virus has a diameter of a hundred and twenty nanometres.'

'It could be a new subtype,' suggested Cummings.

'That's possible,' conceded Phelps with an uncomfortable shrug, 'but we think not. We've carried out an investigation of the nucleic acid content of the virus – that's what's been taking the time – and there are significant differences. That's why we think it's a new virus.'

'All we need,' whispered Cummings to Steven. 'Another bloody African virus.'

'Any ideas about source?' asked someone else.

'None at all,' replied Phelps. 'But if the truth be told, we still have no idea about the source of Ebola either, and we've known about that disease for over thirty years. Ebola's natural reservoir is as much a mystery today as it was when the disease was first reported.'

'Would it be fair to say that this new virus is not as potent as Ebola, in view of the way it was so easily contained? I seem to remember people dropping like flies during the Ebola outbreaks in Zaire a few years back.'

'No, that's an entirely false impression,' replied Phelps. 'And I can't stress that enough. The Heathrow incident was contained with apparent ease because of the expertise of the people involved. The African outbreak you're thinking of was made to appear worse than it actually was by the poor practice in the local hospitals and a lack of knowledge among the staff about how the disease was spread. Using the same syringe needle for several patients was common practice at that time, and still is in many African hospitals. You can work out for yourselves what happens when you get a case of Ebola among them: the disease spreads faster than bad news. Another factor in the Zaire outbreak was nursing care. In African hospitals, basic nursing care tends to be carried out by the patients' families. They, of course, cannot be expected to have any notion of aseptic technique, so they come into contact with contaminated body fluids and then go down with the disease themselves. That's why the African outbreaks appeared to suggest that the virus was airborne and could spread like wildfire.'

'Can we be perfectly sure there's no danger of a general outbreak arising from the Heathrow incident?' asked a female voice.

'Absolutely. The patient, Barclay, was the source of the outbreak, if you want to call it that. The others contracted the disease by coming into contact with his body fluids. Barclay and all the others who died were cremated, so we are confident that the virus died with them.'

'What about the other passengers?' asked a man who identified himself as Chisholm, a professor of virology at the London School of Hygiene and Tropical Medicine.

'What about them?'

'Isn't there a chance that they might still be incubating the disease?'

'No. We're talking about an incubation time of four to ten days. That time has passed and everyone is still okay.'

'It's four to ten days for Ebola,' the professor reminded him.

'A fair point,' agreed Phelps. 'I suppose it is conceivable that this virus might have a longer incubation period than Ebola, but not judging by the rapidity with which the stewardess and the others went down with it after coming into contact with Barclay.'

'But they had direct contact with Barclay,' said the professor, clearly unwilling to let the matter drop.

'What is the point you are making, Professor?' asked Phelps, his voice betraying slight impatience.

'Merely that some of the other passengers might have received smaller initial doses of the virus and therefore might conceivably take longer to go down with the disease.'

'What did you have in mind?'

'A cough or a sneeze from Barclay would have given rise to small fluid droplet particles, which could for all intents and purposes be deemed to be body fluids.'

'I take your point, Professor, and we did consider that aspect, but the surviving stewardess was able to tell us that Barclay did not have any coughing or sneezing fits while he was on board the aircraft, although he did vomit once.'

The professor's silence emphasised his point.

Phelps appeared to develop a slight tic below his left eye. 'Well, as of this morning, all the other passengers are absolutely fine,' he said, hoping to put an end to speculation.

'Am I right in thinking that this new virus appears to have a hundred-per-cent mortality rate?' asked Heathrow's chief medical officer. 'There were no survivors, were there?'

'You're quite right,' said Phelps, 'but thankfully there were only a small number of patients and therefore that is perhaps not significant in a statistical sense. It is true, however, that they all died.'

'So in that respect the disease could be said to be even worse than Ebola?'

'Yes, on the basis of just five cases,' agreed Phelps. 'Ebola itself has a seventy- to eighty-per-cent mortality rate. It would be quite unusual to find anything more deadly than that. Let's hope we've seen the last of this particular bug so we won't get the chance to compare it.'

'And so say all of us,' muttered the man behind Steven and Cummings.

'I take it you have no idea how Barclay himself caught the disease?' asked Fred Cummings.

'None at all, I'm afraid. I understand there is no current outbreak of haemorrhagic fever in Ndanga or its immediate neighbours, so it's all a bit of a mystery.'

Steven left the meeting with Fred Cummings and they went for a drink. 'So what's your interest in all of this?' asked Cummings as they sat down with their beer.

'The foreign secretary's due to visit Ndanga in the next couple of weeks. His people want to be sure there's no outbreak of Ebola or anything like it in the country, so they asked Sci-Med if we could sniff around, see what we could come up with on the unofficial grapevine.'

'And?'

'It seems to be clear from all accounts but, like the man said, it's a bit of a mystery how Barclay went down with it in the first place.'

'Happily, it's not *my* mystery,' said Cummings. 'Salmonella from dodgy restaurants I can cope with, the occasional pocket of TB, seasonal blips of meningitis, yes, but the thought of something like one of these African viruses on the streets of London makes my blood run cold.'

'Or just run,' said Steven. 'From every orifice, I understand.'

'The trouble is, it *is* going to happen one day. I've never been more sure of anything.'

'You don't think we're prepared?'

Cummings took a sip of his beer and thought for a moment. 'There's a real danger of complacency,' he said. 'The Heathrow people did a good job, but the fact is that their problem was confined to the inside of an aircraft. They had all the time in the world to surround the problem and contain it, and they did. All credit to them, but there's a danger of people in my line of work thinking that it's always going to be that easy, or that the virus really isn't that dangerous when it is. The real lesson to be learned from this incident is the fact that a highly trained nurse, equipped with all the protective gear available, still managed to contaminate herself. Despite what Phelps said, it's surprisingly difficult to avoid contact with body fluids, especially in a domestic situation where people tend not to have Racal suits with self-contained air supplies hanging in their wardrobes or boxes of surgical gloves sitting by the kitchen sink. Frankly, it's damned nearly impossible. I think we'd see a very different picture if Ebola or Marburg broke out on a large housing estate instead of in an airliner at thirty-five thousand feet.'

'Put that way, it doesn't bear thinking about,' said Steven.

'And d'you know the worst thing? If it did, the whole medical profession put together couldn't do a blind thing about it. We'd be completely powerless. It would be like the great plagues of the Middle Ages all over again. We'd have to resort to nosegays and prayer books.'

'Then the solution must be to tackle the problem at source,' said Steven. 'Seek out the natural reservoirs of these viruses and destroy them before they spread into the community.'

'Unfortunately their source, whatever it is, lies in Africa and nothing is ever easy in Africa. CDC Atlanta has been trying to establish the natural source of Ebola for decades without success. The Pasteur Institute in Paris is trying to get a handle on it by examining all the data ever logged about the disease, but records are less than scrupulous.'

'I can imagine.'

* * *

When he got home, Steven poured himself a gin and tonic and put a CD on the stereo to fill the room with the soulful tenor sax of Stan Getz. He found two fax messages lying in the tray of the machine and sat down in his favourite chair by the window to read them. They were from two of his contacts in the medical charities, one working with the Red Cross and the other with a voluntary organisation called Medic Outreach. Both stated that, as far as they could ascertain, Ndanga was free of haemorrhagic fever and had been for some time. He faxed back his thanks.

Steven switched out the lights and rested his head on the chair back for a moment to look up at the sky. It was a clear night and he could see the stars – that was why he liked sitting in this chair. He reflected that finding out what he wanted to know had all been surprisingly easy. No one had reported that they didn't know or that they weren't sure. Everyone had said that there was no haemorrhagic fever in Ndanga. Barclay's misfortune in contracting the disease had just been one of these things – whatever that meant, he mused; it tended to be a generally accepted explanation anywhere outside academia. Just one of these things . . . just one of those 'crazy' things, as the song said, or one of those 'unexplained' things that spawned late-night television programmes that invariably never came to any conclusions. To the list he added one of those 'foolish' things, when he realised with a wry smile that this was the title of the current Getz track. But whatever the reason for Barclay's bad luck, he felt confident that he could tell Macmillan in the morning that there was no good reason for the foreign secretary's visit not to go ahead. With a bit of luck, he himself should be able to catch an afternoon flight up to Scotland and be in Dumfriesshire with his daughter by early evening.

Steven's five-year-old daughter, Jenny, lived with his sister-in-law, Sue, and her solicitor husband, Richard, in the Dumfriesshire village of Glenvane where she was being brought up with their own children, Mary, aged eight, and Robin, six. This had been the case since Steven's wife, Lisa – Sue's sister – had died of a brain tumour some two years ago. It had become his practice to visit

Scotland every second or third week and stay the weekend, so that Jenny would not forget who her real father was and he could enjoy watching her grow. Despite her tender years, there was a lot about Jenny that reminded him of Lisa and he took pleasure from that – especially the look in her eyes when she thought that he might be keeping something from her. That was Lisa to a tee and he just melted inside when she did it.

To say that Steven had taken Lisa's death badly would be a gross understatement. Although there had been seven months to prepare for the inevitable after the initial diagnosis, her death had hit him hard, and after the funeral he had given up on just about everything. He hadn't worked at all for over nine months afterwards, preferring instead to seek solace in booze and trying desperately to live in the past by shutting out the present and ignoring the very possibility of a future. But, like most people going through the hell of bereavement, he survived and came out the other side – perhaps not better for the experience, but knowing a great deal more about himself than he had before. He could now look back on his painfully short time with Lisa – a little over four years in all – with great fondness. He still missed her but it was no longer that awful knife-in-the-guts feeling.

The situation with Jenny was not ideal but his job was such that it ruled out arrangements involving day help or nanny care. He had toyed with the idea of finding a more ordinary job so that he would be home every night and could therefore have Jenny living with him, but, if he was absolutely honest with himself, it hadn't gone much further than that and it wouldn't. It might be selfish – in fact, it almost certainly was, he admitted – but he liked working for Sci-Med too much to give it up. Any feelings of guilt he might harbour were comfortably offset by the fact that Jenny seemed very happy living with Sue and Richard and their kids, and they saw and treated her as one of their own.

The Getz track changed to something soulful and almost subconsciously he started to look round the room in the dim light coming from outside. There was a photograph of Lisa in her nurse's uniform – she had been a nurse in Glasgow, where he had met her while on an assignment – and a photograph of the pair of them together when they went on holiday to Skye. He remembered that it had rained solidly for seven days before the weather had afforded them one beautiful day to walk in the Cuillins and appreciate just how lovely the island was. There was a picture of Jenny with Sue's children at the beach in Dumfriesshire, holding hands as they paddled together, their eyes bright with childish joy. There was a picture of himself in uniform and one in civilian clothes with his friend Mick Fielding when they had served in Special Forces together. Mick now ran a pub down in Kent; at least, that's what he'd been doing the last time Steven had heard about him – Mick tended not to keep up with old friends. God help the troublemakers down there, he thought with a smile.

There were a few bits and pieces he had rescued from the family home after his parents died, mainly books, but also a Spanish guitar he had bought when he was seventeen and still played when the notion took him. Not much to show in the way of possessions for a man on the wrong side of thirty-five, he concluded. The music stopped and he got up to pour himself another drink. He turned on the TV to hunt for news.

'The virus that has recently claimed the lives of three airline passengers, a stewardess and a nurse at the hospital where they were treated is thought to be a new one, previously unknown to medical science,' announced the newscaster.

'How the hell did they get hold of that so quickly?' exclaimed Steven.

'This was the conclusion of medical scientists who examined specimens taken from the victims of the Heathrow incident in a maximum-security lab at Britain's biological defence establishment at Porton Down. The source of the virus remains unknown. Health officials when contacted by Sky News in the last hour, however, have stressed that the outbreak posed no threat to the general public.'

Bloody hell, thought Steven. Does everything leak these days?

The report was accurate and had obviously been leaked to the media by someone present at the briefing. Accurate or not, any government assurance that things posed 'no threat' still smacked of the false assurances given during the time of BSE, he thought.

The news editor had decided to pad out the story and had found a microbiologist to interview.

'Dr Marie Rosen is a medical microbiologist at a leading London hospital. Where do *you* think this virus emanated from, Doctor?' asked the interviewer.

'Well, I haven't seen the report yet,' replied the woman. She was dressed in 'sensible' clothes and rimless glasses that sat well down her nose. Her skin looked as if it desperately needed moisturising and her plentiful mop of grey hair suggested she had recently been standing out in a gale. 'But I understand that the aircraft at the centre of this incident had just arrived from Africa. That would seem to be the likely source of the virus. It wouldn't be the first to come . . . "*out of Africa*".' She seemed pleased with her allusion.

'Why do you think this is, Doctor?' continued the interviewer, not bothering to smile. 'Why should new viruses appear all the time in Africa when this doesn't happen anywhere else in the world?'

'I would question whether or not they really are new viruses,' replied Rosen. 'I think it highly likely that they've been there all along, but with so much of the African interior being opened up these days, and people moving around much more than they used to, we're seeing what happens when a vulnerable population are suddenly exposed to agents they have not come into contact with before.'

'A bit like the situation when Native Americans were exposed to measles when the Pilgrim Fathers landed?' suggested the interviewer.

'Quite so.'

'But surely it can only be a matter of time until one of these viruses slips through the net and threatens us all?'

'I think the way the authorities dealt with the problem at Heathrow demonstrates that we can have confidence in the defences currently in place,' said Rosen.

'Maybe you should talk to Fred Cummings,' said Steven under his breath. He watched the rest of the news, then switched off the set. He decided to pack his bag for his trip up to Scotland tomorrow. He made a mental note to buy presents for Jenny and Sue's children after he'd talked with Macmillan in the morning.

FOUR

Manchester, England

Miss Warren looked at the luminous numerals on her bedside clock: it was 2.35 a.m. She tried once more to get to sleep by turning on her side and pressing one ear to the pillow while holding the bedcovers to her other but it was no use; the music was too loud. She didn't know what it was (it was Bruce Springsteen's 'The River') but it had been playing non-stop for the last two hours. She looked up at the ceiling and sighed, feeling more puzzled than annoyed because this was all most unusual; in fact, it had never happened before. It was just not the sort of thing one expected at the Palmer Court flats.

When the music started she had assumed that her upstairs neighbour, Ann Danby, must be having a party. That in itself would be unusual, but maybe it was a special occasion, a birthday, perhaps, or job promotion? But as time went on Miss Warren came to realise that there was no sound of people in the flat above, no clinking of glasses, no party chatter, no intermittent gales of laughter, just that loud, unremitting music.

Although younger than most of the other residents in the flats – somewhere in her mid-thirties, she would guess – Miss Danby had always seemed to fit in so perfectly at Palmer Court. She dressed well, had an executive job – although Miss Warren didn't know exactly what – and was always polite and courteous when they met in the hall. More than that, she was usually the first to pay her resident's fees for grass-cutting and lift maintenance and could always be relied upon to turn up at meetings of the residents' association – which was more than could be said for some of the others.

Miss Warren decided that she couldn't stand the noise any more: she would have to go upstairs and have a word. She got out of bed, put on her slippers and dressing gown, fastening the belt with a firm tug and a large bow. She stopped to glance at herself in the hall mirror and primped her hair before opening the front door and padding along the landing to the doors leading to the fire-escape stairs. She almost turned tail when she heard voices and concluded that perhaps there was a party after all and the guests were now leaving, but then she recognised a man's voice, that of George Dale, Miss Danby's neighbour.

Miss Warren climbed the stairs and pushed open the landing door. George and Lucy Dale turned round. They wore matching dressing gowns in navy with green piping.

'Whatever's going on?' she asked.

'She won't answer the door,' replied Lucy Dale. 'George has been knocking for the past five minutes. The noise is driving us mad.'

'It's not like Miss Danby at all,' said Miss Warren. 'Can you see anything through the letterbox?'

George knelt down with some difficulty, holding his right knee and lowering himself gently. 'Bedroom light's on,' he said. 'God, I feel like a peeping Tom . . . No sign of movement, though. Miss Danby! Are you there?'

There was still no response after several tries.

'She hasn't been well, you know,' said Lucy. 'She told me she thought she had flu coming on when I spoke to her the other day.'

'Do you think we should call the police?' asked Miss Warren.

Lucy looked doubtful. 'I don't like the idea of that,' she said. 'Policemen clomping their big boots all over the place. Maybe she just took a sleeping pill and fell asleep with the music on.'

'If she can sleep through that, she's the only one!' snapped her husband. 'I agree with Miss Warren. I think we should call the police.'

'Oh dear, I hope it won't cause bad feelings,' said Lucy. 'One hears such dreadful things these days about neighbours falling out.'

'We're doing it with the best of intentions,' Miss Warren re-assured her. 'We're worried about her welfare.'

As agreed, Miss Warren called the police when she went back downstairs. She did so in a very apologetic way, as she did most things in life, and was told that a Panda car would shortly be on its way. She gave the operator details of her buzzer number so that she could admit the officers when they arrived and then sat by the window. Her heart sank when she saw the flashing blue light appear. Drama was the last thing she or any of the other residents of Palmer Court would welcome, but at least the police car wasn't making that awful noise.

Miss Warren admitted the two constables and briefed them on what had been happening.

'And you say there was no response at all?' asked the elder, PC Lennon.

'None, and Mr Dale tried several times.'

'Right, then, Miss Warren, leave it to us.'

The two officers went upstairs, their personal radios crackling with the static created in the steel-framed fire escape.

'Nice place,' remarked PC Clark as they climbed.

'You'd need a few bob to live here,' replied Lennon. 'Come back when you're a chief super.'

They went through the same routine that George Dale had before deciding to force an entry. Lennon, the beefier of the two, crashed his shoulder into the door three times before the lock gave way and splintered wood fell to the ground around their feet. The door swung open and the sound level went up even more. The two policemen entered and heard Bruce Springsteen going mournfully 'down to the river'. They made their way slowly through the hall but did not call out, knowing that they could not compete with Bruce.

Lennon signalled to Clark to kill the music and watched as the younger man tried to figure out the controls on the front of the expensive sound system. In the end, he lost patience and pulled the plug out of the wall. A respectable silence was restored to Palmer Court.

'Miss Danby? Are you there?' The two policemen walked through to the bedroom and found a woman on the bed. She was wearing a nightdress and lying on top of the covers with her eyes closed. Her pillow was stained with vomit and her nightdress soaked in sweat.

'Miss Danby?'

They moved closer and saw an empty whisky bottle on the bedside table. An empty pill bottle lay on its side next to it.

'Oh, love, was life really that bad?' murmured Lennon as he felt for a pulse at the woman's neck.

'Is she dead, Tom?'

'Yeah, poor lass. Just shows you, money can't buy you happiness.'

Both men looked around at the expensive furnishings.

'This is my first,' said Clark, looking down at the body. 'She looks just like she's sleeping.'

'She's not been dead that long, she's still warm. Wait until you see them pulled out the canal after a week or lying on the floor in summer for a month because they didn't have anyone to check on them.'

At that moment the 'corpse' moved its head and Clark jumped back. 'Jesus, she's alive!'

'Christ!' exclaimed Lennon. 'I couldn't feel a pulse. Get an ambulance. Miss Danby! Miss Danby, can you hear me?'

The woman groaned quietly.

'Come on now, waken up! D'you hear me, Miss Danby? Waken up!'

'Men . . .'

'What's that? What about men?'

'All men . . . are bastards.'

'Come on now, Miss Danby, waken up. Don't go to sleep again.'

Her head slumped back on to the pillow.

'Shit! Maybe her airway's blocked. It's the sort of thing that happens when drunks throw up. Come on, son, give me a hand here.'

43

Lennon reached into her mouth to clear away any obstruction, while Clark held her on her side. 'Come on, Miss Danby, cough it up, love, cough it up.'

Both men worked at trying to get her to breathe again but she fell back on the bed and was absolutely still.

'Will I try mouth-to-mouth, Tom?'

'Might as well make it a big night for "firsts".'

Clark carried out textbook resuscitation until Lennon told him to stop. 'It's no good, son, she's gone. You did your best but she wouldn't have thanked you for it, anyway. She's got what she wanted. Let's get cleaned up before the cavalry arrive.'

At a little after 4.15 a.m. Ann Danby's body was removed from Palmer Court. Miss Warren, still awake and standing at the window, watched the zipped-up plastic bag being loaded into the waiting ambulance in the courtyard. She swallowed as she saw the doors close and the vehicle move off. 'Goodbye, Miss Danby,' she whispered. 'God bless.'

The body of Ann Danby was taken through silent, deserted streets to the local hospital, where she was formally pronounced dead on arrival by the houseman on duty. She was taken to the mortuary by the night porter on a covered trolley and transferred to a metal tray, which was slid into bay 3, row 4 of the mortuary fridge. The big toe on her left foot was labelled with her name and the date and time of her arrival.

There were no suspicious circumstances as far as the police were concerned: it seemed a clear case of suicide but, as with all sudden deaths, a post-mortem examination would be required before a death certificate could be issued; there could be no funeral without it. Establishing the exact cause of death would be the responsibility of a forensic pathologist. Arranging the funeral would be the responsibility of Ann Danby's parents who at 4.30 in the morning did not yet know of their daughter's death. The task of telling them fell to the two constables who had found her.

'Another first,' said Lennon as they turned into the Danbys' street in a pleasant, tree-lined suburb. 'Wakey wakey, your daughter's dead. Jesus, what a game.'

Clark looked at him sideways. 'I suppose you've done a lot of these,' he said.

'More than you've had hot dinners, my son. Your husband's been involved in a car crash . . . Your wife's been involved in an accident . . . Your son fell off his motor bike . . . We've found a body in the river and we think it may be . . .'

'Will you tell them?'

'Yeah. You can do it next time.'

'Yes, who is it?' asked a woman's voice from behind the door of number 28.

'Police. Could you open the door, please, madam?'

'Do you have identification?'

Lennon pushed his warrant card through the letterbox and the door was opened. A small woman with white hair corralled in a hairnet stood there in her nightclothes. 'It's Johnny,' she said. 'He's had an accident, hasn't he? Oh my God, is he . . . ?'

'No, it's not Johnny, madam. Do you think we could come inside? Is your husband awake?'

With both the Danbys sitting on the couch in the living room and the two constables facing them, the news of Ann's death was broken to them. The fact that it was suicide seemed to come as an even bigger shock than her death.

'I just can't believe it,' said Mr Danby. 'Ann had everything to live for. She was doing so well in her job and up for promotion yet again. Why on earth would she do such a thing?'

'When did you last see your daughter, sir?'

Mr Danby turned to his wife, who was sitting with head bowed and a handkerchief pressed to her face. 'I suppose about two weeks ago. She came to lunch. She seemed absolutely fine. But you spoke to her on the phone the other night, didn't you, Alison?'

She nodded mutely, then after a pause said, 'She thought she was getting flu and might have to stay off work. She didn't like doing that; she was always so conscientious.'

'Your daughter wasn't married?'

'No, she was very much a career woman, Officer,' said Mr Danby.

'No boyfriends?'

'What has that got to do with anything?' snapped Mrs Danby.

Lennon held up his hands in apology and said, 'I'm sorry, I didn't mean to pry. I was just trying to establish if there was anyone who might have seen your daughter in the last two or three days, someone who could throw more light on why she felt driven to take her own life.'

'No one.'

'A close female friend, perhaps?'

A look of anger flitted across Mrs Danby's face as she thought she saw an implicit suggestion in the question, but it faded and she responded with a curt shake of the head before covering her nose and mouth again with her handkerchief. Her shoulders started shaking with silent sobs.

Mr Danby cleared his throat twice before managing to whisper, 'You'll want me to identify her?'

'Yes, please, sir, when you feel up to it.'

'I'm not sure about the procedure in such cases . . .'

'There will have to be a post mortem, sir. After that the body will be released to you. You can go ahead and make arrangements pending the issue of a death certificate.'

'Thank you, Officer.'

'I don't want them defiling Ann,' Mrs Danby blurted out. 'Leave my baby alone!' She broke into uncontrollable sobs, and her husband put his arm round her and tried to comfort her. 'Make them leave her alone, Charles. I don't want them . . . doing things to her.'

Both policemen moved uncomfortably in their chairs as her raw grief reached them. 'I'm sorry, sir,' said Lennon. 'It's mandatory in such cases.'

Mr Danby nodded his understanding and suggested with his eyes that they should leave.

'Christ, that was awful,' said Clark as they drove off.

'It couldn't be anything else,' replied Lennon.

'What a night. What a bloody awful night.'

'You'll have worse.'

'That poor woman. It was as if we just destroyed her life.'

'We didn't. We were just the messengers, disinterested parties in other people's lives. We tiptoe in and then we tiptoe out again – and then we forget.'

'Forget? How can you possi—'

'You do because you're not involved personally and there's no alternative. Either you learn to forget or you get out of the job double quick. Understood?'

'Understood.'

'Come on, I'll buy you a bacon roll.'

Ann Danby was third on forensic pathologist Peter Saxby's list the following morning. 'So what have we here?' he asked in his usual imperious manner as the mortuary technician transferred the body from the fridge transporter trolley to the PM table. The head hit the metal table with a bang and Saxby snarled, 'Must you be so bloody clumsy, man?'

The technician mumbled an apology and melted into the background.

Saxby read from the file he was holding. 'Ann Danby, white Caucasian female, thirty-three, believed to have overdosed on malt whisky and barbiturates. No suspicious circumstances as far as our boys in blue are concerned. Not exactly *Silent Witness* material, is it? Unless, of course, we find a Malaysian *kris* up her arse and two kilos of heroin in her peritoneal cavity, eh?'

The technician smiled dutifully. He didn't like Saxby. He found him crude and insensitive but tried to make excuses for his behaviour, as befitted a soldier of the Salvation Army, something Saxby was unaware of. He waited while the pathologist made an external appraisal of the body and spoke his findings into the microphone that hung above the table. When Saxby had finished, the technician realigned the instrument tray at the head of the table and stood by as the pathologist made the first incision, a long, sweeping cut from throat to groin.

'Well, no heroin,' muttered Saxby when he had opened up the body to expose the internal organs. 'But a hell of a lot of blood. She's been bleeding internally from . . .' He paused while he made a closer examination. 'Just about every-bloody-where. Christ, are you sure this is the right body?'

'Her toe tag says "Ann Danby", and she was the only woman in the fridge,' replied the technician. 'Looks about the right age, too.'

'Yes, thank you for your forensic input,' snapped Saxby.

The technician said nothing and kept his eyes fixed on the table.

'Jesus, she was leaking like a sieve. This wasn't caused by whisky or bloody sleeping pills. Let me see those admission notes again.' Saxby snatched them, smearing them with bloody mucus from his gloves in the process. 'No mention of illness. Shit, I don't think I like this . . .'

'What d'you think was wrong with her?' asked the technician. Normally he wouldn't have dared ask, but the apprehension in Saxby's face gave him the impetus.

'I don't know,' murmured Saxby. He seemed mesmerised by the insides of the corpse. 'I've read about this but I've never actually come across it. I think she may well have been suffering from haemorrhagic fever.'

'What's that when it's at home?'

There was a long pause before Saxby said, 'Suffice to say, the last thing on earth you would want to do to such a case is perform a PM on it.'

'It's dangerous, then?'

'Bloody lethal,' whispered Saxby, turning pale. 'What have I done?'

'Are you absolutely sure about this?' asked the technician.

Saxby shook his head slowly and said, 'No, but I can't think of anything else it could be.'

'So where do we go from here then?' The technician was still calm, in spite of what he was hearing. He had his faith to thank for that. He knew God was on his side.

Saxby came out of his trance and started snapping out instructions. 'We need a body bag. I'll give you a hand getting her into it, then wash down the entire place in disinfectant. When you've finished, dump all your clothes in the steriliser bin and shower for at least ten minutes.'

'What about you?'

'I'm going to talk to the police first and then Public Health.'

Saxby locked the door to stop anyone coming in, and went to the phone. 'I need to talk to the officers who discovered Miss Ann Danby's body last night . . . Even if they are off duty . . . Then wake them up . . . Yes, it is urgent.' Saxby hung up and waited. Six minutes later the phone rang and he snatched it up. 'Sorry to disturb you, Constable Lennon, but this is most important. Did anything last night give you reason to think that Miss Danby had been ill recently?'

Tom Lennon rubbed the sleep from his eyes with one hand while he got his thoughts into order. 'Her mother said that she spoke to her a few days ago and she thought she was coming down with flu, and one of the neighbours said that she had been off work for a couple of days.'

'Thank you, Officer,' said Saxby, his tone suggesting that this was bad news. 'Was there any mention of her having been abroad recently?'

'None at all, but the subject didn't really come up.'

'Do you have a phone number for her mother?'

'Give me a minute; it's in my notebook.'

Saxby tapped the phone impatiently as he waited, then scribbled down the number on a wall pad. He dialled it immediately.

The technician sluiced down the PM table while he listened to Saxby being 'nice' to Ann Danby's parents. At least he didn't say what kind of doctor he was and what he had just been doing, but watching Saxby apologise profusely for his 'intrusion on their grief' and then offering his 'heartfelt condolences' was like watching a man commit an unnatural act.

'Has Ann been abroad recently? . . . She hasn't . . . You're absolutely sure about that? . . . Yes, I see . . . Majorca in 1998.'

Saxby put down the phone and stood there looking thoughtful while the technician, mop in hand, pushed a tide of disinfectant across the floor ever nearer to his feet.

'Progress?' asked the technician.

'Maybe I was a bit hasty in pushing the panic button,' said Saxby. 'She hasn't been abroad for two years, and even then it was only bloody Majorca. I don't think it can be what I thought it was. Bloody odd, though.'

'So all this is unnecessary?'

'Better safe than sorry.'

'What about the samples you took?'

'Send them to the lab in the usual way.'

'And the shower?'

'Won't do you any harm.'

FIVE

Edinburgh

'Yes, what is it, Jean?' snapped Paul Grossart.

His secretary moved back involuntarily from the intercom, surprised at his tone of voice. A change had come over her boss in the last week or so. Ever since the Americans' visit he had been preoccupied and on edge. 'I have a Mr Brannan on the phone for you.'

'I don't know any Brannan, do I?' asked Grossart.

'He's a journalist with the *Scotsman*. He wonders if he might have a few words.'

Grossart paused and swallowed hard before saying, 'Put him through.'

'Mr Grossart?' said a friendly sounding voice. 'Jim Brannan, science correspondent of the *Scotsman*.'

'What can I do for you, Mr Brannan?' said Grossart, adopting a neutral tone.

'There's a rumour doing the rounds that Lehman is making a big cut in its transgenic research initiative.'

'What gives people that idea?' asked Grossart defensively.

'You paid off a number of staff at the end of last week.'

Grossart had to think fast. He hadn't realised that this was a newsworthy event but it was a fact that Lehman had paid off a number of support staff engaged on the Snowball project whose services were no longer required. They were relatively low-grade, and none had been privy to the overall aims of the project, but a couple were part-qualified junior technicians and might have been able to figure out something. 'We are a cutting-edge research

51

company, Mr Brannan,' said Grossart. 'Our priorities constantly have to change with the ever-advancing state of scientific knowledge. The loss of jobs was simply the unfortunate fall-out from a course adjustment we had to make.'

'So Lehman isn't abandoning its transgenic animal work?'

'We remain committed to exploring every avenue of medical research which will benefit mankind,' replied Grossart.

'I trust I can quote you on that,' said Brannan sourly, thinking he could have found a better quote in a Christmas cracker.

'Of course.'

'It was a bit sudden, this "course adjustment", wasn't it?'

'Not at all. We'd been considering it for some months.'

'Right,' said Brannan slowly, sounding less than convinced. 'So nothing went wrong, then?'

'Nothing at all,' said Grossart.

The conversation ended and Grossart took several deep breaths before looking at his watch and doing a mental calculation. He punched the intercom button and said, 'Get me Hiram Vance in Boston.' He tapped nervously on the desk until the connection was made.

'Paul, what can I do for you?'

'They know,' hissed Grossart hoarsely. 'For Christ's sake, Hiram, they know. I've just had the press on the phone asking about the shutdown of the Snowball project.'

'Slow down, Paul,' said Vance, sounding calm and controlled. 'Just take it easy and tell me exactly what happened.'

Grossart gave him the details of his conversation with Brannan.

'Then what the hell are you worried about?' said Vance. 'You said exactly the right thing and it's my guess that will be an end to it.'

'I'm not so sure,' said Grossart hesitantly.

'Trust me,' said Vance. 'A story about a few guys losing their jobs isn't exactly Watergate, is it? By tomorrow it'll be yesterday's news.'

'Brannan knew they were working with transgenic animals.'

'Who isn't these days, in our line of business?' said Vance. 'Relax, Paul.'

'If you say so.'

'One thing worries me, though,' said Vance, sounding less friendly. 'I see our UK share price has dropped sharply.'

'The market here's a bit volatile at the moment,' said Grossart, feeling his throat go dry.

'I certainly hope that's all it is,' said Vance. 'I wouldn't like to think anyone there was trying to unload large numbers of our shares, if you get my drift?'

'I'm sure that's not the case,' lied Grossart.

'Glad to hear it,' said Vance. 'You have a nice day.'

Grossart tried to reciprocate but the line went dead.

Glenvane, Dumfriesshire

It had been a good day and Steven had insisted that Sue and Richard go out to dinner while he babysat: they didn't often get the opportunity, so there was usually one night when he offered to do this on his visits. Earlier, he and Sue had taken the children up to Edinburgh, where they had visited the zoo, eaten ice cream and generally had a fun time. The children had walked like the penguins, growled like the lions and behaved like the chimpanzees all the way home. The afterglow of a happy day was still with him as he watched a film on late-night television while nibbling potato crisps and sipping a Stella Artois. He always found it easy to unwind at the house in Glenvane. It seemed a million miles away from the bustle of London.

The earth was in danger of being hit by a giant asteroid but the missiles launched by the USA were on their way. Men with caps and epaulettes carrying several kilos of scrambled egg watched their progress on a giant screen, but instead of a nuclear impact Steven's mobile phone went off and he hit the mute button on the TV remote.

'Dunbar.'

'Duty officer at Sci-Med here. Mr Macmillan would like you back in London as soon as possible, Dr Dunbar.'

'I'm on leave.'

'Perhaps you'd like to tell him that yourself.'

'What's the problem?'

'Don't know but you could try working the words "shit" and "fan" into a well-known phrase or saying.'

'Gotcha. I'll catch the first flight in the morning.' As Steven spoke, he heard the clatter of a diesel engine outside and saw Sue and Richard get out of a taxi. They were giggling like naughty children and it made him smile.

'Bad news?' asked Sue when she saw the phone in his hand.

'I'm on the first flight to London.'

'Tough luck, old son,' said Richard. 'But I'm glad they didn't take you away earlier, because we have just had a bloody good time.' He slumped down into an armchair with a silly grin on his face. 'We really are very grateful, you know.'

'Not nearly as grateful as I am to you two,' said Steven, thinking on a different plane. 'I couldn't begin to tell you.'

Sue smiled and put her finger to her lips. 'Coffee?'

'I'll make it,' said Steven.

Steven crept out of the house a little before five in the morning, trying to make as little noise as possible. It was dark and there was a damp mist hanging in the still air. He looked up at Jenny's bedroom window and imagined her sleeping there, snug and warm and very much part of a loving family. He blew her a kiss before getting into his car and heading north to Glasgow airport to catch the first British Airways shuttle of the day to London Heathrow.

'They seem determined to deny you a holiday,' said Jean Roberts when Steven arrived in her office.

'Next time I'm just going to disappear without saying where I'm going,' said Steven.

'Strikes me Mr Macmillan will still know where you are. He has an uncanny knack of knowing where everyone is at any given time.'

'Electronic tags would be a better bet,' said Steven. 'I'm going to take a closer look at my shoes when I get home. What's up?'

'I don't know everything but I do know that the government's chief medical adviser, several Public Health people and two senior people from the Department of Health are with him at the moment.'

Steven looked at his watch. 'So I just wait?'

'I suppose so. He knows you're here.'

'I'll grab some coffee next door.'

Steven was sipping his second cup of coffee and reading the clues of the *Times* crossword before committing pen to paper – he had to get at least four before starting to fill it in – when he heard the sound of people leaving next door. A few moments later Miss Roberts popped her head round the door to say that Macmillan was asking for him.

John Macmillan was standing looking out the window when Steven entered and closed the door softly behind him. From past experience he knew that Macmillan took up this pose when he had bad news to impart.

'Any idea why I called you back?' asked Macmillan.

'You're going to tell me there's been another case of haemorrhagic fever,' suggested Steven.

'Guess or inside information?' asked Macmillan, sounding surprised.

'Just a guess.'

Macmillan turned round. 'There are seven new cases in Manchester. One woman has already died.'

'Sweet Jesus!' exclaimed Steven. 'Seven?'

Macmillan walked over to his desk and picked up a sheet of paper. 'The dead woman is Ann Danby, aged thirty-three, a graduate computer expert who lived alone in the city. Ostensibly she took her own life, but she was found to have been suffering from the disease.'

Steven looked puzzled.

'The police were called to her apartment by neighbours

concerned about noise. They found that she'd taken an overdose of sleeping tablets and washed them down with booze, although it's not clear why. Maybe it had something to do with her illness, but when a routine post mortem was performed, she was found to be suffering from the disease. Two policemen, a pathologist, a hospital houseman, an ambulanceman and a medical lab technician have all gone down with the disease and all are dangerously ill. They were all contacts of this woman in one way or another. Public Health are waiting for the next wave, when contacts of these people start falling ill. They are resigned to it spreading further.'

'Classic kinetics of a disease spread by body contact,' said Steven. 'If one gets you six, six will get you thirty-six and so on, like ripples on a pond. I take it this woman was a passenger on the Ndanga flight?'

Macmillan shook his head. 'No, damn it, I'm afraid she wasn't.'

'Then how?'

'That's really why I called you back. The Danby woman was not on that flight, nor has she been out of the country anywhere during the past two years, not since a holiday in Majorca in spring of 1998.'

'But she must have had contact with someone from the Ndanga flight?'

Macmillan shook his head again. He said, 'Public Health have gone through the passenger manifest with a fine-tooth comb. They can't find a connection with the dead woman at all.'

'But there must be one.'

'You'd think so. Apparently the police pathologist started to have doubts during the PM. He thought he was examining a routine drink-and-drugs suicide, but when he opened her up he found that she'd been haemorrhaging badly. Haemorrhagic fever crossed his mind, but when he couldn't come up with an African connection after talking to the woman's parents he didn't sound the alarm for fear of looking foolish.'

'We've all been there,' said Steven.

'The Public Health people have been working round the clock to isolate contacts, but unless we find out – and soon – where the disease originates from, we could be looking at a very unpleasant situation indeed. What do you think?'

'Well, assuming that we're talking about the same disease here – are we?'

'Porton haven't finished analysing the samples from the Manchester cases yet, but it would be a hell of a coincidence if it wasn't.'

'Then obviously the passenger, Barclay, and this woman, Danby, are the prime movers in the affair. We know how everyone else got the disease. We have to find out how these two got it.'

'That's where you come in,' said Macmillan. 'The authorities up in Manchester are going to be working flat out to contain the outbreak. Although there will be an epidemiological team investigating the cause, I want you involved as well, because it's absolutely vital that we establish the source as quickly as possible. I've had this okayed at the highest level, so you'll have a free hand to operate as you see fit. You'll have the support of the police and the Public Health Service should you need them, and of course you'll have access to all the medical and scientific back-up you need. What do you say?'

'Do I have a choice?'

'No.'

'Then I say I'd best get started.'

'Miss Roberts will prepare a background file for you in the usual way. After that, you're on your own.'

'This hasn't reached the press yet?' said Steven.

'Only because the disease doesn't have a name and there's no obvious African connection to scaremonger about, but six associated people going down with something nasty is not going to go un-reported for long.'

Steven had lunch in a city pub, an old-style pub with high ceilings and self-conscious Victorian fittings. He cut an anonymous figure as he sat in a corner, eating a cheese roll and sipping a beer while mulling over the situation. The thing troubling him most was the fact that the Public Health people had failed to establish a connection between the woman in Manchester and the Ndanga flight. If there really wasn't one, it would suggest that there was an original source of viral haemorrhagic fever in Manchester. Not a happy thought. And not a likely one, either, he decided after some consideration. Despite the failure to establish a connection, there just had to be one. Maybe some lateral thinking was called for.

Although the true natural reservoir of Ebola and the other filovirus infection, Marburg disease, had not yet been established, he was aware of a strong suggestion among investigators that animals – particularly monkeys – were involved in the chain of events. If his memory served him right, the very first case of Marburg disease had been contracted in the German town of that name, back in the late 1960s by a worker who got it from an African lab monkey. If by any chance the woman in Manchester had had contact with animals – perhaps as a 'friend of the zoo' or as a voluntary helper or some such thing – that might conceivably be where she had picked up the disease. That would be the best possible outcome, he concluded. It would also be one hell of a coincidence.

Steven returned to the Home Office to pick up his briefing file, which he'd been told would be ready by two thirty if Miss Roberts worked through her lunch hour to collate information supplied by the authorities in Manchester. She obviously had, for a purple folder was waiting for him on her desk when he went into her office. Jean Roberts had gone off to have a late snack but she had left a Post-it note stuck to the cover of the file, wishing him well. He in turn left her one, thanking her.

Steven paused on the pavement outside and thought about taking the file home to read, but then decided on using the facilities of the medical library at the London School of Hygiene and Tropical Medicine, where he had a reader's card. He would have access there to all the reference books and current journals he might need.

The first page of the Sci-Med file was entitled 'Primary Victims'. Humphrey Barclay, he read, had been a middle-ranking civil servant who had been attached to the Foreign Office for the last fourteen years after shorter stints at the Ministry of Agriculture and the DHSS. He had a BA from Durham University in geography and had joined the civil service immediately after gaining his degree, a lower second. Two years later he had married Marion Court-Brown, daughter of a Surrey stockbroker, whom he had met at university. The marriage had produced two daughters, Tamsin and Carla.

Barclay's annual job appraisals suggested that his career had been in the doldrums for the past few years, his performance never being assessed any higher than 'satisfactory' during the past four. Illness had played a part, in that he had suffered intermittently from heart problems, although this had apparently been put right after surgery earlier this year.

Barclay's being sent to Ndanga had been seen as a bit of a test by his superiors to find out if he merited promotion to the next grade after all. Barclay himself had been made aware of this and had been keen to do well, according to his superior, Sir Bruce Collins. Confidential vetting reports obtained from Special Branch suggested that there was no scandal in Barclay's life. He was honest, straight and reliable to the point of being dull. Steven sighed and moved on to the next file.

Ann Danby had been thirty-three at the time of her death; she was unmarried and lived alone in Palmer Court, an expensive apartment block on the West Side of Manchester. She was a graduate of the University of Manchester in computer studies, and worked as an IT specialist with Tyne Brookman, a large academic publishing firm in the city. Her parents also lived in Manchester and she had one brother, John, who lived and worked in London for a public relations firm. By all accounts, she had been settled and content, even if regarded as a bit of a loner by her neighbours

– although university involvement in a whole variety of societies had suggested otherwise. No one interviewed could suggest a reason why Ann Danby should want to take her own life, and the possibility of this action being connected with her illness seemed entirely plausible. She had not been outside the UK since 1998 when she had taken a package holiday to Majorca, apparently alone. She had never been to Africa, nor had she any known connection with anyone who had.

Steven shook his head and sighed again. There was absolutely nothing in these two biographies to suggest an opening course of action. He couldn't see a first move and first moves were all-important, be it the first leg of a journey or the first move in a chess game. Get it wrong and it could be hard to recover lost ground. He moved on to the list of 'Secondary Victims' but found nothing helpful – it was quite clear how these people had contracted the disease. It was impossible not to be struck by the tragedy of so many young lives being wiped out; the stewardess and the nurse had both been well under thirty.

Steven noted down some key points for a plan of action. He saw the impending report from Porton as being critical, because it would establish whether or not the two outbreaks had been caused by the same virus. If, by any chance, they had not – and he sincerely hoped against hope that this might be the case – he would concentrate all his efforts on finding out where Ann Danby had picked up the disease, starting first with any animal connection he could establish. If, as was more likely, the two viruses turned out to be one and the same, he would have to gamble on there really being a connection between Ann Danby and the Ndanga flight, despite the authorities' failure to find one. Either way, Manchester was the place to be. He would travel up there in the morning. In the meantime, he would read up on filovirus infections and in particular the reports on any recent outbreaks of the disease. He started with the 1995 epidemic of Ebola in Kikwit in Zaire where 80 per cent of the 360 cases identified in the outbreak died.

*   *   *

Steven's arrival in Manchester coincided with the newspapers getting hold of the story. 'Killer Disease Stalks Manchester Hospital' was what he read on the first billboard he saw in the station. He bought several papers and flicked through them while he had a weak and slightly cold coffee in the station buffet. The press had the basic story but not much more. They knew that several people connected with the hospital had gone down with an unidentified disease, but they didn't appear to know anything about Ann Danby, the cause of it all. One of the tabloids, however, speculated that the source of the illness might well have been a drug-addicted prostitute who had overdosed and been picked up by the police before being taken to the hospital in question. They went on to cite the problems that Glasgow had suffered recently with a killer disease that struck at drug addicts. That had been shown to be due to the toxin of a bacterium called *Clostridium*. Was this the same thing? the paper asked.

'I wish,' thought Steven. He finished his coffee and took a cab to the City General Hospital, where he was introduced to the medical superintendent, Dr George Byars, a short dapper man wearing a pinstripe suit which emphasised his lack of height and narrow shoulders.

'They tell me you'll be working flat out on finding the source of this damned thing,' said Byars.

'I'm going to give it my best shot,' replied Steven. 'How do things stand at the moment?'

'Not good. The pathologist, Saxby, died early this morning and two of the others, the lab technician and PC Lennon, are dangerously ill. Everyone feels so helpless, but there's nothing we can do other than give them nursing care. They either pull through or they don't.'

Steven nodded and asked, 'Have there been any more cases?'

'Not yet, but Public Health aren't counting their chickens and, frankly, we could be in trouble. This hospital isn't equipped to deal with a big outbreak of a disease like this. We have a special containment unit, but it's really designed to deal with the occasional foreign traveller who goes down with something nasty. As for an . . . epidemic?' Byars seemed reluctant to use the word. 'Forget it.'

'I suspect that'll be the case with most hospitals?'

'Correct. It's been government policy for some time now to close down all the old fever hospitals.'

'So what are you guys going to do?'

'Hope that Public Health have been quick enough off the mark in rounding up the patients' contacts. If they have, they tell us we can expect something in the order of ten to twenty new cases. We plan to re-open two of the wards we closed last year and use them as an isolation unit. We've already got in the Racal suits for the nurses and we're running refresher courses on barrier nursing for the nursing volunteers we've asked for.'

Steven nodded, but the look on his face prompted Byars to add, 'I know, it all smacks of wartime spirit and backs-against-the-wall stuff, but that's the way it is, I'm afraid. We're just not prepared for this sort of thing.'

'At last a use for the Millennium Dome,' murmured Steven.

The comment made Byars relax a little. 'I think we'll be okay as long as there aren't any more wildcards like Ann Danby in the pack. If there are, God knows what the outcome might be.'

'Well, she's my problem.'

Steven was taken on a tour of the hospital special unit, where he had to suit-up before entering and where he could look at the current patients behind glass screens. They did not make for pretty viewing. 'Poor sod,' whispered Byars as they looked at Lennon who was not expected to pull through; he seemed to be bleeding all over.

'You know, it's a funny thing,' said Byars. 'Despite all the bleeding, haemorrhagic fever cases rarely die from blood loss.'

'You've had experience of it before?'

'No,' Byars confessed. 'I read it in a book.'

Steven accepted an invitation to attend a meeting later in the hospital with representatives from the Public Health Service and other bodies concerned with the outbreak, then headed for the police station where Lennon and Clark had worked.

He was seen by a chief superintendent who seized the opportunity to subject him to a short lecture about the dangers his officers on the street were constantly exposed to. It was short because Steven interrupted him with a request to see the shift rota the two sick officers were on at the time of the call to Ann Danby's place. He followed this up with a request to speak with Sergeant John Fearman.

'I've known Tom Lennon for fifteen years,' said Fearman. 'Salt of the earth, he is. That's why I put young Clark with him – I thought he'd teach the lad a lot about what police work's all about.'

'Tell me about that night,' said Steven.

'It's all in the report,' said Fearman. 'We got a call from one of the neighbours about loud music. Tom and Clark attended and had to force an entry to the Danby woman's flat. The rest is history.'

'No, tell me the details.'

'What's to say? Tom thought she was dead when they arrived – he couldn't find a pulse – but then she moved and he yelled for an ambulance. Clark actually tried mouth-to-mouth on her, poor little sod – I suppose that's how he got it. But by the time the ambulance got there she really was dead.'

'You say she moved?'

'Clark was watching her when it happened. She was the first body he'd ever come across, see, and when she moved it gave him the fright of his life.'

'Then what?'

'Tom called immediately for an ambulance and tried clearing her throat. There was vomit on the pillow so he thought her airway might be blocked, but he told me it was all clear when he put . . . his fingers in her mouth.'

Steven and Fearman exchanged glances as they both saw the significance of this action.

'Tom kept trying to wake her up because he thought she'd taken an overdose of pills, as indeed she had, and he thought he was succeeding, too, when she appeared to come round and say something. But it was no use. She died.'

'She said something?' asked Steven.

Fearman shrugged ruefully. 'Tom told me that her last words were, "All men are bastards."'

SIX

Steven said he wanted to take a look at Ann Danby's flat. He had no specific reason in mind but it was vital that he understand as much as possible about her because she was – in the absence of any known contact – the sole cause of the Manchester outbreak. He was told that the police and Public Health people had finished their business there, and was given a key, which had been marked for collection by her parents on the following day; it had been necessary to change the lock after the police's forced entry. He was driven over to the flats in a police Panda car, and he told the driver not to wait, as he might be some time.

'Just like Captain Oates, eh?' said the driver.

'But I'm planning on coming back,' countered Steven.

Palmer Court had little architectural merit, being a rather non-descript block of concrete flats four storeys high with roughcast walls and a flat roof, but it had a well-cared-for appearance. The grounds inside the gates were obviously professionally tended, with manicured lawns and knife-edged borders. The residents' parking bays were white-lined and numbered and the rubbish bins, also numbered, were discreetly stored in a little stable of their own at the side of the building, disguised with climbing plants. The hall-mark of the middle class, thought Steven, a place for everything and everything in its place.

A round-shouldered man wearing a blue serge suit and a grubby-collared shirt, supposedly made respectable by a thin black tie secured with an incredibly tight knot, admitted him to the building. He carried a large bunch of keys on a metal ring as if it were a symbol of his authority and walked with a shuffling gait that suggested his shoes were too large. His complexion spoke of a long association with alcohol but his breath smelled of peppermint. He seemed pleasant enough when he asked Steven his business. Steven showed his ID and said why he'd come.

'Another one, eh,' said the man. 'Poor woman has had more visitors since she died than she ever did when she was alive.'

'That's often the way,' said Steven, keen to engage the man in conversation in case he had useful information. 'People tend to turn up at your funeral when they wouldn't have crossed the street to say hello to you while you were alive.'

'Ain't that the truth,' agreed the man. 'You know, I still can't get over it.' He sighed. 'Poor Miss Danby. She seemed happy enough when I talked to her the weekend before last. She was asking me about a good garage to service her car. I sent her to Dixon's in Minto Street. My brother works there.'

'Then you didn't think she was the sort to take her own life?' probed Steven.

'Who's to say?' replied the doorman, philosophically. He put his head to one side and both hands behind his back to impart his wisdom. 'People often put a brave face on things. Hide the truth from the world, if you know what I mean.'

'Sure,' replied Steven, hoping he wasn't about to be subjected to a series of examples. 'You implied that she didn't have many friends?'

'If she did, very few of them ever came here,' replied the man. 'Having said that, she quite often went away for the weekend but maybe that was work.'

'She didn't say?'

'She was a very private person, was Miss Danby, not the sort to volunteer that kind of information, and I'm not the sort to ask,' replied the doorman.

'Of course not,' said Steven. He asked for directions to the flat.

'Third floor, second door. You can still smell the disinfectant. God knows why they'd want to go and do that.'

Steven had overlooked the fact that the Public Health people would have disinfected the flat thoroughly in the wake of the PM findings. He got the full lingering force of it when he opened the door and entered the hall. They had obviously used a formaldehyde 'bomb' to make sure that the disinfectant got everywhere and that no virus particles were left alive. This was effective, but unfortunate from Steven's point of view, because he hated the smell of formaldehyde and had done ever since his early days at medical school, where the cadavers the students worked on were stored in solutions of the stuff. He put a handkerchief over his nose and mouth until he opened a window in the living room and waited by it until the air had cleared enough for him to take a look around.

The flat was very well furnished but in a pleasantly understated way – good-quality stuff but kept to a minimum so that there was a feeling of light and space about the place. He noted that Ann Danby had an eclectic CD collection, all stacked neatly in purpose-built racks beside the Bang and Olufsen music centre. A closer inspection revealed that they were filed neatly in alphabetical order. Steven moved on to her tape collection and found that the same system applied. It spoke of a tidy, organised mind. Her books, however, were arranged by subject and occupied three tiers of black metal shelving fitted to the wall opposite the window.

Many of the titles were computer- and probably work-related. They took up almost the entire top shelf, while a liking for poetry was demonstrated by the titles to the left on the middle shelf. Keats seemed to have been a particular favourite but Auden, Rupert Brooke and Wordsworth were also well represented. At the end of the poetry section, just before the shelf divider, there were a number of volumes of love poetry. Steven saw a certain poignancy in that in view of the picture the man on the door had painted of a rather solitary, lonely woman.

Steven picked up a little book of Elizabeth Barrett Browning's work and moved through it until he found the one that had been Lisa's favourite. 'How do I love thee? Let me count the ways.' He lingered over the last line, 'And if God choose I shall but love thee better after death', and felt a lump come to his throat. He replaced the book and noticed there was a triangular gap a little further along, as if one had been removed, so that the books to the right of it had flopped back. He looked around the room and noticed a small blue-covered volume lying on the lamp table beside the chair that Ann Danby had used most, judging by the letter and newspaper racks beside it.

Steven went over, picked it up and saw that *The Sonnets of William Shakespeare* had been her last reading companion. He checked for a bookmark, to see if he could find the last poem she'd read, but didn't find one. He did, however, note with some surprise that the flyleaf had been ripped out. It had not been cut out, because a jagged remnant of paper had been left, as if it had been done in anger.

Puzzled as to why such a meticulous woman would do such a thing, he looked for the missing page in the waste-paper basket but found nothing. Then he noticed a piece of paper lying on the window ledge. It had obviously been crumpled up at one point, but had been smoothed out in order to make examination possible. He suspected that the police had found it on the floor but had assigned no significance to it. It was the missing flyleaf. There was some writing in light-blue ink on it. It said simply, 'My love for ever,' and was signed 'V'. The initial had been done with quite a flourish, the sign of an extrovert personality perhaps?

Steven sat down for a moment and wondered why there had been no mention of a boyfriend before. Had this been an oversight or . . . a secret? A secret lover might explain a lot, but why had she kept him secret? Could V be a woman? Not everyone was comfortable with openly gay relationships, even in these enlightened times.

Steven remembered the policeman's recollection of Ann's last words, 'All men are bastards.' Not terribly original but now it made sense, and it was conveniently significant because it suggested strongly that V was a man. The fact that the relationship had been kept secret also suggested that he might be married, but, whatever the personal details, finding out the identity of V was now going to be a priority, particularly if it should turn out that he had been on the Ndanga flight.

Steven put the book back in its place on the shelf and glanced quickly through the other titles. There were a number of biographies, mainly of politicians both past and present, half a dozen reference books, a number of illustrated books about French Impressionist painters and fiction ranging from Tolkien's *Lord of the Rings* to Umberto Eco's *The Island of the Day Before*. The right-hand corner of the very bottom shelf was given over to books on hill-walking. Lakeland, Snowdonia and the Scottish mountains were all featured, but there was also a guide to trekking in Nepal. Why had there been no mention of a love of outdoor pursuits in the file on Ann Danby? Or had she kept that a secret, too? Perhaps this had been an interest that she had shared with V: it might even account for the weekends away. On the other hand, it could be that she had just been an armchair enthusiast for the outdoor life.

The question was resolved when he found hill-walking gear in the walk-in wardrobe in the main bedroom. There were two expensive shell jackets, one in red and one in blue Gore-Tex fabric, and two matching fleeces hanging on the rail beside a range of good-quality business and leisure clothing. A pair of Scarpa mountain boots sat on the floor with boot stockings stuck inside them. A Berghaus rucksack was propped up against the back wall, along with two Leki walking poles.

The smaller of the two bedrooms had been used by Ann as a study, and featured a pine desk and a wide range of computer equipment. There were two small metal filing cabinets and a swivel chair in light-cream leather with a matching footstool. Steven didn't like the thought of doing it, but he would have to search the desk drawers for more information about Ann Danby's life, not least for clues as to who V might be.

The fact that she had been an almost obsessively tidy person proved to be a big help. All her bank and credit card statements were filed neatly together in an A4 binder. There was a separate binder for household bills and another for mortgage and insurance details. Within minutes, he was able to establish that Ann Danby had had no money worries. Her salary, paid directly into her cheque account on the thirtieth of each month, had been more than sufficient to cover all outgoing expenses and had left enough for a monthly transfer of five hundred pounds into a savings account with the Halifax Building Society. This account currently showed a balance of something over fifteen thousand pounds. In addition, she had tended to pay off her credit-card accounts, three in all, in full every month.

Steven paid particular attention to the credit-card statements because of what the doorman had said about Ann going away for the weekends. He could not, however, find any pattern of spending to support this or give any clue as to where she had gone. Did this mean that her trips *had* been connected with work, in which case they would have been paid for through a company account? Another possibility was that someone else – V for example – had been paying.

He found a leather-bound diary in the bottom desk drawer and opened it hopefully, only to find that it was merely an appointments diary. Better than nothing, he reassured himself, and started looking through it to see if the weekends featured. He found that they did, but without any detail: Ann had simply written in the letter V approximately every third or fourth weekend. There had, however, not been any weekend featuring V for the last six weeks then suddenly V popped up on a weekday, the Thursday during the week before Ann Danby died. He had been pencilled in for p.m. and she had put three concentric rings around the initial.

Steven felt a small surge of excitement as he realised that a meeting on that particular day would make V a possible suspect for having given Ann the virus. The subsequent incubation period would have been about right. But what had happened to V himself? Why hadn't *he* gone down with the disease? Steven decided there was no point in wasting time worrying about that at the moment. His first priority must be to find out if there had been any passengers on the Ndanga flight with a first name starting with V. The passenger manifest had not been included in the Sci-Med file, so he requested the information by mobile phone, asking that the list be e-mailed to him as soon as possible.

The sound of a key being inserted in the front door broke Steven's concentration. He had been led to believe that the police and health authorities had no further interest in the apartment. He was about to get up from his seat at the desk to investigate when an elderly couple appeared at the room door.

'Who the devil are you?' exclaimed the man, clearly startled to have found him there. The woman's hands flew to her mouth, her eyes wide with alarm.

'I'm sorry,' said Steven, realising the couple must be Ann Danby's parents. He felt more of an intruder than ever. 'I'm afraid there's been some kind of a mix-up. I'm Dr Steven Dunbar from the Sci-Med Inspectorate. I'm part of the investigating team. The police gave me your key. I understood that you wouldn't be picking it up until tomorrow. I had no idea that you'd be coming here today.'

'The police gave us a key yesterday,' said Mr Danby. 'It was the spare that we were going to pick up tomorrow. It's just one damned misunderstanding after another with you people,' he complained. 'What more is there to investigate, for God's sake? Haven't my wife and I suffered enough?'

'I'm sure you both have,' said Steven sympathetically. 'But there are still some important things to establish. If you can bear with me, I really would like to ask you a few questions now that you're here.'

'Questions, questions, questions.' Danby sighed. 'What d'you want to know this time?'

'Did Ann have a boyfriend?'

'My God,' snapped Danby, 'we've been through all this with the police already. She did not have a boyfriend. Was that some kind of crime that you keep asking about it?'

'Of course not,' replied Steven but he noticed that Danby's wife had diverted her eyes when her husband was answering. It struck him as odd, perhaps the action of someone hiding something. It prompted him to say, 'Are you absolutely sure about that?'

'Of course I'm bloody sure,' said Danby.

'And you, Mrs Danby. Ann never said anything to you about a special . . . friendship?'

'You heard what my husband said.'

Steven nodded but kept on looking at the woman, who was clearly uncomfortable with this line of questioning and more particularly with his persistence. He was more than ever convinced that she was concealing something.

'This is very important. I promise you that anything you might tell me will be treated with the utmost discretion.'

'There were no boyfriends,' stormed Danby. 'Now will you please leave? We've told you people everything we can. Now please leave us alone to do what we have to.'

'And what's that?' Steven asked gently.

'Start clearing away our daughter's effects.'

Steven was uncomfortable with the prospect of having to tell the Danbys that they couldn't do that until he'd finished prying into every corner of their daughter's life, so uncomfortable that he decided to leave. He convinced himself that the chances of the meticulous Ann Danby having left anything around concerning V were remote and he felt optimistic about finding V on the passenger list.

'Of course,' he said. 'I'll get out your way.' Apart from anything else, he mused as he returned to the lobby, if push came to shove, Mrs Danby could probably fill him in concerning V.

Steven took a taxi to his hotel and connected his laptop modem to the phone socket in his room. He made the connection to Sci-Med in London and collected the e-mail containing the passenger list for the Ndanga flight. He scanned it anxiously, and found that there was only one male passenger with a first name starting with V. He was Vincent Bell and he had been sitting in seat 31D.

'Ring a ding ding,' murmured Steven. His second thought, however, was that row 31 was a long way back from where the ill-fated Barclay had been seated in row 5. There did not seem to be a lot of opportunity for contact on board the aircraft. But they could have met at some other point in the journey, perhaps in the queue at the airport or sitting in the lounge, if places like Ndanga had departure lounges. At this juncture, however, it didn't really matter. What did matter was that he trace Vincent Bell as soon as possible. He called Sci-Med and asked for their assistance in getting details about him and they responded quickly, furnishing him with basic information within the hour. They had obtained it from the passenger record compiled by the special reception centre at Heathrow where they had dealt with the incoming Ndanga flight. As one of the passengers not deemed to have been at high risk during the flight, Bell had only been asked to leave his name, address and the name of his GP, but that was enough. Steven now knew that Bell lived at 21 Mulberry Lane, Canterbury. Not the most convenient location from which to conduct an affair with someone in Manchester, but perhaps Bell was a travelling man, drifting up and down the motorways of the land six days a week in his company Mondeo. Alternatively, it could simply be a case of love knowing no bounds. As it often said in the personal columns of the papers, 'good sense of humour essential' but 'distance no object'. He would soon find out for himself: he planned to travel to Kent in the morning.

Steven looked at his watch and saw that he was going to be late for the meeting at City General if he didn't get a move on. He rang down to the desk to order a taxi and had a quick shower before changing. The cab driver was none too pleased at having to wait, but money smoothed the way as usual, and before the journey was over the driver was giving Steven his thoughts on the current outbreak at the hospital.

'Bloody junkies – they should shoot the lot of them. Once a junky, always a junky, that's what I say. All this shit about rehabili-tation is just a bunch of crap, a waste of bloody money. And now they're passing on their diseases to innocent people. Bloody criminal it is.'

'I didn't know drugs were involved in the outbreak,' ventured Steven when he managed to get a word in.

'Drugs are involved in most things these days, mate, take my word for it. Ninety-nine per cent of all crime in this city is drug-related, one way or another.'

'But I don't see the connection with the problem at the hospital,' said Steven.

'The junkies are riddled with disease, mate, all of them. AIDS, hepatitis, salmonella, the lot, and then when they land up in hospital they start giving it to the nurses, don't they? That's how it happens, mate. Those poor girls have enough to contend with without those wasters giving them things. Shoot the bloody lot of them. It's the only answer.'

Steven got out the cab thinking that desert islands might have a lot going for them. He was preparing to apologise for his late-ness as he entered the room, but found to his relief that the meeting had not yet started and there were still two other people to come. In the interim the medical superintendent, George Byars, intro-duced him to some of those present. There were too many names to remember, so Steven tried to memorise them in groups. There were three senior people from the Manchester social work depart-ment led by a short squat man named Alan Morely who obviously had a liking for denim clothes, and a team of five epidemiologists led by a sour-faced, grey-bearded man introduced as Professor Jack Cane. These people seemed seriously academic, thought Steven, narrow shoulders, bad eyesight and an ill-disguised impatience with the perceived stupidity of the rest of the world. There were four senior nurses, including the hospital's nursing superintendent, Miss Christie, for whom no first name was proffered, and finally a small delegation from the Department of Health in London. This last group was fronted by an urbane-looking man named Sinclair who smiled a lot but looked as if he might be good at playing poker.

Steven accepted a mug of coffee but was conscious while drinking it of hostile glances from the epidemiology group and he suspected they might be resentful of his presence. This was a situation he was not unfamiliar with, having encountered it often enough before on assignment. Outside investigators were seldom welcomed with open arms by those already on the ground.

As a consequence, he had simply learned to be as self-sufficient as possible. If anyone offered help it was a bonus. John Donne's assertion that no man was an island might well be true, but over the years he had become a pretty accomplished peninsula. In his view, team players – those whom society set so much store by – moved at the pace of the slowest member of the team. That the earth went round the sun was discovered by Galileo, not by a team or a group led by him.

The two missing people arrived; both were senior doctors from the special unit.

'We've lost another two,' said one by way of explanation.

'The two you thought this morning?' asked Byars.

'Yes.'

'Any new cases?'

'No, but assuming a ten-day incubation period at the outside – it was actually less for the Heathrow people – we've still got four to go. Touch wood, things are looking good at the moment.'

'Then I think we have cause for optimism,' said Byars. 'How have the barrier nursing courses been going, Miss Christie?'

'Very well. There was a good response to the call for volunteer nurses, as I knew there would be. I think we can safely say that we are on top of things at the moment.'

'Well done.' He turned to Morely and asked, 'How about contacts? Any problems there?'

'All the friends and relatives we've seen seem to understand the gravity of the situation and are reconciled to staying indoors for the ten-day period. We've had no real opposition at all,' said Morely. 'I think the same goes for the community nurses?'

One of the nursing staff took her cue and agreed that this was the case.

'Excellent,' said Byars. 'How about the academics? Any progress in establishing the source of the outbreak, Professor?'

'Not yet,' admitted Cane. 'But we had one interesting piece of news this afternoon. Porton say that the Manchester virus is identical to the Heathrow one.'

SEVEN

Steven returned to his hotel with positive feelings about the meeting. He would have felt less happy with the news about the Manchester and Heathrow viruses being identical had it not been for his findings at Ann Danby's flat. As it was, it just seemed to confirm that Vincent Bell was the link, something he should be able to establish beyond doubt next day. If he did, and if the medical teams in Manchester continued to keep tight control over the outbreak, there was a good chance that the whole affair might be consigned to history by the end of the following week.

The only loose end left would be how Humphrey Barclay had contracted the disease in the first place. It might not be relevant in a practical sense if the outbreak could be eradicated without knowing, Steven conceded, but he suspected that the question was going to niggle away at him for some time. If the answer lay in Africa, as it seemed it must, that was probably where it would remain. It would be yet another secret of the Dark Continent.

Steven flew down to London first thing in the morning and picked up a hired car from the Hertz desk at Heathrow. Traffic on the A2 was as bad as he expected, but he still managed to make Canterbury by lunchtime, and he left the car in one of the large car parks outside the city walls. He took a walk along the main thoroughfare in bright winter sunshine, looking for a street guide to tell him where Mulberry Lane was, but also because he wanted to take a look at the old city again.

It was a while since he'd been there and he had a soft spot for Canterbury, having spent many of the summer holidays of his youth working on an uncle's fruit farm out in the Kent country-side. He saw the area as quintessentially English, different from the North he was more used to, England's brain rather than its brawn. The cathedral's huge presence still dominated the city and seemed to influence everything in it from the names of the narrow streets to the contents of its bookshops, the weight of its history almost tangibly forming a bridge between past and present. A chattering group of choristers from the cathedral school, unself-conscious in their cassocks, passed by and reminded Steven that Christmas was little more than a month away. They'd be singing carols soon.

Mulberry Lane, when he eventually found it, comprised a row of pretty little cottages backing on to the River Stour. It would not have looked out of place in a scene from *The Wind in the Willows* and he half expected Ratty and Mole to appear at any moment, arguing about nothing too important. He found the cottage he was looking for and walked up its meandering gravel path to knock on the heavy wooden door. After a short delay a stocky man with dyed auburn hair combed over a freckled, balding scalp opened the door and looked him up and down. He was wearing an apron with vintage cars on it and wiping his hands on a tea towel.

'Mr Bell?' asked Steven.

'No, who wants him?' asked the man. His voice had a lisp.

'My name's Dunbar. I'm an investigator with the Sci-Med Inspectorate. I'd like a word with Mr Bell.'

The man turned away and called, 'Vincent! There's a big handsome policeman here to see you. You'd better have a good story, love, I can tell you.' He turned back to Steven and said, 'And you'd best come in.'

Steven stepped inside the cottage, suspecting that his beautiful theory was about to turn to dust. Vincent Bell entered the room and with one word, 'Hello,' managed to blow even the dust of it away. Bell was overtly homosexual; he was clearly not Ann Danby's secret lover.

'What can I do for you?' asked Bell. He put admiring emphasis on the word 'you'.

'I understand you were a passenger on the ill-fated Ndanga flight recently, Mr Bell?' said Steven, not at all sure what he was going to do now.

'I was indeed and d'you know, I still wake up sweating when I think about it, don't I, Simon? There but for the grace of God, I say.'

'You haven't been unwell at all yourself?'

'No, love, right as rain. Can I tempt you to some lunch? We're just about to have ours.'

Steven was taken unawares by the offer, but with his theory shot to pieces and not having anything else to say he replied almost automatically, 'That would be very nice, thank you.'

He sat down at the table and was treated to carrot and coriander soup and a smoked mackerel salad, prepared by Simon and accompanied by chilled Australian white wine.

'Now, what else would you like to know?' asked Bell.

The truth was, nothing, but Steven asked a few questions out of politeness. 'Did you have any contact at all with the sick passenger, Humphrey Barclay?'

'No, thank God. He was in a right state, by all accounts.'

'How about a woman named Ann Danby?'

Bell looked blank. 'No, sorry. Was she on the flight, too?'

'No, she lives in Manchester.'

'Poor woman. Where does she come into it?'

'I don't think she does any more,' said Steven resignedly. 'Have you visited Manchester recently, Mr Bell?'

'Not recently, not ever, if truth be told – and let's keep it that way, that's what I say,' replied Bell, getting a nod of agreement from his partner. 'They say it rains there all the time.'

Steven smiled and said, 'Don't think me rude but can I ask you why you were in Ndanga?'

'Business, love. African arts and crafts. Simon and I run a business marketing African carvings and artwork through zoos and wildlife parks. We needed some new lines so I went over to get them. Got some super carved rhinos. Would you like to see them?'

Steven said that he should really be going, as he had a lot to do. It wasn't strictly true but he did have a date with depression about his wasted journey and for that he needed to be on his own. He had been wrong. Whoever V was, he certainly wasn't Vincent Bell.

The sky had darkened during the course of lunch and it started to rain as he walked back to the car. It suited his mood. He sat for a while in the car park, pondering on the fickleness of fate and wondering what his next move was going to be. Bell was the only male passenger on the manifest with a first name beginning with V, but there had been a couple of females whom he'd dismissed at the time in the light of Ann Danby's valediction about men. He wondered if he'd been wrong to do that. Her comment, he supposed, could have been unconnected with the end of her love affair . . . but he still thought not. That would be just too much of a coincidence. He decided against visiting the females on the list for the time being. Instead, he would have a try at making Ann Danby's mother reveal what she knew about her daughter's relationship. Something told him that she knew exactly who V was.

Steven spent the night in his own flat in London before flying back up to Manchester in the morning. His spirits weren't exactly high when he boarded the aircraft, but when he opened out the newspaper he'd been handed by the flight attendant, they hit rock bottom.

'IS IT EBOLA?' asked the headline.

The story, concentrating on the Manchester outbreak, showed that the paper had identified the source of the outbreak as Ann Danby. It emerged that Ann's mother had telephoned the paper, outraged that her daughter had been portrayed variously as a prostitute and a drug addict by the tabloids, when in fact she was neither. Having got that message across, she had gone on to tell the paper about the questions the authorities had been asking her and her husband. The paper had latched on to queries concerning Africa and connections with people on the Ndanga flight. 'FIVE DEAD IN LONDON, FOUR IN MANCHESTER. HOW MANY MORE?' it wanted to know. It followed up by accusing the authorities of covering up the truth and then drew parallels with the BSE crisis: 'HAVE THEY LEARNED NOTHING?'

'Shit,' murmured Steven, causing the man in the seat beside him to turn and say, 'Nasty business. Is it me or do we get a new disease every time medical science cures an old one?'

'Certainly seems that way,' agreed Steven, but he was thinking that his chances of speaking to Mrs Danby had just gone out the window: journalists from all the other papers would be camping outside her door. When he arrived he went directly to the City General, where he had to wait while a hospital spokesman, grasping his moment of fame and sounding like the returning officer in a by-election, made a statement to the waiting press and TV crews at the gates. 'What we can say at this moment is that the disease is definitely not Ebola,' he concluded. 'Thank you all for coming.'

'How can you be sure at this stage?' yelled one of the pack.

The spokesman gave a superior little smile and said, 'Because the scientists at Porton have assured us that—'

'Porton? Porton Down? The biological weapons establishment? Are you telling us that Porton Down is involved in this?' yelled the reporter.

The spokesman paled. 'This was just a routine—'

'Jesus!' exclaimed the journalist, scribbling furiously. Questions started to rain down on the hapless man. He held up his hands with about as much success as Canute addressing the waves. Everyone wanted to know about Porton Down's interest in the virus.

Steven slipped past the throng and showed his ID to a policeman on the gate, who waved him through with a wry smile. 'Talk about a feeding frenzy,' he said. 'That lot make sharks look like tadpoles.'

Steven found George Byars holding an impromptu meeting in

his office with the head of the Public Health team, Dr Caroline Anderson, and her deputy, a frizzy-haired young man named Kinsella. He was invited to join them.

'Problems?' asked Steven.

'We thought we were almost out of the woods but we're not,' said Byars. 'One of the contacts went walkabout last night.'

'Not necessarily the end of the world,' said Steven.

'The lady in question is the eighteen-year-old sister of the ambulanceman who's lying in the special unit; she sneaked out last night and went to a city-centre disco,' said Caroline Anderson.

'But if she was feeling well enough to go dancing—' Steven said.

'She's feeling ill this morning,' interrupted Kinsella. 'She's got a headache and she thinks she might be coming down with flu.'

'Oh, I see,' murmured Steven, realising the implications.

'I thought we'd convinced all the contacts to wait out the incubation period,' said Caroline.

'You can't convince teenagers of anything they don't want to be convinced of,' said Byars, as if from painful personal experience.

'We were just discussing whether to put out an appeal for all the kids who were in the disco to come forward or . . . whether we should hold back at this stage,' said Caroline.

Steven mentioned what he'd heard the spokesman saying at the gate.

'Damnation!' exclaimed Byars. 'He was supposed to go out there and reassure everyone that it wasn't Ebola. Now it sounds like he's convinced them it's something worse; the virus from the black lagoon. This makes things even more difficult.'

'If I go by the book,' said Caroline, 'I should call the kids in, but do we really think that we can convince a couple of hundred teenagers that they should stay indoors for the next two weeks? My feeling is that we'll just sow the seeds of panic and alarm.'

'Well, it's your call, Caroline,' said Byars quietly.

'I know,' she said with a wry smile. 'I'm not trying to pass the buck. There were two hundred young people in that disco last night. Do I put out an appeal for them to come forward, just so that I can tell them that they've been exposed to a deadly virus that we can do nothing at all about? Or do I hold off until we know more?'

She didn't expect an answer and none was forthcoming.

'Like I say, it's your call,' reiterated Byars.

'I'm not convinced that an appeal would do anything other than cause absolute panic among the kids,' said Caroline. 'I'm going to take a chance and hold off until we know there actually is a problem.'

'After all, we're not sure yet that this girl has the disease,' said Kinsella. 'It could still turn out to be flu or even just a hangover.'

'Then it's decided: no appeal?' asked Byars.

'It's decided. I'm going to leave it for the moment,' said Caroline. 'Maybe we'll know more about the girl's condition tomorrow.'

Byars reminded them that there would be a full meeting at three in the afternoon on the following day, and Caroline and Kinsella left.

When they had gone, George Byars asked Steven about progress in tracing the source of the outbreak.

'I thought I'd found the link between the two outbreaks, but it turned out I was wrong,' confessed Steven.

'Professor Cane's not been having much luck either. This damned virus seems to have appeared out of nowhere.'

'No,' said Steven, 'it didn't do that. That's the one thing we can be absolutely sure about.'

On the way back to his hotel, Steven asked the taxi driver to take him round by the street where the Danbys lived. As he had anticipated, a scrum of cameramen and news reporters were camped outside the bungalow, forcing the cab to slow down to squeeze between carelessly parked vehicles.

'What's *your* interest in this?' asked the taxi driver, his tone betraying irritation.

'Just curious,' replied Steven.

'Poor sods have enough to worry about without rubber-neckers like you turning up.'

'You're probably right,' agreed Steven distantly.

'If you want my opinion—'

'I don't,' snapped Steven, and they completed the journey in an uncomfortable silence.

When he got to his room he ordered coffee and sandwiches from room service and leafed through the Sci-Med file again, looking for anything he might have overlooked. He suspected that it would be a couple of days before press interest in the Danbys died down enough to give him a chance to speak to Mrs Danby. He needed something to do in the interim and his attention finally came to rest on the firm that Ann had worked for, Tyne Brookman, the academic publishers in Lloyd Street. He should have thought of that before, he told himself. Ann might have had a special friend or colleague on the staff there, someone she might have confided in. It was something definitely worth pursuing, but first he would hire a car. It was beginning to look as if he would be here for some time. He asked the hotel desk to arrange it, and a Rover 75 was duly delivered to the car park within the hour.

After a brief consultation with a street map in the hotel reception, Steven drove out of the car park to circle round the south side of the town hall on Fountain Street, intending to enter Lloyd Street. At the last moment he saw that entry was blocked at that end, as it was part of a one-way system, and had to skirt round the block on Albert Cross Street and enter from the west, off Deansgate.

The premises of Tyne Brookman were located in a Victorian building, three storeys high and black with the grime of a century's traffic. The high ceilings were at odds with the poor lighting arrangements, resulting in an ineffectual dull yellow light in the entrance hall and making the place depressingly gloomy. The frosted-glass door marked Reception in black stick-on letters jammed against its frame when Steven turned the handle. It juddered open when he applied a deal more force.

'It sticks,' said the young girl behind the desk, stating the obvious.

Steven showed his ID and asked if he might speak to someone in charge.

'Mr Finlay's out and Mr Taylor's at his brother's funeral,' replied the girl.

'Someone else perhaps?' ventured Steven, wondering why so many firms put an idiot at the interface between themselves and the public.

'Can you give me some idea what it's about?' asked the girl.

'Did you know Miss Danby, who worked here?'

'Not well. She worked in computers.'

'Then how about someone in computers?' he suggested.

'I could try Mrs Black – she works in computers,' said the girl. She posed it as a question and Steven nodded. He looked about him while she made the call. Tinsel had been hung on the plain yellow walls. It fell in vertical strips at intervals of a metre or so. A single smiling reindeer galloped above posters advertising the firm's latest books, pride of place going to *A Molecular Understanding of Protein Interactions* and *A European View of American Corporate Law*.

'A couple of blockbusters there,' said Steven when the girl had finished on the phone. She looked at him blankly, then said, 'Mrs Black will see you. She's on the floor above, in room 112.'

Mrs Black turned out be an extremely attractive fair-haired woman in her mid-thirties wearing a white blouse over a navy-blue pencil skirt. She got up from her desk and offered her hand when Steven entered. 'Hilary Black. What can I do for you, Dr Dunbar?' she asked in a friendly and pleasantly cultured voice.

'I'm not sure,' admitted Steven. 'I'm trying to build up a picture of Ann Danby's life so I'm doing the rounds, speaking to people who knew her. I take it that would include you?'

'She was our systems manager.'

'And you are?'

'I'm now our systems manager; I was Ann's assistant.'

'I see. Did you know her well?'

'She was extremely good at her job.'

'That isn't quite what I asked.'

'We had the occasional after-work drink together, a pizza once in a while, that sort of thing, colleagues rather than friends.'

Steven nodded and asked, 'How would you describe her?'

Hilary Black sat back in her chair and took a deep breath. 'Pleasant, responsible, reliable, intelligent, discreet . . .'

'Lonely?'

'Lonely? No, I don't think so. Ann wasn't lonely. Loneliness suggests a state that's forced on one. That wasn't the case with Ann. People liked her. She kept them at a distance through her own choice.'

'What did you think when you heard that she'd taken her own life?'

'I was shocked. We all were.'

'How about surprised?'

'Yes . . . that too,' agreed Hilary but less surely.

'You hesitated.'

'Ann had something on her mind, something that had been getting her down for at least a month before she died. She hid it from most people, simply because she was used to hiding most things from people, but working together I could tell that she was worried or depressed about something, though she wouldn't say what.'

'You asked her?'

'Yes. I wanted to help but she wouldn't let me. That was Ann, I'm afraid. But now I come to think of it, I remember thinking at one point that she had got over it. It was one day during the week before she died because she came in that day and was all smiles again. But it only lasted the one day.'

'You can't remember what day that was, can you?' asked Steven.

'Give me a moment.' Hilary opened her desk diary and flicked through the pages before tracing her forefinger slowly down one of them. 'It would have been a Thursday,' she said. 'Thursday the eighteenth of November.'

'Thank you,' said Steven. Thursday, 18 November, was the day that had been marked in Ann's appointments diary as the day she was due to meet V – for the last time, as it turned out.

'Mean anything?' asked Hilary.

'Not on its own.' Steven smiled. 'But the pieces are building. Did Ann have a boyfriend?'

'Not that she ever admitted to.'

'That's an odd reply.'

'All right, no, she didn't have a boyfriend,' said Hilary.

'But she did?' ventured Steven.

Hilary conceded with a smile. 'Maybe she did. I had my suspicions. I think he was probably married.'

'I don't suppose she ever let slip a name?'

'I thought she did once but then she covered it up so well that I sort of dismissed it as my imagination.'

'Go on.'

'I was telling her about an interview I'd seen on television with Michael Heseltine. John Humphrys was asking him about the Millennium Dome and she said something like, "Wotsisname says that's a load of rubbish about urban regeneration," and I said, "Who's Wotsisname?" She sort of blushed and said, "Oh just someone I was talking to." I know what you're going to ask now but I don't think I can remember the name. It was just a passing moment.'

'If I were to tell you that his name begins with V?' said Steven.

'Yes,' agreed Hilary, her eyes lighting up. 'I remember now. It was Victor.'

EIGHT

'You haven't said why you want to build up a picture of Ann,' said Hilary. 'I take it it's her illness rather than her suicide that you're interested in?'

Steven agreed that it was.

'It's incredible, the papers are saying it was Ebola.'

'It's not that.'

'But something just as bad?'

Steven nodded. 'Could be.'

'But how would someone like Ann get something like that? She wasn't exactly a jet-setter. I only knew her to go abroad once, and that was a few years ago.'

'That's what I have to find out,' said Steven.

'And you think that this man, Victor, might have something to do with it?'

'I have to explore every avenue, as they say,' said Steven. 'Tell me, were you aware that Ann went hill-walking?'

Hilary looked blank. 'No, did she? That's news to me. She didn't strike me as the sort.'

Steven felt that he'd just made progress. If the hill-walking had been kept secret, it was probably something that Ann had done with Victor. 'Do you think I could see where she worked?' he asked.

'Of course. I decided not to move in there, so you're in luck. Her office hasn't been touched.'

Steven was shown into an office three doors along the corridor. It felt cold and unwelcoming, like a disused cellar.

'Brrr, the janitor's turned the heating off in here,' said Hilary as she clicked on the lights. 'Maybe I should just leave you to it?'

Steven was left standing alone in the office that had been Ann Danby's. It was large, square and high-ceilinged, like all the other rooms. It reminded him of a primary school classroom of yester-year. It had two tall windows that looked out on to a brick wall less than twenty feet away. Steven walked over and looked down at the cobbled lane below, and saw litter blowing about in the breeze and the lights of the early-evening traffic on the main road at the end providing intermittent illumination. He sighed at the thought of working in such a place, sat down at the desk and switched on Ann's desk lamp. The yellow pool of light was a welcome island in a sea of gloom.

Steven found the same meticulous attention to detail in Ann's office as he had found in her flat. Each project she had worked on had its own box file on the shelves above her computer, and the first page in each gave details of where on the computer the master files were stored and where back-up files could be found. She had recently been working on the design of a new payroll system for the company, and the amount of detail listed suggested that Hilary Black would have little trouble in carrying on where Ann had left off. A second project had been concerned with providing computer-generated graphics for the illustrations for a book on Italian Renaissance architecture, which was due to be published by the firm in the late spring.

There was very little in the way of personal effects: no letters or cards that were not concerned with work, and the desk diary had been used exclusively for work-related appointments and meetings, with one exception. Ann had entered details of an appointment to have her hair done on Wednesday, 17 November, at 5.30 at a salon called Marie Claire. The date was interesting; it was the day before she had been due to meet Victor.

There were a number of prints on the walls which Steven presumed were Ann's own: they were mainly of popular Canaletto and Monet paintings but there was a less well known Rory McEwan watercolour of African violets that he paused to admire. The attention to detail was awe-inspiring. He could understand why Ann had liked it. On a bookcase there were a couple of framed photographs featuring Ann herself at company functions. One of them he'd seen at her flat. It was the one where she was wearing a pink suit and shaking hands with a man wearing a chain of office while a number of other men in suits looked on with fixed smiles. In the other she was in a group of people watching a lady with a large hat cutting a ribbon to declare something or other open, although it wasn't clear what.

'A very private lady,' murmured Steven when he had finished. He put out the lights and went along to Hilary Black's office to return the key.

'Find anything?' she asked.

Steven shook his head. 'Not really. She didn't exactly put her personal stamp on things. There are a couple of photographs . . .'

'Our centenary celebrations last year,' said Hilary. 'We put on an exhibition of our published work in the big room on the ground floor. You know the sort of thing, a celebration of all the titles we'd published. Local dignitaries came along and it was opened by the countess of something or other.'

Steven smiled at the irreverence.

'Hardly anyone came, apart from university types. I guess they're about the only ones who understood the titles, anyway,' said Hilary.

'I don't see many of your books on the shelves at WH Smith,' agreed Steven.

Hilary held up a book that had been lying on her desk. '*The Weaponry of Ancient Rome*. It's not exactly the heart-warming story of a boy and his dog, is it?'

Steven smiled and thanked her for her help.

'Any time.'

'One more thing. Can you tell me where I'll find a hairdresser called Marie Claire?'

'Not your kind of place, I would have thought, but it's not too far from here. Turn left when you go out the front door then take the second on the right.'

Steven left the building to find cold, wet drizzle falling. It was putting a fuzzy halo round the streetlights and changing the sound of the car tyres as the evening rush hour got under way. He decided to leave the car where it was and find the salon on foot, which he succeeded in doing without much trouble. He welcomed the blast of heat that hit him when he entered, if not the smell of setting lotion and hair lacquer. He brushed the rain from his hair and turned down his jacket collar as he closed the door behind him.

'I'm afraid we're closing shortly,' said the woman at a semicircular reception bar. 'Would you like to make an appointment?'

Steven stated his business, showed his ID and was introduced to the owner, a busty blonde woman who was fighting a losing battle with the years by hiding behind an excess of make-up. She invited him through to the back. 'How can I help exactly?' she asked in a hoarse voice that suggested she smoked a lot.

'Does the name Ann Danby mean anything to you?' said Steven.

'We've been talking about nothing else all day!' exclaimed the woman. 'There was a story in the papers this morning saying that she was the cause of the outbreak at the hospital. She was in here having her hair done only a couple of weeks ago. I just hope to God *we're* going to be all right. They're saying it's that African thing. My God, I was the one who did her hair.'

'I'm sure you have nothing to worry about,' said Steven. 'Can you remember anything at all about her visit?'

'What sort of thing do you mean?'

Steven went for broke. 'She didn't happen to say why she was having her hair done, did she?'

The woman thought for a moment before replying. 'She didn't say much at all as I remember. Very reserved, she was, or anally retentive, depending on how you look at it. I found it difficult to get a word out of her, but I think she did say in the end that she was going out for dinner. Yes, because I automatically asked her if it was somewhere special and she said, yes . . . the . . . Magnolia, that was it, the Magnolia.'

Steven said, 'I'm a stranger in town.'

'It's a posh place up near the Bridgewater Concert Hall – costs the earth but the food's good. I just wish someone would take *me* there.'

Steven saw the none-too-subtle invitation in her eyes. 'I'm sure they will,' he said diplomatically. He thanked her for her help, and left. He found the concert hall easily enough, but had to spend some time searching for a parking place.

When he eventually got to the Magnolia it had not yet opened its doors to the public; it had just turned six thirty. The lights inside said that there were people about, so Steven knocked on the door. He had to repeat the exercise twice before the slats of the blinds on the door were parted and a hand pointed to the card listing opening times. Steven showed his ID and pointed to the door lock with an opening gesture.

'This really is most inconvenient,' said the man who opened up. 'We've got a full house tonight and we're very busy. Can't whatever it is wait?' He was a stout man with an olive complexion that suggested Mediterranean origins, although he spoke English well enough.

'Sorry, no. It shouldn't take long,' said Steven and stepped inside. The door was locked again behind him and the slats closed. 'I just need to ask you a few questions. You are?'

'Anthony Pelota. I'm the owner. Make it quick please.'

'Did you know a woman called Ann Danby?'

'Never heard of her.'

'She had dinner here on the evening of November the eighteenth.'

'Lots of people have dinner here, but I don't know them personally,' snapped Pelota.

Steven described Ann, and Pelota gave a patronising little smile. 'That would apply to eighty per cent of the women who walk through my door,' he said.

Steven had to concede that the gravitational pull of a place like the Magnolia on executive women in their thirties and their partners would be considerable. 'Can I see your bookings for November the eighteenth?' he asked.

Pelota shook his head. 'No, you can't,' he said. 'That's confidential.'

Steven felt irked. 'Am I missing something? Are you a doctor or a priest?' he asked.

Pelota's smile faded. 'No,' he said, 'but we are known for our discretion here at the Magnolia. Our clientele expects no less.'

'I'm very discreet,' said Steven, 'and I have no interest at all in who's screwing who in Manchester but I would like to see the reservations for November the eighteenth, please.'

'And if I refuse?'

'You'll be obstructing me in the course of my duty.'

'Then what?'

'Proceedings may be taken against you.'

'It strikes me that that kind of publicity might do me no harm at all.' Pelota smiled.

'Your choice,' said Steven, keeping a poker face.

Pelota blinked first. He shrugged and fetched the reservation book from the corner of the cocktail bar and flicked through the pages. Steven watched his expression change as he found the page for the 18th. Something akin to alarm flickered across his face and he frowned as if he had just realised something worrying or unpleasant. 'I'm sorry,' he said. 'I can't help you.'

Steven sensed that further pressure was not going to work – Pelota had obviously made his mind up – so he simply said, 'Then you must take the consequences, Mr Pelota.' He turned to leave but as he got to the door he turned in response to a tearing sound and was in time to see Pelota remove the page from the book.

'Taking discretion a little far, aren't you, Mr Pelota?' he said calmly. 'Just makes me wonder all the more what you have to hide.'

Steven walked back to his car, concluding that, in spite of what Pelota had done, the visit had not been an entire waste of time. He had learned something valuable. Not only was Victor married, but he was also someone with a bit of influence in this city; he was someone important.

On the way back to the hotel he considered what further action, if any, to take against Pelota, now that the man had destroyed what he wanted to see. He could, of course, have him charged with obstruction, but what good would that do, apart from satisfy the desire for revenge? There was no place for pointless payback gestures in his line of work. That was for schoolboys and amateurs. Professionals substituted logic and reasoning for spite and petulance. If the page had been destroyed, Pelota would have to tell him the names that had been on it. It was as simple as that and, with his objective so clearly defined, all that remained was to think how best to go about persuading the man to do just that. It would require a little thought.

Steven was woken by a telephone call at three in the morning. It was Caroline Anderson. 'The girl we spoke about earlier has been brought in to City General,' she said. 'I'm afraid it's the real thing.'

'Damnation,' said Steven.

'It gets worse. Her brother, the ambulanceman, died at one thirty this morning, and four other contacts have called in to report that they're feeling unwell.'

'Just when you take down your umbrella . . .' said Steven.

'It starts to pour,' agreed Caroline. 'Anyway, the meeting has been brought forward to 9 a.m. Everyone is requested to attend.'

'Thanks for telling me,' said Steven.

At 5 a.m. his mobile bleeped twice to herald an incoming text message. It came from Sci-Med and said, 'Read your e-mail, encryption code 5.' He connected his laptop to the phone line and downloaded the message. He rubbed his eyes while the unscrambling program made sense of it. It was short and to the point. 'New case of haemorrhagic fever confirmed in Perth, Scotland. No established connection with Heathrow or Manchester outbreaks. Details to follow.'

Steven stared at the screen, as he read and reread the words 'No established connection'.

'Another bloody wildcard,' he whispered. An epidemic without a source was every epidemiologist's worst nightmare. He tried re-assuring himself that things always looked worse in the wee small hours of the morning, but a filovirus outbreak with no traceable source could wipe out thousands.

The details of the Scottish case arrived before Steven left for the hospital. The victim, Frank McDougal, a forty-year-old assistant bank manager, was already dead. He had died in Perth Royal Infirmary after being taken there in response to a 999 call from his wife. His wife, his eighteen-year-old daughter, a nurse in A&E and a hospital porter had all since gone down with the disease and were in isolation at the same hospital. Public Health were doing their best to locate and isolate contacts.

McDougal had not been abroad since his last holiday in Cyprus last July. He had no connection with anyone on the Ndanga flight, or indeed with anyone in Manchester. His condition had been diagnosed three days after admission to the hospital with suspected viral pneumonia.

'Shit,' murmured Steven. Apart from anything else, he was alarmed that it had taken three days before the Scottish doctors realised what was wrong with McDougal. Something would have to be done about this situation. An alert would have to be sent out to all A&E departments. Hospital staff had to be warned to be on the lookout for filovirus cases. GPs would also have to be alerted.

There were a lot of worried faces in the room when Steven arrived at City General, and his was one of them. The new case was on everyone's mind, with some people learning about it only on arrival. Steven made his point about the need for forewarning. 'It took three days in Scotland,' he stressed. 'The virus can do a lot of damage in three days.' Everyone was in agreement except the Department of Health group led by Sinclair.

'Perhaps a confidential memo to heads of A&E units might be in order,' Sinclair conceded. 'But we must guard against anything that will cause widespread public alarm.'

'Is an epidemic really preferable?' insisted Steven. 'The warning must go out to all front-line personnel. *All* A&E staff and GPs must be included.'

'With respect, Dr Dunbar, I think this area is outside your remit,' said Sinclair with a smile that reminded Steven of the Cheshire Cat in *Alice in Wonderland*.

'It's not outside mine,' Caroline Anderson intervened. 'And I agree with Dr Dunbar. All clinical staff must be warned to be on the lookout.'

'I'll relay your comments to the appropriate ears, of course, but any sort of national decision must be taken at ministerial level,' said Sinclair.

'And probably in both parliaments.' Steven sighed.

'I beg your pardon?' said Sinclair.

'The Scots have their own parliament,' Steven reminded him. 'I presume the DoH in London has been keeping the Scottish Health Minister informed of events?'

The look on Sinclair's face told Steven that he had scored a direct hit in spite of the blustering reply, 'I'm sure all relevant parties have been kept informed of the current situation.'

'It's just a great pity that the staff on duty at Perth Royal Infirmary when McDougal was brought in or his GP were not "relevant parties",' said Steven.

'Ah, such clarity of hindsight,' said Professor Cane, with a sideways sneer at Steven. 'I don't think we can blame our London colleague here for not wanting to cause undue public alarm. The public are subjected to an endless stream of scare stories as it is, and it's not as if we're talking about an epidemic here.'

'I think that's exactly what we are talking about,' said Steven. 'And that's foresight, not hindsight. I take it you and your team have made no more progress than I have in establishing the root cause of these outbreaks, Professor?'

'My team is exploring every avenue, based on the data we have collected. I'm confident that the rigorous application of epidemiological methodology will prevail over more . . . unconventional means.'

'Can we take that as a no?' said Steven, ignoring the insult. 'That leaves us with three outbreaks of a fatal disease and no idea where it's coming from. If things continue like this, we'll be faced with a country-wide epidemic within weeks.'

'But they won't,' insisted Cane. 'This is not the Third World. Medical science is on our side. Panic would be a bigger enemy than the virus.'

'Hear, hear,' said Sinclair.

'There is a middle course,' said Steven. 'Simply saying, "Trust us," is not enough. We have to make sure that hospitals and surgeries are on the lookout for this thing. Containment is an absolute must.'

'Won't the notifiable disease system ensure that anyway?' asked the social work chief, Alan Morely.

'This disease isn't on the list,' said Byars, sounding slightly embarrassed. He responded to looks of disbelief by adding, 'Simply because it's a new virus. The authorities don't know what to call it, I suppose.'

'Might I suggest that "the authorities" put it on the list?' asked Steven. 'Even if they have to call it Mary Jane for the time being?'

'In due course,' said Sinclair.

The ensuing silence made Sinclair's words hang in the air.

'Gentlemen, I think we really must move on to more immediate matters,' Caroline Anderson interceded. 'We've had one new case and there are four new possibles.'

'All of whom are now here in the hospital,' said George Byars, 'but there is a limit to how many more we can cope with in terms of ward space and nurses trained in the appropriate techniques.'

'It's more than likely that these will be the last cases,' said Cane. 'It'll all be over by Christmas.' He laughed at his own joke and his team dutifully followed his lead. Steven couldn't help but think that the last time someone in authority said that, it had been followed by five years of world war.

'I still think we should be at least thinking about contingency plans, in the unfortunate event that we're faced with a more lengthy outbreak than we had anticipated,' said Byars, tiptoeing through a minefield of egos.

'I must say I agree,' said Miss Christie, the nursing director. 'I think it would be an idea to broaden our nursing base for the courses to include nursing volunteers from other hospitals.'

'We might also like to talk to the local council about suitable vacant accommodation that could be pressed into service – in the unfortunate event that the need should arise,' said Byars.

Cane shrugged as if he wanted nothing to do with such considerations, and looked at his watch. He said, 'I'm due to speak with my Scottish colleagues about the outbreak in Perth in ten minutes. We're hopeful of being able to establish a link.'

'Good luck,' said Steven.

'And so say all of us,' added Byars. 'I suggest we all meet again tomorrow morning to assess the situation. Miss Christie, I suggest you contact your colleagues at other hospitals with your idea, and perhaps Mr Morely might speak to relevant council officials about the accommodation issue – purely as a precautionary measure.'

Steven left the meeting with Caroline Anderson. When they were free of the others he said, 'You look like a woman in need of a cup of coffee.'

'I'd sell my soul for one right now,' she replied.

'There'll be no charge.' Steven smiled.

They sought out a local hotel and sat down at a window table in the breakfast room, where they both ordered black coffee and toast.

'What's the problem?' asked Steven, seeing that she was pre-occupied.

'That damned disco,' replied Caroline. 'I've got a bad feeling about it now that the girl's gone down with the disease. I'm beginning to think I should have put out that appeal yesterday.'

'You called it as you saw it and, for what it's worth, I think it was the right thing to do. The appeal wouldn't have made any difference in practical terms. It's not as if you were going to be able to take two hundred people off the streets and lock them away for two or three weeks. The best you could have hoped for was persuading them to stay at home for the period when they're going to infect the people they're most likely to infect anyway: their families.'

Caroline looked at him and smiled. 'Thanks for the support. But I still feel bad because . . . because I . . .'

'You didn't play it strictly by the book, and that makes you vulnerable should the shit start to fly.'

'I suppose that's it exactly,' agreed Caroline. 'You sound as if you're familiar with the feeling.'

'Story of my life,' said Steven. 'Doing what's right isn't nearly as easy as people imagine. In your case the book might say that frightening two hundred kids to death is a good idea, but you and I know differently, especially when dealing with a disease we can do nothing at all about.'

'Thanks. I appreciate your support.'

'Actually, there's something else I'd like you to do that isn't strictly by the book,' he said.

'Hence the coffee.' Caroline smiled.

'That had nothing to do with it,' said Steven firmly. 'Do you think you could spare one of your people to carry out an inspection of a restaurant in town?'

'I suppose so,' said Caroline, a bit guardedly.

'On a daily basis until I say stop?'

Caroline's eyes opened wide. 'Are you serious?' she asked.

'Never more so.'

NINE

Edinburgh

Paul Grossart hitched up the waistband of his trousers as he approached the desk of the George Hotel. He had lost weight recently and his clothes were starting to hang badly on him.

'I'm having dinner with Mr Vance,' he told the receptionist, thinking that eating dinner was the last thing he wanted to do. Food just wasn't high on his agenda these days.

The girl, wearing corporate uniform with a distinctive Scottish theme, pushed her hair back with both hands and checked a small lined notebook in front of her. 'Mr Vance's party is in a private dining room this evening, Mr . . . ?'

'Grossart.'

'Mr Grossart. William will take you up, sir.' She smiled, and summoned the short stocky porter lurking by the stairs and Grossart was led to a small dining room, where he found Vance sitting talking with two other men. His first impression was that the men were not scientists; they were dressed too well.

'Come in, Paul,' said Vance, getting to his feet. 'I thought it best if we met on neutral ground this time round. Drink?'

Grossart asked for a gin and tonic, which Vance ordered before introducing him to the strangers. 'Paul, this is Clyde Miller, a crisis-management specialist, and this is Dr Lee Chambers, one of our in-house physicians and a specialist in infectious diseases.'

Grossart shook hands with both men and sat down.

'How are things?' asked Vance.

Grossart looked at him as if it were an obscene question. 'You *know* how things are,' he retorted. 'Both my people at the field station have called in sick – that's why you're here, damn it. Look, Hiram, this thing has gone far enough. I think we should come clean and be done with it.'

Vance looked at him coldly and said, 'Not an option, I'm afraid. We're all in this together and there's no going back.' He spoke with such finality that Grossart was speechless for a moment.

'And just what the hell do I do about my people in Wales?' he asked when he'd recovered.

'Nothing,' said Vance. 'Absolutely nothing. That's why Clyde and Lee are here. They'll be on their way to Wales first thing tomorrow morning and they'll take charge of everything. They'll see to it that your folks get the best of treatment, should they need it. They'll want for nothing, I promise. All you have to do . . .'

Grossart looked at him expectantly.

'All you have to do is stall the families when they start asking awkward questions. We'll have to sever direct communications with the field station until the situation resolves itself one way or the other, so they're bound to start complaining.'

'And what the hell do I tell them when they do?' complained Grossart.

Vance leaned forward in his seat, all trace of good humour gone from his face. 'You use your initiative, Paul, that's what you do. I fucking well pay you enough!'

Manchester

The first snow of the winter fell on Manchester. It quickly turned to brown slush on the city streets, but the parks and gardens managed to hold on to their blanket of white long enough for Steven to see the irony of a white coat being worn by such a black day. Twelve new admissions were made to City General, thankfully all of them known contacts, while three more people in Perth went down with the disease, again, known contacts of the dead man, McDougal.

Jack Cane avoided eye contact with anyone when he admitted quietly at the morning meeting that no connection between the

Manchester and the Scottish outbreaks had been established, nor was one likely to be. His team had worked all day and right through the night with their opposite numbers in Scotland, but had failed to find a link.

'The damned thing seems to have come out of the blue,' said a weary-looking Cane.

Steven took no pleasure in seeing that all Cane's self-confidence had disappeared and he seemed a broken man.

Cane's comment heralded thirty seconds of silence, before George Byars said, 'So it seems fair to say things aren't looking too good this morning.'

'One of my nurses in the special unit reported sick this morning,' said Miss Christie. 'I think it's serious. She sustained a needlestick injury last week while changing a saline drip. The patient was only semi-conscious at the time: he moved at the wrong moment and the needle went right through her suit into her arm.'

'I'm sorry,' said Byars quietly. The others also murmured muted words of sympathy as if suddenly and painfully aware of how helpless they all were against the virus.

'This is bound to affect morale among the nurses,' said Miss Christie. 'Protective clothing is all well and good in a laboratory, where the virus sits obediently in a glass test tube, but when the reservoir is a delirious patient with flailing arms and blood and vomit leaking out of him, that is a completely different situation.'

'I don't think we can speak highly enough of your nurses, Miss Christie,' said Byars. 'And I am only too aware that the medical staff in this situation are largely redundant. The nurses are the only factor standing between the patients and death. Please make sure that they are aware of our high regard for them, and pass on our thanks.'

Miss Christie nodded and said that she would.

'The papers aren't exactly helping when it comes to morale,' said one of Cane's team. 'Have you seen the latest?' He held up a front page that said, 'Killer Virus Stalks City'. 'Talk about scare-mongering.'

'People are beginning to panic,' said Morely. 'You can feel it in the air. Fear is breeding anger, and they're looking for someone to blame.'

'Perhaps an appeal for calm?' suggested one of the senior nurses. 'Local radio and television?'

'You'd be as well holding up a big sign that says, "Panic!"' said Caroline Anderson. 'People tend not to pay attention to that sort of thing any more. They've been conned too often in the past.'

'And what has the good Dr Dunbar come up with this morning, might I ask?' said Cane.

'Almost as little as you and your team, Professor,' replied Steven, but he was pleased to see that Cane still had some fight left in him. 'But I do have a lead that I'm following up, for the Manchester outbreak at least.'

Cane swallowed and seemed embarrassed at the revelation. 'Are you going to share this with us, or do Sci-Med investigators prefer the Lone Ranger approach?'

'Whatever gets the job done, Professor,' replied Steven evenly. 'Ann Danby had a boyfriend. I'm currently trying to find out who he was.'

Cane looked at the other members of his team, who shook their heads in unison. 'My people seem to disagree,' he said. 'That's an avenue we've already explored thoroughly.'

'She kept it pretty much a secret but she did have one,' insisted Steven. 'I can even tell you his name; it's Victor. He's almost certainly married and has a high-profile job here in Manchester.'

'But you're the only one who knows about this Victor,' said Cane with a barely disguised sneer in his voice.

'No, I think a couple of other people do,' replied Steven evenly. 'It's just a question of persuading them to confide in me.'

Caroline Anderson looked at Steven wide-eyed, as if suddenly realising why she had been asked to put pressure on Pelota. Steven acknowledged her look with a slight shrug and a raising of his eyebrows.

'And are you proposing that this man gave the disease to Miss Danby, Doctor?' asked Cane.

'I think it's entirely possible. I can't say more than that.'

'Then I'm sure we'll all await developments with bated breath,' said Cane.

'As it appears to be the only lead we have, I wish you luck, Doctor,' said Byars. There was a murmur of agreement from all the others except Cane and his people, who had gone into a huddle to murmur among themselves. 'Might I remind everyone,' continued Byars, 'that we are all in this together. There is absolutely no room for petty feuds and academic jealousies.'

'Hear, hear,' said Cane, who obviously knew that the implied criticism had been levelled at him.

'We must keep our nerve and pull together if we are to defeat this thing,' said Byars.

'I'm afraid that matters may be taken out of all our hands in the next few days,' said Sinclair, speaking for the first time that morning. 'My masters tell me that a government crisis-management team is being put together as we speak. If things don't improve by the weekend in terms of case numbers, they'll be brought in to take over control. There's also talk of asking the Center for Disease Control in Atlanta, Georgia, for help.'

'You're bringing in the Americans? That's going over the top, don't you think?' complained Cane.

Sinclair gave his practised diplomatic smile and said, 'I don't think I'm giving away any secrets in telling you that HMG does not want to be seen dragging its heels in this affair.'

'So they've come up with a grand gesture?' said Cane.

'CDC Atlanta have more experience than anyone else in handling outbreaks of these African viruses,' countered Sinclair.

Caroline Anderson collared Steven when the meeting broke up. 'So that's why you asked for the harassment of a law-abiding citizen,' she said.

'Ann Danby had dinner at his restaurant with the elusive Victor the week before she died,' explained Steven. 'Pelota knows who he is but refuses to tell me. Have your people been to see him yet?'

'Yes,' replied Caroline. 'He wasn't at all amused.'

'Good,' said Steven. 'What worries me most right now is the possibility that Victor is a healthy carrier of the disease and doesn't even know it.'

'That *would* be the stuff of nightmares, all right,' agreed Caroline, 'but carrier status has never been shown for filoviruses.'

'I'm clinging to that straw too,' said Steven. 'But that would mean either that he was incubating the disease when he gave it to Ann – in which case why hasn't he turned up as a patient? – or that he was recovering from it and didn't even know he'd had it, which sounds equally unlikely.'

'Beats me,' said Caroline.

'Let's rattle Pelota's cage a bit more,' said Steven.

Things had not improved by the weekend: in fact, they had got worse. Thirty new cases had been admitted to City General between Thursday and Sunday, stretching the nursing staff and ward facilities to breaking point. The only comfort was that all the new cases were contacts of known cases; there were no new wildcards. The depressing thing from Caroline Anderson's point of view was that three of the new cases were contacts of the girl who had broken quarantine to go to the disco.

The government crisis-management team arrived on Saturday, as did an 'advisory' team from CDC Atlanta – two virologists and an epidemiologist. Steven decided to stay out of what he thought might be a recipe for internecine strife but was pleased to see that one of the crisis-management team was Fred Cummings. He arranged to meet him at his hotel on Sunday evening.

By Sunday, the newspapers had decided to upgrade the outbreak to epidemic status. They ignored the official figures required for such an accolade, but no one argued too much. People were dying, so what you called it was irrelevant. Five had died in the last two days and eleven more were on the critical list. Politicians had now decided that the press attention being focused on Manchester merited their presence, and fluttered northwards like moths to a flame to voice their opinions to a frightened public. While government ministers praised the relevant local authorities, opposition spokesmen accused them of bungling ineptitude and cover-ups.

Steven was watching a regional news bulletin on TV in his hotel room before leaving to meet Fred Cummings when a debate between a Labour health minister and a Manchester Conservative MP, introduced as the 'shadow spokesman on health matters', became very heated. The Labour man maintained that the outbreak had been handled in textbook fashion from the outset. The Conservative asserted that he had 'proof positive' that it had not, and that the spread of the disease could be blamed fairly and squarely on the shortcomings of the Public Health Service in the city.

When challenged, he started to relate the story of the disco girl. Steven closed his eyes in dread.

'How could a girl who was suffering from the early stages of a killer disease, and whom the authorities had already listed as a known contact, very much at risk of contracting the disease, be allowed to visit a crowded city disco?' the MP wanted to know. 'And afterwards, what steps did the authorities take to warn the people at risk in the disco? None, absolutely none.'

The government man was forced on to the defensive, claiming weakly that he was 'unable to speak about individual cases'.

The exchange gave Steven a bad feeling; this would be a natural story for the papers to pick up on in the morning and if that happened Caroline Anderson was going to be very vulnerable.

Fred Cummings was wearing one of his usual loud sports jackets when Steven found him in the bar of his hotel. He was also wearing a bright-blue tie with horizontal yellow stripes. Steven wondered for a moment if the man was colour blind but changed this to a positive thought – it made him easy to find in a crowded bar.

'So it's the streets of Manchester, not London,' said Steven by way of greeting.

'I take no comfort from that,' said Cummings, getting up to

shake Steven's hand. 'I thought your involvement in this was over.'

Steven explained that he had been reassigned to investigate the source of the outbreak.

'Some guys get all the good jobs,' said Cummings. 'Heathrow, Manchester and now Scotland, and not even the suggestion of a link anywhere, as I understand it.'

'About sums it up,' agreed Steven.

'Makes you think,' said Cummings, looking thoughtful.

'Makes you think what?'

'Terrorism,' said Cummings.

'Are you serious?'

'Three unconnected outbreaks of a previously unknown virus with a high mortality rate? It's got to be a possibility, don't you think?'

'Frankly, I didn't even consider it,' admitted Steven. 'But now that you've made me, you're right, it is a possibility, albeit a remote one in view of them using individuals as prime targets – a London civil servant, a Manchester computer expert and a Scottish bank manager.'

'Good thinking, Dunbar,' conceded Cummings. 'Just testing. So, give me the low-down on the game and the players.'

Steven filled Cummings in on the management team handling the outbreak so far, and gave his frank opinion of those involved. His conclusion was that he thought the whole thing had been handled well by people who knew what they were doing.

'Who's been in charge of epidemiology?' asked Cummings.

'Professor Jack Cane.'

'Sourpuss Cane? Always looks as if someone has put vinegar in his tea?'

'I've certainly not seen him smile much,' agreed Steven. 'But then he resents my involvement.'

'That sounds like Jack: everything gets done by the book. He is to imagination what Tony Blair is to socialism, a complete bloody stranger.'

Steven laughed. 'I take it you don't rate him,' he said.

'The guy who was bottom of the class at medical school has to end up working somewhere,' said Cummings.

'He's got a chair,' Steven pointed out.

'He married the vice-chancellor's daughter,' countered Cummings. 'A woman with no dress sense, if I remember correctly.'

Steven almost choked on his drink.

'Still, mustn't speak ill of the brain-dead,' said Cummings, getting up to fetch more drinks. When he came back, he asked, 'How about the Public Health woman, Anderson?'

'She's very good but I'm worried about her,' replied Steven. 'Unlike your friend Cane, she doesn't always play it by the book. She dared to use common sense at one stage and I think she's about to pay dearly for it.' He told Cummings about Caroline's decision not to publicise the girl's visit to the disco and about the television news earlier.

'Doesn't look good,' said Cummings. 'The gods might well demand a sacrifice.'

And so it proved on Monday. The papers, as Steven had feared, couldn't resist making Caroline Anderson a scapegoat. She was blamed for the spread of the disease in the city through her lack of 'decisive action at a crucial time', as one of them put it. 'Public Health Chief's Blunder Threatens City', crowed another. Caroline was forced to resign by three in the afternoon.

Steven called her to say how sorry he was.

'They didn't listen to a word I said,' she complained, obviously bemused by the rapidity of events. 'They'd all made up their minds before they even saw me.'

'I don't suppose it's much help right now, but you made the right decision,' said Steven.

'Thanks, but I get the impression people are trying to avoid me this afternoon.'

'Embarrassment,' said Steven. 'They don't know what to say.'

Steven had scarcely put down the phone when it rang. 'All right, you win, Dunbar,' said a voice he didn't recognise.

'I'm sorry, who's this?'

'Just get these Public Health bastards off my back and I'll tell you what you want to know. They're ruining my business.'

The penny dropped: it was Anthony Pelota.

'We close at midnight tonight – assuming anyone turns up after what you bastards have been doing to me. Come round then and I'll tell you.'

'It's a date,' said Steven, elated at the prospect of making progress at last. Another comforting thought was that he might not have to tackle Ann Danby's mother after all. In his book, Ann and Charles Danby seemed two decent people whose life had been turned upside down by their daughter's death. He suspected that respectability had always been a cornerstone of their lives and now they had to cope with the fact that not only had Ann taken her own life, but she was being cited as the cause of a virulent disease. On top of that, she had been wrongly labelled a drug addict and a whore by several tabloids. The Danbys really didn't need him questioning them all over again about their daughter's sex life.

At six in the evening Steven telephoned his own daughter, Jenny, to apologise for not having been up to see her at the weekend. He spoke first to his sister-in-law, Sue, to find out how things had been going.

'No problems at all,' she assured him. 'Jenny was disappointed, of course, that you couldn't come, but the school's planning a Christmas fair and the kids are making the decorations, so that's being keeping all three of them occupied. Jenny's been made responsible for green stars.'

'A big responsibility,' said Steven.

'You'd better believe it,' said Sue. 'I'll put her on.'

Steven felt the usual lump in his throat when Jenny came on the line with a cheerful, 'Hello, Daddy.'

'Hi, Nutkin, how are you?'

'Busy, busy, busy. I'm making stars for the school hall, beautiful green ones.'

'Then I'm sure they'll be the best green stars anyone's ever seen,' said Steven, 'and I look forward to seeing them when I come up there. I'm sorry I couldn't make it this weekend, Jenny.'

'That's all right, Daddy. Auntie Sue said you were busy with sick people, trying to make them better. We prayed for them at school this morning. Miss Jackson said they were very ill.'

'They are, Nutkin, and the sooner I find out where the germs are coming from, the sooner people will stop falling ill.'

'Best get on then. Bye, Daddy.'

'Bye, Nutkin. Love you.'

'Love you too, Daddy.'

Sue came back on the line. 'Any idea how long the epidemic down there is going to run?' she asked. 'There were three more cases declared in Perth today.'

'Something tells me it's going to get worse before it gets better,' said Steven. 'Frankly, we're no nearer finding the source of it today than we were at the outset.'

'That's not a happy thought.'

Steven agreed. He had a word with Sue's kids, Mary and Robin, before hanging up. They asked if they could go to the zoo again the next time he came to Scotland and his 'Maybe' was taken as a cast-iron promise.

The streets around the Magnolia were dark and almost deserted when Steven got there just after midnight. The earlier snow had given way to a clear starlit night which had brought a hard frost to the pavements, and they glistened as he walked from his parking place to the restaurant. The lights were on inside but just like last time the blinds were shut and a 'Closed' sign hung on the door. He knocked on the glass but this time there was no response. He tried several more times before beginning to think that Pelota had changed his mind.

'Shit!' he murmured. More in frustration than anything else, he gave the door handle a sharp twist, and to his surprise the door opened. He stepped inside, paused and called Pelota's name. Still no response. He looked around. The restaurant was warm, the table lights were all on and Mozart was playing gently in the background. He went to the back of the restaurant and pushed open the kitchen door. He found Pelota lying on the floor in a pool of blood.

'Sweet Jesus!' he exclaimed. He bent down to examine the body, which was curled up in the foetal position and facing away from him. The amount of blood convinced Steven that Pelota must be dead, but he was wrong: Pelota gripped his arm weakly and turned to face him. His eyes were wide and his lips drawn back over his teeth in agony. He tried to talk but blood was frothing from his mouth and Steven saw a kitchen knife embedded in his stomach.

'Don't try to speak, old son,' said Steven, freeing himself from Pelota's grip and fumbling for his mobile phone. He punched in three nines and asked for an ambulance and then the police. He gave the bare minimum of information, knowing that his skills as a doctor were pressingly in demand if Pelota was to survive. He stripped off his jacket, rolled up his sleeves and donned a pair of plastic kitchen gloves before grabbing some clean table linen and getting to work on stemming the blood flow.

Stomach wounds were bad, and Pelota's was particularly awful in that there had been intestinal damage: the contents were oozing out into his peritoneal cavity, increasing the danger of infection many-fold. Steven spoke automatically to the man as he worked, assuring him that help was on its way and all would be well soon. Pelota passed out and Steven felt for a carotid pulse; it was still there, but weak.

The last time Steven had dealt with such a wound he had been sheltering in a hollow in the desert while on operation in the Middle East. His patient on that occasion had been a fellow soldier whose insides had been opened by a grenade booby trap. The soldier had died because sophisticated help had been a long way away. Pelota's chances would only be marginally better if he reached hospital in time. He had already lost an enormous amount of blood.

Mozart's 'Eine kleine Nachtmusik' gave way to the even more beautiful sound of an ambulance on its way. The wail of a police car joined the chorus. The thought of police involvement made Steven start thinking about the criminal aspects of what had happened, as well as the measures necessary to keep the wounded man alive. Pelota had a bone-handled kitchen knife protruding from his stomach and presumably he hadn't put it there himself. Was it conceivable that the attempted murder had had something to do with his decision to tell Steven who Ann Danby's lover was? It was a chilling thought. What could be so important about keeping a love affair a secret? What depended on it? A marriage? A career? A reputation? All three?

The ambulance stopped outside the door and two attendants entered the restaurant, carrying emergency equipment. They froze when they saw the man on the floor. 'Jesus Christ!' said one. 'What the fuck?' said the other.

'He's been stabbed in the stomach; there's intestinal damage. He needs intravenous fluid quickly.'

'Who are you?' asked the first attendant suspiciously.

'I'm a doctor and this man needs help fast.'

'No one said anything about this amount of blood. You'll have to wait for a specialist crew.'

Steven couldn't believe his ears for a moment. 'What?' he exclaimed.

'There's a special service operating for high-virus-risk cases,' replied the man, looking down at Pelota.

'This is nothing to do with the virus,' exclaimed Steven. 'He's been stabbed, for Christ's sake, and if he doesn't get to hospital soon he's going to have no chance at all of making it.'

'We'll call a special equipment vehicle,' replied the man, leading his colleague outside and leaving Steven speechless. As they left, two police officers from a Panda car came in.

'Shit! Nobody said it was a bloody murder,' complained the first.

'At the moment it's an attempted murder,' said Steven through gritted teeth. 'He's still alive but he has to get to hospital.'

112

Another police car drew up and two CID officers entered. 'Would you please step away from the victim, sir,' said the first.

Steven looked up from holding an improvised linen swab against Pelota's wound. 'If I step away he'll die,' he said. 'Your call.'

'I'm sure the ambulancemen know what they're doing, sir. So if you'll please just step back . . .'

'The ambulancemen are calling an ambulance,' said Steven evenly. 'I'm a doctor, and right now I'm the only thing between him and that great big kitchen in the sky.'

One of the ambulancemen came back into the restaurant and said, 'It'll be ten minutes. All the specials are out on shouts at the moment.'

There was a brief conversation between police and ambulancemen while Steven continued trying to stem the blood. The ambulancemen were adamant that they weren't going to touch anyone exuding that amount of blood, certainly not without the special protective anti-virus suits.

'So give me your equipment,' said Steven.

The two men looked doubtful.

'C'mon, for Christ's sake. I've got to get a drip into him. He isn't going to last ten minutes like this.'

The ambulancemen opened up their special equipment bag and Steven rummaged among the contents. 'I need saline,' he snapped. One of the men went to fetch it from the vehicle outside. Steven took the saline pack from the man and attached the giving set to it, asking one of the policemen to hold the plastic reservoir above the patient while he inserted the shunt needle into Pelota's arm.

The minutes passed like hours as Steven worked and the emergency services watched. The show came to an end when Pelota's head rolled to one side and his eyes opened but didn't see. Steven felt desperately for a pulse and found nothing. He let his head slump against his chest for a moment before looking slowly up at the others and saying, 'He's dead.'

TEN

It was after three in the morning when Steven finished talking to the police. He couldn't tell them much, apart from the fact that Pelota had been about to help him with his own inquiries, but hadn't got round to it, thanks to the intervention of a kitchen knife. In theory, he wasn't obliged to tell them anything at all, but Pelota had been murdered and police forces tended to resent anyone hiding behind rank or position where murder on their patch was concerned. Steven had no wish to antagonise those he might need help from in the near future, so he had given them all the information he could. The idea, however, that Pelota might have been killed to stop him revealing V's identity he kept to himself for the time being. The police said that they would keep him informed of any progress and gave him a lift over to where he'd left his car earlier.

He drove slowly back to the hotel, where he immediately made for the mini-bar and splashed a miniature of Bombay gin into a tumbler. He added only an equivalent amount of tonic before downing it quickly. What a night, he thought, what a fucking awful night. He threw himself down on the bed and looked up at the ceiling. If only Pelota had survived long enough to say something, things might have been so different. He might well have been talking to Victor by now and on his way to fitting a very large piece of the jigsaw into the puzzle.

But Pelota had died, thanks to those bloody obstinate jobsworths and their bloody union rules ... Steven stopped himself going down this road, recognising that he was being unfair because of pent-up anger and frustration. Ambulancemen were only human like everyone else, and this was the real world, not the realms of TV drama where nurses were angels and doctors saints and the emergency services were crewed solely by self-sacrificing heroes.

The simple truth was that people were people and these days, in Manchester, the virus was uppermost in everyone's mind. The men were probably right to take the stance they had. In fact, maybe it had been his own fault for not giving the emergency operator more information about Pelota's condition; but he simply hadn't had time. Pelota would have died there and then if he'd delayed in order to give details. Oh fuck, what did it matter now, anyway? He was back to square one with a vengeance, and apportioning blame wasn't going to help – as if it ever did. He ran a bath and poured himself another gin, weaker this time.

Lying in the suds, he began to have doubts about his whole approach to the investigation. Quite early on, he had decided that Victor was going to be a crucial player in the game and had concentrated his efforts on finding him. That had been reasonable when it was a case of just two outbreaks of the virus, but perhaps he should have reconsidered when the Scottish outbreak had occurred. Now, at four in the morning, it seemed highly unlikely that Victor could be the missing link to both outbreaks. There was an unpleasant fact to be faced: Victor might be a red herring.

The water had gone cold. Steven stood up and towelled himself vigorously, still wondering about a change in tactics. Even if Victor did turn out to be a red herring, he would still have to find him in order to establish that fact for sure. Of course, if Victor was Pelota's killer, the police might well find him first. In the meantime, and just in case they didn't, he would continue the search.

Although he had never met Ann Danby, he had a soft spot for her. There was something about her and her circumstances that got to him. He wasn't sure why, but he felt an empathy with her. Maybe it was the lack of any real presence in her existence, her lack of personal possessions. People liked her but no one knew her. Her flat had been like a room in a hotel, comfortable but totally impersonal. The same applied to her office.

Everyone had been kept at a distance, except, of course, Victor. She'd been the soul of discretion as far as Victor was concerned, to the point that she had not even kept any mementoes or souvenirs of their time together. There had been no letters from or photographs of the man she had clearly felt so much for, only a book of sonnets with a false declaration of undying love. In fact, there had been very few photographs of anything at all in Ann's flat, come to think of it. He could recall seeing only two, and one was a duplicate of a print she kept in her office.

That thought brought Steven to a jarring halt. Why? he wondered. Why, if Ann hadn't bothered with photographs as a general rule, had she kept two prints of the same one, one in her flat and one in her office? It wasn't as if there was anything remarkable about the photograph; it was just the standard line-up at the formal opening of a dull exhibition. Nothing remarkable or special at all about it . . . unless of course . . . Victor was in it!

Excited at the prospect, Steven decided to drive over to Tyne Brookman as soon as the working day began and ask Hilary Black who the people in that photograph were.

'Well,' said Hilary with a smile, 'Marie Claire didn't change too much about your hairstyle. I thought maybe blond highlights and a quiff . . .'

For a moment Steven couldn't think what she was talking about and then he remembered that the last thing he'd asked her was for directions to Ann Danby's hairdresser.

'I chickened out.' He smiled.

'What can I do for you this time?'

'The photographs in Ann's room. I'd like you to tell me the names of the people in them.'

'I'll just get them,' said Hilary. She left the room and was back a few moments later with both photographs. She put them on the desk and then stood beside Steven.

'This one,' said Steven, pointing to the print of Ann shaking hands with the mayor.

'This is Cedric Fanshaw, our managing director.' Her forefinger moved along the row. 'Tom Brown, our chief editor, Martin Beale, who organised the exhibition, and William Spicer, our local MP. This is the mayor, Mr Jennings, and, of course, Ann.'

Steven looked closely and pointed at Spicer. 'I've seen him before and quite recently,' he said. 'He was on television.'

'A rising star in the shadow cabinet,' said Hilary. 'I think Health is his current bag.'

'That's it,' said Steven. 'He was arguing with a Labour minister about the handling of the outbreak here. He was accusing the authorities of incompetence, and destroying the career of your director of Public Health.'

'Did he deserve it?' asked Hilary.

'He's a she, and no, she didn't. Spicer reckoned the time was right for a scapegoat so he threw Caroline Anderson to the wolves in order to up his profile and further his own career.'

'How unlike a politician,' said Hilary acidly.

'Quite so. Is he married, do you know?'

'Yes, I remember his election leaflets carrying pictures of his wife doing good works, handing out buns to the poor or knitting socks for AIDS victims, that sort of thing. Can't remember her name, though.'

'You're absolutely sure his name is William?'

'Well, yes. I didn't vote for him but he is my MP. I live in silent-majority-land where they're still in mourning for Margaret Thatcher. They'd vote a chimpanzee in as long as it was wearing a blue rosette and had a strong policy on law and order.'

The description made Steven think about Ann Danby's parents. 'So how come you live there?'

'I met my husband at university, where we shared ideals and principles about social justice. We were going to change the world.' Hilary smiled at the memory. 'He finished up by ditching me so he could marry his boss's daughter and become a director of the firm but I got the house out of it, in "a nice area".'

'Life,' said Steven sympathetically.

'I wouldn't have believed people could change so much.'

'The rebels of today usually turn out to be the bald fund managers of tomorrow,' said Steven.

'And with that sobering thought . . .' Hilary smiled.

'Yes, I mustn't take up any more of your time. Thanks again for your help.'

'You're still piecing together Ann's life?'

'Still trying.'

'The outbreak doesn't seem to be slackening off.'

'Things could get a bit worse yet,' said Steven.

'You look tired, if you don't mind my saying so,' said Hilary.

'I had an exciting night,' said Steven.

'Lucky you,' said Hilary.

As he drove back to his hotel, Steven thought again about the men in the photograph. It was a pity that Spicer's name was William and not Victor, because he would have fitted the bill nicely. He supposed that he might be attractive to women in a Tory MP way – chubby face, wavy hair, cheesy smile. He was married, had a high-profile job and was clearly ambitious. Steven decided that it would be worth asking Sci-Med for more information about him anyway. He still felt there had to be a reason why Ann had kept that particular photograph in both her flat and her office, and, apart from the mayor and the MP, she could see the others in the office on any old day of the week. He realised that he hadn't bothered to ask the mayor's first name. Ann might have had a thing about gnarled men in their sixties with small Hitler moustaches who wore heavy gold chains – a bondage thing, maybe? No, forget the mayor.

Steven e-mailed his request for information about Spicer to Sci-Med, then downloaded and decoded the information he had requested earlier about the Scottish outbreak. He spent the next hour going through it, searching for a possible link – however tenuous – with either of the other two outbreaks but failing to find one. He was preparing to drive over to City General when the information on Spicer came through.

The first line of the report made Steven feel that life was suddenly worth living: William Victor Spicer had been a Conservative Manchester MP for seven years.

'Well, well, well,' murmured Steven. 'Got you, Victor!' He read on. The MP had been educated at Ampleforth College before reading Classics at Cambridge and then joining his father's export/import business. He had been appointed export manager with the company and had at one point survived a Board of Trade investigation into the nature of certain items being exported to Arab countries as 'automotive spares'.

A year later he had been adopted as Conservative Party candidate for the Manchester seat which he now held. He had been adopted in the face of stiff competition, because it was generally regarded as a safe Tory seat, and his father, Rupert, was believed to have played a significant role in securing junior's selection. Spicer senior had long been an influential character in the local business community and Conservative Party Association.

'The son shall also rise,' murmured Steven. Spicer was married to 'Matilda, née Regan' and they had a daughter, Zoe, aged seven. He was currently acting as a spokesman on health matters and was widely tipped as a future minister. He supported Manchester City and enjoyed hill-walking. Steven felt that a little gloat might be in order. There was now no doubt in his mind that he had found the elusive Victor.

Spicer had recently returned from an expedition to Nepal, where he had narrowly escaped death through illness. Steven could feel the pulse beating in his temples as he read the story. Spicer and three companions, one European and two Nepalese, had fallen violently ill with altitude sickness when several hundred miles from the nearest civilisation. Spicer was the only survivor when another walking party had eventually come across them.

'Altitude sickness, my backside,' whispered Steven. 'It was haemorrhagic fever, my son, and you lived to tell the tale.'

It made perfect sense. Spicer had fallen ill with haemorrhagic fever while in Nepal but he'd survived and come home to infect

Ann Danby with the virus, which he was still harbouring inside him. It was odds on that he had infected her when they made love on the Thursday when they'd last met, but then it looked very much as if Spicer had ditched her and she had ended up taking her own life.

The spotlight was now swinging away from Ann and the question was no longer how she had got the disease – he'd answered that one. What he had to find out now was how Spicer had contracted it. Steven could see one big plus in this change of emphasis. Unlike Barclay from the African flight and the Scotsman McDougal, Spicer was alive. He was the one prime mover in this affair who could answer questions. This was a cause for elation.

However, it was not going to be plain sailing. Spicer would have to be handled with kid gloves. He'd probably start off by denying any involvement with Ann Danby so Steven would have to win his trust and assure him of complete discretion in the affair, whatever he felt about the man on a personal level. The object of the exercise would be to gain Spicer's co-operation in finding out how he had contracted the virus, not to blow his career out of the water or destroy his marriage.

Steven wondered how best to contact Spicer and concluded that there must be a good chance that the MP had remained in Manchester after his televised spat with the Labour man, just to see if any more political points could be scored by decrying the current handling of the crisis. His Manchester home address and telephone number were included in the Sci-Med report.

Steven picked up the phone and dialled.

A woman answered. She had a plummy contralto voice and Steven immediately had an image of her standing at the gate of her home announcing to a waiting gaggle of reporters that she would be standing by her man in spite of everything. He dismissed the thought and asked, 'I wonder if I might have a word with Mr Spicer?'

'Who's speaking please?'

'My name is Steven Dunbar.'

'My husband holds surgeries on the first Saturday of each month, Mr Dunbar. Perhaps you'd like to go along to one of them? I'll just check when the next—'

'I'm not a constituent, Mrs Spicer,' interrupted Steven. 'It is Mrs Spicer, is it?'

'Yes.'

'I'm an investigator with the Sci-Med Inspectorate. It's to do with the current virus outbreak.'

'One moment, please.'

'William Spicer,' said the voice from the TV programme.

Steven made his request for a meeting.

'I really don't see how I can help,' said Spicer, sounding puzzled.

'Don't worry, I think you can, Mr Spicer,' said Steven cryptically.

'Oh, very well. Come on over tomorrow morning at eleven. I can give you fifteen minutes.'

Steven put down the phone.

At five in the evening, with confirmed cases standing at fifty-seven and eleven more deaths reported, Fred Cummings rang Steven to say that a state of emergency had been declared in the city.

'Justified?' asked Steven.

'No, it's political. HMG are determined to appear on the ball, so we're taking this step, with the support of the CDC Atlanta team, to divert attention from the fact that City General can't take any more virus patients. We're going to start using a couple of disused churches to accommodate new cases.'

'Churches?' exclaimed Steven.

'Yes. I know it's unfortunate and I know Joe Public won't like it, but it makes sense. There's no point in trying to squeeze virus patients into other hospitals where they're not going to benefit anyway because there's nothing anyone can do for them except give them nursing care. They'll just be a danger to everyone concerned. It makes much more sense to house them together, away from other patients and the community and concentrated in an area where trained staff can cope.'

'How are you doing for trained staff?'

'It is becoming a problem,' admitted Cummings. 'We're almost stretched to the limit but we've had a good response to a request for volunteers. Nurses who've left the profession in the past few years have been calling in to offer their services. We've had retired GPs volunteering to help and Caroline Anderson has been working as a volunteer down at one of the churches.'

'Good for her,' said Steven. 'I wondered what she was going to do. Which one?'

'St Jude's on Cranston Street.'

'Maybe I'll go round and see her. She got a raw deal.'

'The vagaries of public life,' said Cummings.

'You didn't say what emergency measures you were bringing in,' said Steven.

'Closure of public places like cinemas, theatres, night clubs and restaurants in the first instance, asking people not to make journeys that are not absolutely necessary, and a leafleting campaign about simple precautions to be taken in avoiding the disease. We're also going to have to insist on cremation of the dead from the outbreak within twenty-four hours. Apart from the mortuary space problem, the bodies are just reservoirs of the virus.'

'It sounds as though you think it might be airborne, after all,' said Steven.

'We still can't be sure,' said Cummings, 'but it's hellishly infective if it's not. Contacts are going down like David Ginola in the box. We could be looking at over two hundred cases before we're through, and that's providing there are no new nasty surprises.'

'Then the new cases are all still contacts?'

'That's the one good thing,' said Cummings. 'There are no new wildcards.'

'Thank God for that.'

'One other thing,' said Cummings. 'Three patients have recovered, so at least we know now that it's not a hundred per cent lethal.'

'Good,' said Steven. He felt sure that he could think of a fourth. 'What's the state of the Scottish problem?'

'Eight cases, three deaths, but they're containing it well. I understand they don't have any high-rise housing schemes to worry about. People have more room to breathe up there.'

'Let's hope their luck holds.'

Steven drove down to St Jude's church and found a police cordon round it. It comprised a series of no-parking cones and striped ribbon tape except for an area near the front entrance, which was guarded by two constables and where ambulances had access. He showed his ID and was permitted to enter. As he walked in through the stone arch he found himself thinking that this was the first time he'd ever entered a church and found it warm. Industrial fan heaters had been pressed into service to raise the temperature to hospital standards. Large signs in red warned against proceeding any further without protective clothing.

At the reception office, he found two tired-looking nurses sitting drinking tea, with an open packet of Jaffa Cakes on the table in front of them. He said who he was, then asked if Caroline Anderson was on the premises.

The older nurse looked at her watch and said, 'She's due for a break in ten minutes. Would you like to wait?'

Steven said he would, but declined her offer of tea. 'How are you coping?' he asked.

'We're running just to stand still,' replied the younger nurse. 'It's a rotten feeling.'

'I can imagine. What about the building itself?'

'Every time I go through there,' said the first nurse, nodding towards the nave of the church, 'I feel like I'm stepping into a scene from Dante's *Inferno*. It's an absolute nightmare.'

The other nurse checked her watch and said to her colleague, 'We'd best get ready.' She turned to Steven and said, 'It takes us a good five minutes to get into these suits. Just wait here, and Caroline will be with you when she's had her shower.'

The older nurse popped a last Jaffa Cake into her mouth and said, 'Once more into the breach . . .'

'Good luck,' said Steven.

Five minutes later Caroline Anderson came through the door accompanied by a woman in her late thirties, whom she introduced as Sister Kate Lineham. Their hair was wet and they were wearing fresh white uniform jackets and trousers. Their faces glowed from the shower.

'What on earth are you doing here?' exclaimed Caroline.

'I came to see you and find out what *you're* doing here,' said Steven with a smile.

'I volunteered,' replied Caroline. 'They stopped me doing what I do best, but they couldn't stop me doing this. I understand all about cross-infection and I can mop up blood with the best of them, so why not?'

'I take my hat off to you,' said Steven.

'You could always take your coat off as well and give us a hand,' said Caroline. 'We're short on staff around here.'

'Are you serious?'

'You're a qualified doctor?'

'Sure.'

'Well, throw your degree in the bucket. These people don't need your medical skills, just simple nursing care and good aseptic technique. Think you could manage that?'

'I can try,' said Steven. 'Where do you want me to start?'

It was the turn of the two women to be surprised. 'Really?' exclaimed Caroline. 'I was only joking.'

'I wasn't,' Steven assured her.

'I'll get you a suit. Oh, and we may both be doctors, but in this "hospital" we do what Kate here tells us. She's a specialist nurse in infectious diseases. Comfortable with that?'

'No problem,' replied Steven.

'We're back on in fifteen minutes. We'll show you the ropes.'

Caroline found a Racal suit for Steven and briefed him on the respirator function. 'We're using a portable entry/exit system the

Swedes developed for dealing with just such a situation,' she said. 'Basically it's just a clean-side/dirty-side system with a shower inter-face. Anything you take through there you don't bring back out again. Okay?'

Steven nodded.

'It's just a matter of trying to keep the patients as clean and as comfortable as possible,' said Kate. 'The only medical procedure we carry out is the replacement of lost fluids, and that's the most dangerous thing of all. Many of them are delirious, so we tend to do it with one of us holding the patient and the other inserting the needle. We've had to resort to tying some of them down to make sure the shunt stays in.'

'The human rights people won't like that,' said Steven wryly.

'Well, they can come and do it their way, and we can all go home and watch the telly,' said Kate.

ELEVEN

Steven made a final adjustment to his respirator and checked for gaps between his cuffs and gloves. Satisfied that all the seals were in place, he followed Caroline and Kate through the improvised air-locked entry port into the nave of the church. He found that the nurse who had likened it to a vision of hell wasn't far wrong. In spite of the nursing staff's best efforts there was still lot of blood around. He had to remind himself that this was Britain in the twenty-first century and not the bloody aftermath of some medieval battle whose fatally wounded had been gathered in a church for the last rites.

Kate showed him where the supplies of swabs and saline and the safe-disposal bins were; many bins were already full to overflowing. She then led him over to the first group of four beds in a line that stretched the length of the church. They were occupied by two young men, a middle-aged man with a salt-and-pepper beard and a man in his seventies. All of them were seriously ill and none was fully conscious, although one was restless and threw his head from side to side as if in the throes of a nightmare. Kate signalled that Steven should start by tending to the elderly man, which he did.

He worked his way along the line of patients, doing his best to make them as comfortable as possible but also finding himself, reluctantly, on a voyage of discovery. The cries of the sick, although muted to a certain extent by his helmet and visor, were still clearly audible and they echoed up to the roof beams and off the old stone walls. They competed with the laboured sound of his own breathing to provide a soundtrack of hell inside his plastic bubble.

He found himself feeling relief that most of the patients were either comatose or only semi-conscious, because he suspected that reassurance and comforting words might well be beyond him. He felt pity and compassion, but revulsion, too. This was a revelation, because it was a gut-wrenching revulsion that threatened to overwhelm him. He wanted to throw up and make a run for it.

Such feelings brought guilt into the equation. He'd always known that he was no Mother Teresa but this . . . this was something else. He switched to autopilot, which he reckoned was the only way he was going to get through the shift. He cleaned up the blood and the vomit, he changed urine- and faeces-soiled bedding and clothing, and all without allowing himself to think too much about it. A job needed doing so he was doing it, period.

Occasionally he sneaked a look at Kate and the other nurses, and felt that they were showing much more care and compassion. Caroline, who was as unused to this kind of work as he was, looked to be doing a thoroughly professional job. He was probably being every bit as gentle, but what was going on in his head worried him. He had an awful suspicion that the nurses weren't thinking the things he was. He was simply operating as a robot that had been programmed to handle eggs without cracking them. He suspected that they felt true compassion.

Steven worked for five hours with only one break of twenty minutes before the night shift came on duty. He was the last to leave the area, as he was the only male worker on the shift and there were no separate showers. When it at last came to his turn, he lingered in the plastic shower cubicle for a long time, leaning on the front panel, head bowed as he sought comfort from the clean, warm water that tumbled over his skin. He fought to come to terms with all that he had seen and with all that he felt.

'You did well,' said Kate when he finally emerged on the clean side of the barrier. 'You too, Caroline, but you're getting to be an old hand round here.'

'Thanks,' said Caroline. She looked exhausted, having worked ten hours that day.

'Well, I'm off home to see my old friends, G&T,' said Kate

with a smile as she slipped on her coat and gathered her belongings together. 'Will I see you tomorrow, Caroline?'

'I'll be here.'

'Nice meeting you, Steven. Thanks for your help.'

'It was little enough,' said Steven. 'Nice meeting you, too.' They shook hands and Kate left without a backward glance.

'She's nice,' said Caroline.

Steven nodded.

An ambulance drew up outside with a new patient and Steven and Caroline stood to one side to allow the spacesuit-clad attendants to bring the stretcher inside. Caroline made sure the night nurses were aware of the new arrival before following Steven out into the cool night air. 'Where are you going to eat?' she asked.

'I'll get something at the hotel,' said Steven. 'I'm not really that hungry.'

'I felt that way too after my first shift. You have to eat something. I could do us both an omelette. What d'you say?'

Steven nodded. 'Sounds good,' he said, but the truth was that he was more interested in the company than in food; he wasn't ready to be alone with his thoughts. He followed Caroline's car through the city streets to the terrace where she had a modern detached house on a newish housing estate. It backed on to the railway, a fact that made itself apparent when a commuter train passed by on an embankment some ten metres above street level.

'My own train set,' said Caroline as she fumbled for her keys. 'Come on in.'

Steven stepped into a warm house where the central heating hummed comfortingly and the living room was quickly transformed into a cosy refuge from the outside world with the switching-on of lights and the closing of curtains. 'Drink?' Caroline asked.

'Gin would be good,' said Steven.

'For me, too. Why don't you fix the drinks and I'll make a start in the kitchen,' said Caroline. She pointed to the drinks cabinet and Steven got to work.

'You live alone, then?' said Steven when he took Caroline's drink through to her.

'I do now,' replied Caroline. 'Mark and I parted when he found out I couldn't have children. We've been divorced two years now. He re-married last month. She's an air stewardess.'

'I'm sorry,' replied Steven quietly, slightly taken aback at Caroline's frankness and not knowing quite what to say.

Caroline took the matter out of his hands. She turned and said, 'So what's bugging you?'

He automatically went on the defensive. 'Nothing,' he replied evasively. 'I guess I was just a bit shocked by what I saw down at the church.'

Caroline looked directly at him and said doubtingly, 'A bit shocked? I was watching you. The man who came out of that church was different from the one who went in.'

Steven took a sip of his drink as a delaying tactic but found that he had no heart to continue sparring. 'I suppose I found certain things out about myself that I didn't like,' he confessed.

'Then I suggest you get them off your chest before they take up residence,' she said. 'That kind of a lodger can make your life a misery.'

He gave a wry smile. 'I've managed to kid myself for years that the reason I never practised medicine as an ordinary doctor was because I needed more excitement in my life. I needed a physical challenge, travel, adventure, any old excuse. Today I found out that it was a lie. I've been fooling myself. I was running away from the truth.'

'Which is?'

Steven found the words hard to come by. After a few moments he said, 'I don't think I like people enough to practise medicine the way it should be practised. I don't think I have it in me to care enough.'

'You were doing a good job down at St Jude's; I saw you.'

'But the feeling wasn't there.'

'Do you think the patients would have noticed if the "feeling", as you call it, had been there?'

Steven shrugged and thought, before saying, 'I suppose not in a practical sense. I guess most of them were out of it, anyway, but quite frankly I spent most of the time wanting to run out of that place and keep on going.'

'But you didn't. And that's the important thing. You did exactly what the rest of us were doing.'

'I got through it. That's different.'

'That's what we were probably *all* doing,' insisted Caroline.

'The nurses seemed to take it in their stride.'

'It's their profession. They have a professional face.'

'But so should I.'

'No,' countered Caroline. 'You have a medical degree but you're an investigator and let me tell you, if you manage to find out where this damned virus is coming from, you'll have done more good than all the rest of us put together. Horses for courses.'

Steven was unconvinced. He shrugged and finished his drink.

'Believe me, Steven Dunbar,' said Caroline, 'in my time I've come across a few cold-fish doctors who lacked any vestige of human concern for the sick, but you are not one of them. A little too self-critical, perhaps, but your heart's in the right place.'

Steven smiled for the first time and took the empty glass she held out.

'Let's have another,' she said.

Steven wasn't sure whether it was the gin or Caroline's words that made him feel more relaxed but he enjoyed his omelette and the Californian white wine that appeared on the table.

'Can I ask what your plans are now?' he asked when they moved with their coffee to the fireside.

'I'm not sure. I know I'm not really supposed to be involved in the outbreak any more but I still feel that I am, if you know what I mean. It was *my* city, *my* responsibility. When it's over I suppose I'll have to start applying for Public Health jobs some-where else and start again.'

'The MP who forced your resignation . . .' said Steven.

'Spicer? What about him?'

'He's the "Victor" I've been looking for.'

Caroline's eyes opened wide. 'You're kidding!'

Steven shook his head. 'Nope, he's the man.'

'Well, what d'you know? What goes around comes around.'

'I'm going to see him tomorrow and tackle him about his relationship with Ann Danby.'

'You still think it was him who gave her the disease?'

'I'm almost certain,' Steven said. He told her about the ill-fated expedition to Nepal. 'I don't think it was anything to do with altitude sickness,' he said.

'But even supposing it really was haemorrhagic fever, how on earth did he manage to become infected with the same filovirus strain as the Heathrow man and the chap up in Scotland?'

'That's what I have yet to find out,' said Steven. 'And getting Spicer's co-operation isn't going to be easy. He's a politician so he's bound to try and bluster his way out of trouble. Can I count on you if I need help in fitting the bits into the puzzle?'

'Of course,' replied Caroline. 'If I'm not here I'll be down at St Jude's.'

Steven spent a restless night, with visions of the scenes he'd witnessed intruding on his dreams. He was glad when day broke on a grey December morning with a peculiar colouring to the clouds suggesting that there might be more snow on the way. He had plenty of time before his meeting with Spicer, so he had breakfast in the hotel dining room and settled down to read the morning papers before leaving. The Manchester outbreak was still the lead story in all of them as it had been for the last few days. This in itself meant that their editors were now trawling the outer limits for new angles on the story.

'Only the Beginning', suggested one, which painted a scene of new plagues arriving almost on a monthly basis from the African continent. Another gave considerable space over to church leaders for their view of things, the wickedness of man ending up carrying the can as usual. Special prayers would be said at churches all over the nation on the following Sunday, the paper announced. More extreme religious views were also accommodated with a report of an obscure sect announcing that the outbreak heralded the end of the world – something they had mistakenly predicted would happen at the dawn of the new millennium. God had decided to go for a slow, lingering death rather than a sudden decisive end, they maintained. 'In his infinite mercy,' added Steven under his breath.

He arrived at Spicer's house a few minutes before eleven. It was a substantial Victorian villa in a pleasant area with the upper floors commanding uninterrupted views across the city from its elevated position. He walked up the short drive, his feet crunching on the gravel, and rang the bell, noting, as he waited, the sleek green nose of an XK series Jaguar protruding from the double garage at the side of the house.

The door was opened by a blonde, Nordic-looking girl who smiled, showing perfect white teeth. 'Hello,' she said. 'What you like?'

'Hello,' replied Steven. 'I have an appointment to see Mr Spicer. My name is Dunbar.'

'It's all right, Trudi,' said a woman coming up behind the girl. 'I'll see to it. I'm Matilda Spicer, Mr Dunbar. Do come in. Trudi's our au pair,' she said as she showed Steven into one of the front rooms. 'Victor will be with you shortly.'

'I thought your husband's name was William, Mrs Spicer,' said Steven.

'It is, but he prefers friends and family to call him by his middle name. When he first went into politics his electoral agent thought that Vic Spicer sounded like a used-car salesman so he's William to the voters.'

Steven smiled and she left him on his own.

There was a piano in the room, an old upright finished in walnut with brass candleholders bolted to the front. The lid was open and Steven looked at the music that was propped up on the stand above the yellowing keys: it was Debussy's 'Claire de lune'. He deduced that the Spicers' daughter must be learning to play.

There were framed photographs on top of the piano; the largest featured the family with Matilda seated in front, cradling her daughter, while Spicer stood behind with a protective hand on his wife's shoulder and a good, jutting jawline in evidence.

The door opened and Spicer came in. He wore a dark-blue suit with a red-striped Bengal shirt and a maroon silk tie. His wavy fair hair was brushed back and rested comfortably on his collar at the back, making him look younger than his forty-two years. He had a brusque, business-like attitude.

'I can only give you a few minutes,' he announced. 'I have to be on television at midday. I take it you have some kind of identification?'

Steven handed over his ID card.

'You're a doctor?' said Spicer.

'I'm an investigator first,' replied Steven.

'Let's talk in my study,' said Spicer. 'But, as I said on the phone, I can't imagine how I can help you with your inquiries.'

Spicer led the way through to his study and sat down behind his desk, indicating that Steven should sit down on one of the two seats on the other side of it. Steven noticed that the man was adopting what he suspected might be a well-practised pose. He was leaning back in his leather chair with his legs crossed, his elbows resting on the arms and his fingers interlaced while he tapped his thumbs together. Statesmanlike or what? thought Steven. More family photographs sat on the desk, making him wonder whether Spicer had requested an interior designer to do out the place in 'family values'.

'I take it you are familiar with the chain of events that led to the current virus problem in Manchester, Mr Spicer?' asked Steven.

'As I understand it, it all started with this Danby woman,' said Spicer. 'What should have been a minor outbreak has now escalated out of all proportion, thanks to the bungling of those in charge.'

'You, of course, would have handled it differently,' said Steven, almost falling at the first hurdle because he had allowed Spicer to anger him by referring to Ann, his former lover, as 'this Danby woman'.

Spicer seemed a little taken aback. 'Not me personally, of course – I have no training in such matters – but that's no reason to tolerate incompetence in those who are supposed to have.'

Steven bit his tongue. He needed this man's co-operation, he reminded himself. 'I understand that you were in Nepal recently and that you were very ill while you were there,' he said.

'What's that got to do with anything?' asked Spicer.

'Can I ask who diagnosed your illness?'

Spicer shrugged and said, 'There was no diagnosis as such, because we didn't have a doctor with us. I survived; my three companions didn't; that was the bottom line. When I got back to civilisation and described the symptoms of the illness – those I could remember! – it was generally agreed that it had been a severe form of altitude sickness.' He looked at his watch and said testily, 'Look, I really can't give you much longer. Would you please come to the point?'

'I don't think you had altitude sickness at all, Mr Spicer. I think you were suffering from viral haemorrhagic fever.'

Spicer looked as if he couldn't believe his ears. 'Haemor . . . ?' he spluttered. 'You mean the disease that's out there in the city? What utter nonsense. Are you out of your mind?'

'I think you contracted haemorrhagic fever and survived,' continued Steven. 'You're one of the few. Then you came home and passed on the disease to your lover, Ann Danby.'

Spicer paled and for a moment looked like a cornered animal, then he went on the offensive. 'Oh, I get it,' he rasped. 'You're one of these Labour leftie shits who've come up with a little scheme to attack me and save your minister further embarrassment.'

Steven said coldly, 'I am neither leftie nor rightie, nor am I Liberal or Monster Raving Loony. In fact, you won't catch me at a polling station until they put a box marked "None of the Above" on the ballot paper. My experience over the years has taught me to distrust politicians of all shades and hues, Mr Spicer. Now, shall we continue?'

'Dunbar, I am going to see to it personally that you—'

'Save your breath,' interrupted Steven. 'Bluster isn't going to work with me. Why don't you just tell me the truth and save us both a lot of time, assuming you can still recognise it after seven years in parliament?'

'How dare you!' stormed Spicer.

'I dare because I *know* that you had an affair with "the Danby woman" as you had the gall to call her a moment ago. She was a decent woman, by all accounts, and she ended up taking her own life over a little shit like you.'

'I know nothing at all about her,' insisted Spicer, fighting to get his temper under control.

'You gave her a book of Shakespeare's sonnets and inscribed the fly leaf, "My love for ever, V."'

'My name is William.'

'You like to be called Victor, Victor.'

'I tell you, I didn't know the woman,' repeated Spicer, red in the face.

'It was your handwriting; I had it analysed,' lied Steven, sensing that he had the upper hand.

The blood drained from Spicer's face and he sat motionless for a moment before leaning forward slowly to rest his arms on the desk. He finally hung his head and said quietly, 'All right, I did know Ann. These things happen. I'm only human, damn it.'

Steven was not prepared to concede the point.

'We met at some bloody awful exhibition her employers were putting on and it just sort of went on from there. It was stupid, I know, but like I say, these things happen. You're not going to pretend that they don't?'

'I wouldn't dream of it,' said Steven evenly.

There was a slight knock on the door and it opened immediately. Matilda Spicer put her head round and said, 'I hate to interrupt you boys but you're going to be late, darling.'

Spicer didn't look up. He said in a strained croak, 'Matilda, would you telephone the TV people, make my apologies and say that I will be unable to appear today.'

'Is everything all right?' she asked worriedly.

'Fine, fine. I'll explain later.'

The door closed and Spicer said, 'You do realise what this will do to my wife? It will destroy her.'

Steven looked at Spicer as if examining a particularly uninteresting species of pond life. 'My only concern lies in finding out where this virus came from,' he said. 'A lot of people have died. I need you to tell me everything you know.'

'What can I tell you if I didn't even know I had it?' spluttered Spicer.

'First, I need you to give me a blood sample so that it can be tested for antibodies to the virus. That will establish beyond doubt—'

'That I was the cause of the outbreak?' completed Spicer. He sounded shaken, as if realising the full implications for the first time.

'Here in Manchester, yes,' said Steven.

'And if I refuse?'

'That's not an option,' said Steven.

'But it's not conclusive yet, is it? It could be negative. I mean, it could still turn out that I had nothing to do with the outbreak or Ann getting the disease?'

'Theoretically,' agreed Steven, 'in the way that six million people could suddenly visit the Millennium Dome in the next four weeks. You used to go hill-walking with Ann?'

'I took it up last year. Ann was new to it, too. We both enjoyed it.'

'You saw her on a number of weekends and then there was a long gap in her diary. That was when you went off to Nepal?'

Spicer nodded.

'When you came back you had dinner with her on Thursday the eighteenth, and that was the last time you saw her?' said Steven.

Spicer hesitated, as if searching for words. He said, 'When I was close to death in Nepal I came to see just how much my wife and daughter meant to me. I decided to end it with Ann when I came back. You can understand that, can't you?'

Steven nodded, then asked, 'How did Ann take it?'

'Very badly.'

'But you still made love to her that night,' said Steven flatly.

Spicer swallowed. 'It was impossible not to,' he said. 'She was all over me. God, I'm only human.'

Once again, Steven did not concur. 'That was the night you gave her the virus,' he said.

'Christ, I wasn't to know,' said Spicer. 'How the hell could I?'

'You made love to her, then you left her, and Ann took her life a few days later. Sound about right?'

'Give me a break. I didn't know the silly cow was going to do anything like that, did I?'

Steven's right hand balled into a fist but he kept control. 'I suppose not, Mr Spicer,' he said. He let a few moments go by before saying suddenly, 'So why did you kill Anthony Pelota?'

'What the hell are you talking about?' blustered Spicer.

Steven stared hard at him, suggesting total imperviousness to bluster. After a few seconds' silence he noted with some satisfaction that Spicer's expression was changing; his defiance was being undermined by a decidedly hunted look.

'I know Ann ate at the Magnolia that Thursday,' continued Steven flatly. 'Pelota was about to tell me who her dinner companion was. It was you, wasn't it?'

'So what if it was? There must have been twenty other people there that night,' retorted Spicer.

'They didn't kill Pelota, Spicer, you did, and you didn't wear gloves when you stuck that kitchen knife in him, did you?' Steven was taking a gamble; he saw from Spicer's expression that he was right. 'Was he blackmailing you?' he demanded. 'Was that it?'

All the fight went out of Victor Spicer and his shoulders sagged. Almost inaudibly, he said, 'The little wop called me to say that someone had been making inquiries. He made a great play of how discreet he'd been and then suggested that I might care to show my gratitude.'

Steven nodded impassively.

'We agreed on five hundred pounds but when I went along there he raised the price to a thousand, and I just lost it. I knew that that wouldn't have been the end of it. The red mist came down. We argued and fought. I grabbed the knife. You know the rest. What happens now?'

Steven said, 'If you answer all my other questions, I'll give you some time alone with your wife to prepare her for what she'll have to face, then I'll have to call the police. You do realise that your wife has been at risk of contracting the virus too?'

Spicer's eyes opened like organ stops. 'What d'you mean?' he stammered.

'The virus remains in the body fluids of someone who recovers from a filovirus infection for some time afterwards; that's how Ann got it. If you've made love to your wife since your return, well, you can work it out.'

Spicer took a few deep breaths before saying, 'As it happens, I haven't . . . because of my illness . . .'

'No need to worry, then,' said Steven, but to his puzzlement he noticed that Spicer's expression was not one of relief.

TWELVE

Edinburgh

Karen Doig left Paul Grossart's office feeling as if the bottom had fallen out of her world. She walked slowly down the stairs in a daze and out through the front door without really seeing anything or anyone. It was raining heavily but she didn't notice as she walked hesitantly across the car park to where she'd left the car. Not even the deep puddle that lapped over her shoes as she unlocked the door seemed to register with her. She sat stock-still and stared unseeingly through the windscreen for fully five minutes before driving off.

Karen's mother, Ethel Lodge, who had come over to baby-sit her granddaughter, Kelly, opened the door as Karen drew up outside her house, a smart semi-detached villa on the new Pines estate on the outskirts of Edinburgh.

'You're drenched, love,' fussed her mother. 'Give me your coat or it'll drip all over the place. I'll hang it up in the kitchen. Go and warm yourself by the fire. The kettle's just boiled. I'll make some tea.'

She brought through two mugs of tea and handed one to Karen. 'Well, what did Mr Grossart have to say for himself?' she asked. 'Any news?'

Karen looked at her with tear-filled eyes. 'Oh yes,' she said quietly, 'Peter's left me. He's run off with Amy Patterson.'

'Who the hell's Amy Patterson?' exclaimed Ethel, sinking slowly into a chair.

'The scientist Peter went to Wales with.'

'I don't believe it.'

139

'That's what Mr Grossart told me,' said Karen. 'He said he was sorry but there was nothing he could do about it. If Peter didn't want to talk to me about what had been going on, that was his prerogative. The company couldn't involve itself in domestic matters.'

'But this is absolutely crazy!' exclaimed Ethel. 'You two are so happy together.'

'That's what I thought too,' said Karen distantly. 'I can't . . . believe he's done something like this.' She buried her face in her hands, and her shoulders heaved as she sobbed silently.

'Oh, love, there has to be some mistake, Peter wouldn't do something like this. You two have everything going for you and you know how much he dotes on Kelly. What did this man Grossart say exactly?'

'I asked him if he knew why Peter had stopped phoning me and why there was never any answer from the number I'd been given for the Welsh field station. I was worried and angry . . . I demanded an explanation . . . and he gave me one. He said that the pair of them had gone off together and he'd no idea where. He'd only just heard about it himself.'

Ethel Lodge looked at her daughter, sharing her distress as only a mother can. 'I don't believe any of this,' she said. 'People don't just do things like this without having anything planned beforehand. Peter didn't give you any cause to suspect that anything was wrong, did he?'

Karen shook her head. 'No,' she whispered, 'absolutely not.'

'Well, you can't live on love alone, despite what the songs may say. You need money and clothes and food and a roof over your head. Have a look in the wardrobe and see what he took with him, then phone the bank and find out if he took out any money.'

Karen looked at her mother, seeing in her an inner strength she hadn't realised was there.

'You do love him, don't you?' asked Ethel.

'Yes.'

'Then start fighting, girl.'

Karen checked her husband's wardrobe and found that most of his clothes were still there. He'd taken just what he said he was going to take, 'the bare minimum', as he had put it, because there was 'no one to impress at the field station, apart from the animals'. As soon as she remembered it, the thought planted a seed of worry in Karen's mind. Maybe the loneliness of being marooned in rural North Wales when the days were short and the nights were long had brought Peter and whatsername together. But even if it had, surely it would have just been a physical thing? Peter wouldn't have abandoned her and Kelly over something like that . . . would he?

'Anything missing?' asked her mother when she went back downstairs.

'Nothing,' said Karen.

'Good. Get on to the bank.'

Karen did as she was told and contacted the bank to ask about account balances. 'Nothing taken out,' she reported.

'Drink your tea,' said Ethel. 'It's getting cold.'

Karen sipped her tea.

Ethel stared out at the rain-swept garden. 'Do you know this Patterson woman?' she asked.

'I think I may have met her once at a works barbecue in the summer.'

'Did she seem the type?'

'What type?'

'You know what I mean.'

'I thought she was a bit mousy, to tell the truth, a typical blue-stocking, all ethnic skirt and glasses. Didn't strike me as Peter's type at all. She and her husband went on about their bird-watching trips. Peter can't tell a thrush from an ostrich.'

'Then she's married, too?'

'That's a point. Maybe I should get in touch with her husband?'

'You certainly should,' agreed Ethel. 'It'll be interesting to find out if he's as surprised as you.'

The sound of crying came from upstairs. 'Oh, Kelly,' murmured Karen as she leafed through the phone book. 'Give me a moment.'

'I'll see to her,' said Ethel. 'Sounds like the afternoon nap's over.'

Karen started dialling her way through the Pattersons in the local book, asking each time if she had the right number.

She was on her eighth call when a man's faltering voice said, 'I'm afraid Amy's not here at the moment.' He sounded upset.

'Are you Amy's husband?' she asked.

'Who's that?'

'Karen Doig, Peter's wife. I take it you've heard?'

'I just can't believe it,' said Patterson.

'You didn't suspect?'

'No, nothing. Paul Grossart's call came completely out of the blue. You?'

'The same. Look, maybe the company's wrong about this,' said Karen, her confidence growing by the minute. 'Peter didn't take any extra clothes with him and he hasn't touched our bank account.'

'So what are you suggesting?'

'Just because the pair of them have disappeared doesn't necessarily mean that they've run off together. Maybe that's an assumption on the company's part.'

'I hadn't even considered that,' admitted Patterson.

'Nor had I until this very moment.'

'My God, they could have been involved in some kind of accident or be lost somewhere in the hills . . . or anything!'

'I think we should go to the police,' said Karen. 'Right now.' She turned to look at her mother to see if this were possible. Ethel nodded, and Karen and Patterson arranged to meet outside the police station in fifteen minutes.

'Thanks, Mum,' said Karen as she put down the phone and started rushing around.

'It won't hurt your father to get his own tea for once,' said Ethel. 'Off you go.'

Karen recognised Ian Patterson as soon as she saw him. She remembered the thin, serious man who had been wearing a T-shirt with 'Save the Planet' on it at the summer barbecue. Today he was wearing a waxed cotton jacket over a Shetland sweater, dark-green corduroy trousers and thick-soled brogues. They didn't shake hands and Karen could only just manage a wan smile. 'Shall we go in?' she asked.

They had to wait in line in the police station, which smelt vaguely of disinfectant, its institution-green walls adorned with a variety of warnings and posters promising rewards for information. It was an alien world, thought Karen as she waited patiently while the man in front tried to explain why he couldn't produce his driving licence.

She had to step back as the man, having been given a further twenty-four hours, wheeled round sharply and barged his way out. She stepped forward to the desk and explained to the middle-aged sergeant why she and Patterson were there.

'Nothing we can do' was the verdict he offered almost before she'd finished. He closed the daybook with a slap as if to emphasise his point.

'What do you mean?' exclaimed Karen, taken aback at his offhandedness. 'You've got to do something. It's your job. Two people have gone missing!'

'They're both adults. If they choose to go off together, it's not against the law. I'm sorry but we can't get involved in domestic matters like this,' said the sergeant.

'But they didn't "choose to go off together",' exclaimed Karen. 'They've disappeared and they could be lying injured somewhere. Surely you don't want that on your conscience? Can't you contact the Welsh police and ask them to check?'

A queue was building up, making the sergeant uncomfortable. He picked up the phone and after a short conversation he said, 'Inspector Grant will have a word with you, madam. He'll explain our policy on these matters.'

Karen and Patterson were shown into a small office which lacked light, space and anything resembling charm. They were invited to sit on two hard chairs and Karen felt that they had been called to the headmaster's study to account for some misdeed. This time, Patterson had a go at explaining what had happened, with interjections from Karen where appropriate. At the end of it Grant nodded sagely and said more or less what the desk sergeant had. 'The police really can't become involved in domestic matters.'

'But can't you see that it's only an assumption on the company's part that Peter and Ian's wife have run off together? They could just as easily have had an accident or be lying injured somewhere out on the hills.'

Grant looked at her thoughtfully. 'This man who told you they'd run off, you said his name is Grossart?' he asked.

'Paul Grossart at Lehman Genomics. He's the managing director.'

'Phone number?'

Karen recited the number and Grant wrote it down. He got up and went to another room. When he came back he said, 'I'm sorry but there really is nothing we can do.'

'What did Mr Grossart say?' demanded Karen. 'Did he offer you one scrap of evidence that Peter and Amy had run off together?'

Grant looked uncomfortable. 'Well, no,' he admitted. 'But employers do get a feel for these sorts of things. I know it's difficult for you, and I do sympathise, but frankly this sort of thing happens much more often than you'd think.'

'Then you won't help us?'

'Not so much won't as can't,' said Grant. 'As the law sees it, they're both adults and this is a free country.'

Karen ran out of adrenalin. Her shoulders sagged and she felt a wave of hopelessness wash over her. Tears started to run down her face and she hung her head.

It seemed to have an effect on Grant. 'Did they both take their cars with them to Wales?' he asked.

Karen shook her head. 'No, the company provided transport.'

'The same for your wife, sir?'

Patterson nodded. 'They travelled down together.'

'Mr Grossart hasn't reported the loss of a company vehicle,' said Grant thoughtfully. 'Where is this field station?'

Karen looked blank. She looked at Patterson, who shrugged.

'Neither of you knows?'

'I don't think Peter knew exactly,' said Karen, feeling embarrassed about it.

'Amy didn't say, either,' said Patterson.

'So you couldn't write to them or send them anything, even if you had wanted to?'

'I suppose not,' agreed Karen. 'Not that the need arose. I suppose we could have sent things to them through the company. We had a telephone number, though. I used to speak to Peter every night at the beginning.'

'And me with Amy,' said Patterson.

Grant said, 'That's something. Have you got the number?'

Karen checked her handbag and handed over a piece of paper. Grant excused himself and was gone for several minutes. When he came back he said, 'I've checked with Mr Grossart about the transport. He thinks they travelled to Wales in a company Land-Rover but he's not sure.'

'Not sure?' exclaimed Karen and Patterson in unison.

Grant's look suggested that he might share their surprise. 'He's going to get back to me with details of the vehicle and registration number and whether or not they want to report it missing.'

Karen and Patterson went quiet for a moment while they digested this information.

'I have to stress once again that there's nothing we can do in a situation like this, unless of course the vehicle is reported stolen, but . . . in the interests of . . . crime prevention, shall we say, I might just pass on the registration number to our Welsh colleagues. If the vehicle should still happen to be in North Wales, they might care to stop the driver and enquire about ownership and destination.'

'Thank you,' said Karen.

Ian Patterson added his thanks. 'It's really the not knowing,' he said.

'As for the telephone number Lehman gave you,' said Grant, 'it's ex-directory so I can't pass on the information to you.' As he spoke, he pushed across the desk a piece of paper with an address on it.

'Of course not,' said Karen, slipping the paper into her handbag. 'Thank you for seeing us, Inspector.'

'Sorry I couldn't be more help,' said Grant, getting up to show them to the door.

Outside on the pavement, Karen looked at the paper and read out, 'Plas-y-Brenin Experimental Field Station, near Capel Curig, Gwynedd, North Wales.' She looked at Patterson. 'I'm going there,' she said with sudden resolve. 'I have to know for sure. Well, what d'you say? Are you coming?'

'All right,' he said. 'I'm game. We'll use my car – it's a four-wheel-drive.'

Next morning Karen dropped Kelly off at her mother's along with a bag full of the essentials required for looking after a seven-month-old baby. She gave Ethel a big hug and said, 'I can't thank you enough.'

'That's what grannies are for.' Ethel smiled, cuddling Kelly. 'Didn't you know?'

'I'll call you as soon as we get there.'

'Take all the time you need. And take care!'

Karen nodded and ran to her car. It was already seven-thirty and she was due to meet Ian Patterson back at the house at eight. Despite her fears, she was only a few minutes late in getting back after the stop-go frustration of driving through rush-hour traffic. She swung her car into the small run-in in front of the garage and locked it, then ran up to the house to collect the overnight bag she had left ready behind the front door.

Patterson was sitting waiting in a dark-green Toyota Land Cruiser adorned with wildlife stickers and one proclaiming his membership of the RSPB. For some reason the fact that he was 'Saving Whales and Dolphins' registered with Karen as she climbed into the passenger seat and she wondered idly how.

'Sorry I'm a bit late,' she said. 'Kelly was playing up.'

'No problem,' said Patterson. He took off from the kerb and headed south.

'How long do you think it will take?' asked Karen.

'I reckon from the map it's about three hundred miles,' replied Patterson. 'Normally about five hours but I'm not sure about this trip. I don't know what the mountain roads are like; I've never been there before. How about you?'

'I once went to a Girl Guide camp in Llandudno,' said Karen. 'We went by train. I remember it rained a lot.'

'We'll just have to play it by ear,' said Patterson.

They stopped for coffee in the Scottish borders and again for lunch at a service station on the M6, although neither of them was particularly hungry. It just seemed like a welcome gesture of normality. Patterson ate a bacon roll while Karen pushed a salad around her plate, trying to make it look smaller than when she started.

Patterson asked, 'How are you feeling about all this?'

'Scared,' admitted Karen. 'I just don't know how I'm going to cope if we find out that they really have run off together. You?'

Patterson shrugged and said, 'About the same, I think. I just can't bring myself to imagine life without her. We were talking about having a baby only the week before she went to Wales. This whole thing just doesn't make sense.'

Karen took comfort in yet another snippet of information that didn't fit with Peter having deserted her.

'There's something else that worries me,' said Patterson. 'If they really have had an accident or got into some kind of trouble . . . it's been about five days since I last heard from Amy and it's winter in the Welsh mountains.'

They took this as their cue to get up and head back to the car.

The dark clouds that had been building and threatening most of the way down the M6 turned to torrential rain as they turned west into Wales along the M56. The wipers struggled to cope as they made their way to the junction with the A55 North Wales coast road. After an hour or so the strain of driving in such appalling conditions made Patterson turn off into the car park of a roadside café. He said, 'Let's have some hot coffee and take a look at the map.'

The air in the café was heavy with the smell of cooking and wet waterproofs. Steam drifted up from the service counter and condensation streamed down the windows.

They sat down at a red plastic table and opened the AA road atlas that Patterson had brought in with him.

'I reckon our best bet is to turn off at Llandudno Junction and head south through the Vale of Conwy,' he said. 'Then, if we turn west through Betws-y-coed on to the A5, that'll take us right to Capel Curig. We can ask for directions from there.'

Karen agreed.

It was dark and just after five in the evening when Patterson brought the Land Cruiser to a halt outside a hotel in Capel Curig in the heart of the Welsh mountains. The rain was still hammering down. They dashed across the cratered surface of the car park to seek sanctuary in the entrance hall, which was warm and dry but deserted. They looked around for a bell to ring but without success. Karen leaned her head through the hatch at Reception and called hopefully, 'Hello!' There was no response.

Patterson opened a door and popped his head round. 'Dining room,' he said as he closed it again.

They followed a sign saying Cocktail Bar but found it, too, deserted. 'Do you think they've dropped the bomb?' asked Karen.

'The state of some of the furniture in this place might support that theory,' said Patterson.

Karen saw his point. A variety of rickety tables sat in front of black plastic bench-seating with occasional slash marks across it. The ashtrays were full and a half-empty pint glass of stale beer stood on the bar counter.

The sound of coughing came from somewhere upstairs, followed by slow, heavy feet on the stairs. A small, fat, bald man appeared in the bar with a cigarette in the corner of his mouth. He said something in Welsh.

'We're not Welsh,' said Patterson.

'What'll it be?' asked the barman, removing the cigarette.

Karen showed him the paper with the field station address

on it. 'We're trying to find this place,' she said. 'Can you help us?'

The barman took the paper in short stubby fingers and squinted at it. 'You'll be from the papers, then?' he said.

'No, why should we be?' asked Patterson.

''Cos it burned down last night,' replied the man. 'It's a pile of bloody ashes, they tell me.'

Patterson and Karen looked at each other in disbelief. 'Was anyone hurt?' Karen asked in trepidation.

'No. They reckon the place was empty, which makes it a bit of a bloody mystery if you ask me,' said the barman. 'Not exactly the weather for spontaneous combustion, is it?'

'Did you see much of the people who worked there?' asked Patterson.

The barman shook his head. He held up the paper Karen had given him and said, 'This may say "near" Capel Curig, but it's a bloody long drive up into the mountains.'

'When was the last time you saw anyone from the field station?' asked Patterson.

'Must be . . . last summer, I'd say.'

'So you didn't see anything of the two scientists who came to work there about four weeks ago?'

'News to me,' said the man.

'Can you tell us how to get there?' asked Karen.

'But there's nothing left,' said the barman.

'We'd still like to see it.'

The barman gave them directions and they went back out to the car. Karen offered to drive. 'If you're sure,' said Patterson, who'd had quite enough of driving in miserable conditions for one day.

When they reached the junction the barman had warned them about, Karen strained to see through the windscreen. 'He said it was just after here . . . on the left . . . there it is.' She swung the Toyota on to a rough mountain track, and they began to bump their way slowly up an ever-steepening incline that was rapidly turning into a river with the rainwater streaming off the mountains.

'I'm not even sure why we're doing this,' said Patterson.

Karen thought for a moment, then said, 'We are going to the place where the people we love were last known to be,' she said. 'Anything else starts from there.'

It took them nearly fifty minutes to negotiate the track and reach the charred ruins of the field station. Karen kept the engine running and the headlights on while they surveyed the remains in silence.

'Do you have a torch?' she eventually asked.

Patterson reached over into the back and brought up a large rubber-handled torch.

Karen switched off the engine. She killed the headlights but left the sidelights on to provide a reference point in the darkness.

'What a mess!' exclaimed Patterson as they walked among the ruins. 'I suppose they couldn't get a fire engine up here.'

'If they even knew about it,' added Karen.

'All the same,' said Patterson thoughtfully, 'the fire did a remarkably thorough job. Makes me wonder what they were storing here – aviation fuel, by the look of it.'

Karen saw what he was getting at. There was practically nothing recognisable left in the shell of the building. She moved to the side and said, 'Bring the torch over here.'

Patterson brought up the beam to illuminate a burned-out car. Despite the rain, it still smelled strongly of burning rubber. 'Looks like a Land-Rover,' said Patterson.

'Do you think it's the one Peter and Amy used?'

'So why is it still here?' said Patterson. 'They'd have needed transport to get away.'

'It's not exactly hitch-hiking territory, is it?' agreed Karen.

The moment was interrupted by the sound of a labouring engine. 'Who the devil?' exclaimed Patterson.

They turned to face the track, and a few moments later two headlights topped by a flashing blue light appeared. A North Wales Police Land-Rover drew up and two yellow-jacketed policemen got out.

'What's your business here?' asked one aggressively. He shone his torch directly at them.

Karen put her hand up to her eyes and said, 'My husband was working here.'

'And my wife,' added Patterson.

'You must be the two from Scotland, then?' asked the policeman, changing his tone.

'How did you know that?'

'We had a call from Lothian and Borders Police asking us to keep an eye out for a Land-Rover owned by some outfit called Lehman Genomics. Turns out it's this one here,' he said, pointing to the wreck. We identified it from the VIN number on the chassis.'

'So what does that tell us?' asked Patterson.

'Not much,' said the policeman. 'The only comfort I can give you is that the building was unoccupied at the time of the fire.' In the ensuing silence he added, 'You've come a long way. I'll have a word with the local taxi firms in the morning, if you like.'

'Thank you,' said Karen, still looking at the ashes.

THIRTEEN

By mid-afternoon William Victor Spicer had been taken into custody, charged with the murder of Anthony Pelota, and Steven was nearing his wits' end trying to establish how Spicer had managed to contract the disease. The MP had not been anywhere near Africa in the past five years and could recall no recent dealings with anyone who had. Absolutely nothing in what Spicer had told him in their long interview even hinted at a new line of inquiry.

His worst fears about the man being a red herring, rather than the common factor in the virus outbreaks, looked like being realised. Humphrey Barclay, Victor Spicer and Frank McDougal still appeared to be independent, unconnected sources of filovirus outbreaks. He called Fred Cummings and arranged to meet him over at City General. He needed a sounding board and Caroline was working down at St Jude's; her answering machine had just told him so.

'You did well in getting to Spicer,' said Cummings when Steven told him about the morning. 'Cane's people didn't even know he existed.'

'But it hasn't got me anywhere. Spicer has just replaced Ann Danby as the wildcard in the pack. We're left with a virus that looks as though it's breaking out at random.'

'But we both know better than that.'

Steven nodded. 'But I am beginning to wonder.'

'You'll find the link,' said Cummings encouragingly. 'It's out there somewhere, as someone used to say.'

'Thanks a lot.' Steven smiled. 'So what's happening in the real world?'

'More and more cases, and it's been spreading out of the city, as we knew it would. People move around, and with the best will in the world we're not going to put a stop to that with a city population of over two and a half million. All the medical services have been put on the alert for it nationwide, so there's a better chance of snuffing it out than there was here in Manchester at the beginning. There are no new wildcards as far as we know, but there are still a few cases we have to work on to establish the line of contact.'

'What are CDC up to?' asked Steven.

'They're having a re-think about whether this particular flilovirus might be airborne after all.'

'Shit,' said Steven.

'They're reaching the same conclusion we did: that there are just too many people going down with it for it to be body-fluid transmission alone.'

'So what happens now?'

'We ring-fence the city and burn down all the houses,' replied Cummings, adding, in response to Steven's expression, 'It's ironic, really, but that's what they do in the African outbreaks and it's very effective.'

'But not an option.'

'I think a curfew is the best we can manage. We've got to stop people mingling in public places. We've closed the big things like cinemas and football grounds, but so many small businesses got exemptions from the last order that it ended up making very little difference. People are more frightened now, though, and that's going to work in our favour.'

'Fear is our friend,' said Steven.

'A good soundbite,' said Cummings. 'I'll make a note of it.'

'How about resources?'

'No problem about equipment. The Americans and Swedes have been flying in state-of-the-art stuff. I think the CDC people see us as a bit of a testing ground for what they've been preparing for in a big American city for years. The Swedes have prided themselves on being expert in mobile facilities ever since Linköping in

1990. That aside, we have a growing nursing-staff problem as I think you've seen for yourself?'

Steven nodded.

'There's a country-wide call going out for volunteers, preferably those with infectious-disease experience but they're a dying breed. Most of the old infectious-disease hospitals have been closed down over the last ten to fifteen years.'

'I guess we didn't need them with all these old churches lying around empty,' said Steven sourly. 'They're ideal. All we need do is tack a crematorium on the back and they're tailor-made for the job.'

Cummings looked sidelong at him and said kindly, 'Don't let it become your problem, Steven. You've got to stay detached from the nitty-gritty and concentrate on finding the source. There must be one.'

Steven said, 'It's hard to remain detached when people are dying around you and you haven't a clue where to look next.'

'It'll come to you. It sometimes takes more courage not to become involved.'

'How's Sourpuss Cane doing?'

'He's all but given up,' replied Cummings. 'Going strictly by the book, as he's done all his life, has yielded precisely nothing. Your coming up with a boyfriend for Ann Danby whom he and his lot failed to spot and the government calling in help from CDC were severe blows to his pride. It's my guess he's about to realise that he needs to "spend more time with his family" and resign.'

'Another resignation?' said Steven. 'Not good for morale. Who's taken over from Caroline at Public Health?'

'Her number two, Kinsella. He's okay but Caroline already ran a good department; he's just taken up the reins. Pity Spicer played politics with Caroline's job. She was a big asset.'

'Right.'

Steven returned to his hotel and started to work his way once more through all the data he had gathered on the people classified as wildcards. Yet again he searched for a common factor he might have overlooked but yet again he and his computer failed to spot one. 'More data,' he murmured. 'Must have more data.'

He rang Sci-Med and asked for more information about the people involved. No, he couldn't be more specific, he told them, just send anything they could come up with, however trivial. Better too much information than too little.

Steven thought long and hard about what Cummings had said about not becoming too involved. It made sense, and he acknowledged that, but his gut instinct was telling him something else. It was telling him that waiting for inspiration was something that could be done anywhere. It might just as well be down at St Jude's.

Assuming that Caroline and Kate would take their mid-shift break around the same time they had on the previous evening, Steven drove down to the church and waited for them to emerge. He waited fifteen minutes before the pair of them appeared with hair wet from the shower and dark rings under their eyes from tiredness.

'I really didn't think I'd see you here again,' said Caroline quietly.

'I find I have another free evening,' said Steven, using bravado to combat what he really felt.

'Good for you,' said Kate. Caroline echoed this but her eyes said that she understood just how big an effort it was for him.

When the two women returned to work after after their break, Steven joined them as an extra pair of hands. If anything, conditions in the old church had got worse overnight. Patient numbers had risen sharply; there was an extra line of beds, making three in all and housing something in the region of sixty desperately ill people.

'We're having to use the old vestry as a mortuary,' said Kate Lineham. 'The crematoria are finding it difficult to cope. There's a bit of a backlog.'

Steven swallowed and gave a slight nod.

'Let's go to it, guys,' said Kate.

Steven worked a five-hour shift as he had the night before and left with Caroline again, feeling drained but very conscious that Caroline had worked twice as long as he had.

'I think I have a tin of corned beef in the cupboard at home,' said Caroline, 'and maybe some beans. What d'you say?'

'You temptress, you,' said Steven, feeling again that he could do with some company. 'But I'm sure I could get us both dinner at my hotel if you'd like?'

Caroline shook her head and said, 'No, I'm all in and I must look it. Let's go home. You can take me to dinner when this is all over.'

'That's a date.'

'What on earth possessed you to come back to St Jude's, feeling the way you do?' asked Caroline while they waited for the beans to heat.

'I'm still a doctor. I couldn't stand by when staffing levels are as bad as they are,' replied Steven. 'My precious feelings are a luxury the situation can't afford.'

Caroline gave a nod of understanding, perhaps tinged with admiration, and asked, 'Did you find it any easier today?'

'I've just thrown up in your bathroom, if that answers your question, but you've been doing much more than me. How are you coping?'

Caroline swallowed as she thought about the question, and Steven saw vulnerability appear in her eyes for the first time. It disappeared when she tried to disguise it but then it returned and remained. It brought a lump to his throat.

'We had nineteen deaths today,' she said quietly. 'We piled them up in the vestry . . . one on top of the other . . . like sacks of potatoes. Somebody's daughter, somebody's son, all waiting in a heap to be collected . . . and burned. I never thought I'd see anything like that in England in this day and age.'

'When did you last have a day off?' asked Steven gently.

'None of us without family commitments are taking days off until we get some extra nurses down there,' said Caroline.

'You'll make yourself ill,' said Steven.

'Maybe I deserve to be. Maybe if I'd put out an alert after that girl went to the disco, it really would have made a difference.'

'Nonsense,' said Steven. 'We've been through all that. You made entirely the right decision in the circumstances. You have nothing to reproach yourself for, absolutely nothing. That MP just used you and the circumstances to get himself noticed – self-seeking little bastard.'

'Thanks . . . but I'm not entirely convinced.'

Steven's assurances were interrupted by his mobile phone going off in his jacket pocket. He went out into the hall to retrieve it and took the call there. When he returned Caroline could see that something was the matter.

'What's wrong?' she asked.

'They think there's a new wildcard case in Hull,' Steven replied, still stunned at the news. 'Sci-Med are sending details, but Public Health have been unable to establish any contacts. They seem to think that this is the best example yet of a case occurring spontaneously.'

'Shit.' Caroline sighed. 'Where's all this going to end?'

Steven looked at her bleakly for a moment, then said, 'It will end when we wipe out the source, isolate all the contacts and stop the spread, just like with every other outbreak. We have to believe that.'

Caroline nodded slowly but she seemed preoccupied.

'Don't we?' Steven prompted.

'Of course,' came the weak reply. 'I'm sorry. I'm just so damned tired. I'm not thinking straight.'

'And no wonder.'

'Tell me a joke, Steven. I feel as if I haven't smiled for weeks.'

'Know the feeling,' said Steven.

'C'mon, tell me a joke.'

He thought for a moment then began, 'There was this little baby polar bear sitting on a rock, watching the ice floes drift by. Suddenly he looked up at his mother beside him and asked, "Mum, am I a polar bear?" "Of course you're a polar bear," said his mother and she patted him on the head. A short time later the little bear repeated the question and got the same response. A short while later the little bear asked the question yet again. By now his mother was losing patience. "Of course you're a polar bear," she snapped. "I'm a polar bear, your father's a polar bear, your brother's a polar bear. We're all polar bears. Now, what is this nonsense?" "Well," sighed the little bear, "it's just that I'm fucking freezing!"'

Caroline's face broke slowly into a grin and then she started to laugh. She laughed until her sides were splitting, and Steven feared she might be becoming hysterical, but it was just that the joke had acted as a release valve for all her pent-up emotions. 'Oh, my God,' she said with the tears running down her face. 'Spot on, Dunbar. Bloody brilliant.'

'Glad to have been of service, ma'am,' said Steven. 'Anything else I can help you with?'

'You can pour us both a drink and make the world go away for a couple of hours.'

It was late when Steven got back to his hotel but he downloaded the new information from Sci-Med on to his laptop and worked his way through it. He put to one side the extra information he'd requested on Barclay and the others while he concentrated on the new wildcard. It was easy to see how Public Health had reached their conclusions about the new case, because the patient was Sister Mary Xavier, a Benedictine nun living in an enclosed, contemplative order. The sisters had little or no contact with the outside world, and Public Health had established that Sister Mary had neither been outside the walls of the convent nor met with anyone from the outside world during the past several months.

Initial puzzlement gave way to the more positive feeling of excitement: Mary Xavier must hold the key to the mystery. She was a nun: there would be no secret boyfriends, no casual liaisons with strangers, no trips abroad and no possibility of contact with rogue animals. If he could find out how Sister Mary Xavier had contracted the illness, he would solve the whole puzzle of the outbreaks.

He learned that the sick nun had been born Helen Frances Dooley in the town of Enniscorthy in the Republic of Ireland, where she had been orphaned at the age of four. She was now thirty-six and had been in the enclosed order for the past eleven years. She had fallen ill eight days ago and the GP who looked after the sisters had been called in when her condition deteriorated. He recognised the problem immediately, after all the recent publicity, and raised the alarm. Public Health had seldom had such an easy time of it when it came to the isolation of patient and contacts. The nuns had already done that themselves. It was, after all, their way of life. The authorities had, however, called in one of the Swedish mobile laboratory units to deal with contaminated diagnostic material and the team had already established that Sister Mary was suffering from the new strain of filovirus.

Steven started out soon after breakfast and made good time over the ninety miles or so to Hull, but it took him almost as long again to find the convent, which was in a small wooded valley about eight miles north-west of the city. It was not signposted: there was no need for it to be, as the sisters did not welcome visitors or intrusion into their privacy. When he eventually found the old building, which looked as if it had been a rather grand residence at one time, he found that the police had cordoned off the approaches with chequered ribbon tape.

Two officers were sitting in a police Panda car out of the rain. He could also see the Swedish mobile lab at the side of the building. Steven showed his ID to the officers and asked what was happening. He was told that the patient was being looked after in the west wing of the building on the ground floor, which had been sealed off from the other areas. A separate entrance had been fashioned by the Swedish lab team, who had adapted the old French windows on that side of the building to create a secure tunnel. Apart from the sisters who were looking after Sister Mary, the others were going about their normal daily routine and had requested that there be as little disruption to their lives as possible.

Steven walked up to the main, stone-arched entrance and

knocked on the heavy wooden door. There was no answer, but for some reason he didn't expect there to be. He turned the brass handle and entered a dark, musty-smelling hall with threadbare carpets and large, forbidding furniture. Only the cross on the wall said that it wasn't a suitable residence for Count Dracula.

An elderly nun crossed the hall at the junction at the end, head bowed, hands in her sleeves, but she didn't notice Steven standing there and was gone before he could say anything. He continued slowly up to the junction where corridors diverged left and right and stopped there. Not wishing to pry any further, he waited at the intersection for someone else to appear. Eventually a young nun, wearing thick-lensed glasses and looking painfully scrawny despite her voluminous robes, came towards him.

'Who are you?' she asked, sounding annoyed. 'You shouldn't be in here.'

'I'm sorry. No one answered my knock. My name is Steven Dunbar. I'd like to speak to Mother Superior if that's at all possible?' He handed the nun his ID and she held it up close to her face, turning slightly to catch more light as she read it.

'Wait here. I'll ask Reverend Mother.'

Steven watched the girl knock on a door about twenty metres down the corridor to the right. She disappeared briefly, then re-appeared and beckoned him with an exaggerated circular motion of her arm. Steven reckoned that this was because she couldn't actually see him at that distance. He walked towards her and was shown into a small, perfectly square room with a vaulted ceiling, where the Reverend Mother got up from behind a carved rosewood desk to greet him – although doing so made little difference to her height. Steven saw that she had a purple birthmark covering most of the right side of her face and a large blind cyst disfiguring the left.

Her voice, however, was mellifluous and pleasant. 'Dr Dunbar, how can I help?'

'I'm trying to find out how Sister Mary Xavier contracted her illness, Reverend Mother. I need to ask you some questions about her movements and whom she might have come into contact with recently.'

'As I told those who came before you, young man,' she said, 'Sister Mary's movements were confined to this house and the sisters here were her sole companions.'

'But with respect, that isn't possible, Reverend Mother,' insisted Steven. 'There has to be a link with the outside world, otherwise the implication would be that the virus originated here in the convent, a spontaneous creation.'

'All things are possible with the Lord, Doctor.'

'Are you suggesting that the Lord created a virus specifically to kill Sister Mary Xavier?' said Steven, mildly irked at the platitude and the terminal complacency of the deeply religious.

'I don't think that He would necessarily construe it that way.'

'How would He construe it, Reverend Mother? Viruses like the one infecting Sister Mary cannot exist outside a living host. Their only function is to kill.'

'Perhaps their only function known to us, Doctor.'

Steven conceded gracefully. 'You say you've already been asked about Sister Mary's movements?' he asked.

'The people from the Public Health Service were as adamant as you that our sister must have been in contact with the outside world during the last few weeks, but the simple truth is that she has not been outside these walls for much longer than that. Neither has she had contact with anyone other than the sisters and perhaps the priest who comes to hear our confession. I myself can guarantee that.'

'I take it the good father is keeping well, Reverend Mother?'

'Apart from being concerned about Sister Mary Xavier's health, Father O'Donnell is as well as any seventy-year-old can reasonably expect to be.'

Steven wondered if the Reverend Mother was reading his mind. The intelligent look in her eyes said that she might well be and that was why she had volunteered the priest's age. He decided against asking for an antibody test on him. 'As a matter of interest, when *did* Sister Mary Xavier last go out into the world, Reverend Mother?' he asked.

'Ours is a contemplative order, Doctor. We tend not to go out into the world at all. Rather, we pray for it and everyone in it.'

'I see,' said Steven. 'Then the sister has not left these walls in over a decade?'

'It would not be quite true to say that,' replied the nun. 'Sister Mary did not enjoy good health. The doctors decided last year that she needed an operation so she went into St Thomas's Hospital in Hull for a few days some nine months ago to have it done. The Lord saw fit to return her to us fit and well.'

'Good,' said Steven. 'What exactly was wrong with her?'

'She lacked energy and tired easily; she often had to struggle for breath,' replied the nun. 'She gave us cause for alarm on more than one occasion and came dangerously close to collapse, but since the operation she's been as right as rain, praise the Lord.'

'She'll need all her energy to fight this virus,' said Steven.

A knock came to the door and a sister appeared to say that Reverend Mother was required immediately: Sister Mary Xavier was asking for her.

'Of course,' said Steven as she excused herself. He watched the two women bustle off down the corridor to the west wing, and then left the building. He sat in his car, wondering how someone who had not been outside the convent for nine months could possibly have contracted viral haemorrhagic fever. As he admitted defeat, a single bell began to toll and he knew instinctively that it was the death knell for Sister Mary Xavier.

FOURTEEN

Listening to the sombre sound of the bell, Steven wondered if it might not be tolling for all he had been taught about the mechanics of viral infection. None of this made any sense. Viruses needed a living host to maintain them and allow them to replicate. They did not have the wherewithal to lead an independent existence, not even as a simple sleeping spore, in the way that some bacteria could. Sister Mary Xavier *must* have contracted the infection from a living source, or else the textbooks would have to be re-written. The thought brought a wry smile to his face. Textbooks were always being re-written: it happened every time a fact emerged to take the place of expert opinion.

Steven was determined to keep thinking along logical lines. None of the other nuns was ill so Mary Xavier must have picked up the virus outside the convent. That left the unpleasant little fact that she hadn't been outside the convent in the last nine months. Steven cursed in exasperation and leaned forward to rest his forehead on the top of the steering wheel while the tolling of the bell and the patter of the rain on the roof continued to mock him.

On impulse, he decided to drive into Hull and ask at St Thomas's Hospital about the nature of Sister Mary's illness and subsequent operation. He couldn't see how it would help, but he would be amassing more information about a wildcard patient and, until such times as answers were forthcoming, no one could say what was going to be relevant and what was not. In the meantime, doing anything was better than doing nothing.

*   *   *

Mr Clifford Sykes-Taylor, FRCS was not at all sure about divulging information about his patient, and said so in no uncertain terms. He treated Steven to a monologue about slipping standards of patient confidentiality and the erosion of the patient–doctor relationship. He was a short, tubby man but with all the self-confidence in the world and a booming voice that belied his size. A spotted bow tie assisted in his quest to establish presence.

Steven imagined that he might have to stand on a box at the operating table, but certainly no one would have trouble hearing him.

'I do have the authority to ask you for this information,' said Steven calmly.

Sykes-Taylor sighed and said, 'The authority, yes, of course, the authority, always the authority. Well, I'm not at all happy about authority's role in this. I see it as a betrayal of my patient's trust, and in my book my patient comes first. So far you haven't given me one good reason why I should tell you anything.'

'I'll give you three if you like,' said Steven. 'One, like you I am a doctor, and the information will go no further. Two, I have the legal right to compel you to give me it if necessary. Three, your patient is dead; she died an hour ago.'

Sykes-Taylor looked surprised and then alarmed. 'I hope you're not here to suggest that my surgery played any part in her demise?' he said, suddenly suspicious and defensive.

A surgeon's epitaph for his patient, thought Steven. 'No, Mr Sykes-Taylor, I'm not suggesting anything of the sort,' he said. 'But I would like to know why Sister Mary Xavier required your services in the first place.'

A look of relief spread over Sykes-Taylor's face. 'People sue if you as much as look at them the wrong way these days,' he said, managing a half-smile for the first time. 'Bloody legal insurance has gone sky-high this year, I can tell you. I sometimes wonder why I bother operating on the buggers, for all the thanks I get.'

Steven wondered what had happened to agonised concern about patients' interests, but didn't think it in his own interest to say so because Sykes-Taylor had got up to open his filing cabinet. He returned to his desk and flipped open a bulky cardboard file, slipped on half-moon glasses and began reading.

'Ah yes, the good sister had a heart problem – she'd had it for the past five years or so. It manifested itself in the usual way, a lack of energy, breathlessness, that sort of thing. She was initially diagnosed as having a weak mitral valve – it was operating at around seventy per cent efficiency, but until the beginning of the year she wasn't considered a high-priority case. At her check-up in December last year, however, it became apparent that the valve was becoming weaker and the stenosis worse: we thought there was a chance that it might fail completely, so we listed her for corrective surgery. She was brought in in February. She wasn't in hospital long and the operation was straightforward and, as far as we were concerned, very successful. She left here feeling like a new woman and, to my knowledge, she hasn't had any problems since – apart from the fact that she's now dead.'

'Nothing to do with her heart,' said Steven.

'Thank God for that,' said Sykes-Taylor.

The milk of human kindness is not strained, thought Steven. *It droppeth as the gentle rain from heaven . . .*

He drove back from Hull feeling thoroughly depressed. He had felt sure when he set off that morning that this would be the day when he made definite progress but now here he was, driving back through the rain with an apparently insoluble puzzle for company instead of an answer.

As he entered the outskirts of Manchester and headed towards the city centre he saw newspaper stands featuring the word 'Disaster' prominently as the 'hook' on their advertising hoardings. Intrigued, he stopped and bought a paper, only to find that the story was the commercial disaster of Manchester's Christmas. City stores' takings were down by more than 60 per cent on the previous year. Fear was keeping people away from the shops. *Good*, he thought. *Let's have an old-fashioned Christmas, folks – just like the ones we used to know.*

There hadn't been time the previous evening to go through all the new material from Sci-Med on the wildcard patients, so Steven applied himself to it as soon as he got in. There was a lot on Humphrey Barclay, ranging from school reports to his dental records. He had been fined twice for speeding over the last ten years, and had spent three days in hospital in 1997, having a wisdom tooth removed.

This last piece of information reminded Steven of something in the original Sci-Med file about Barclay having been ill more recently, that being the reason for his poor rating at annual appraisal time. He looked out the file and found that Barclay had undergone heart surgery in the early part of the current year. Like Sister Mary's operation, it had been straightforward and he had made a full recovery. No further details were available.

Steven's satisfaction at having found some common factor, however tenuous, between two of the wildcards was greatly tempered by the fact that it hardly seemed relevant. Both Barclay and Mary Xavier had undergone successful surgery in the past year and both had made a full recovery. So what? Almost half-heartedly he thought he'd better check Ann Danby's file and, to his no great surprise, he found no mention of surgery in her medical records, and the record seemed complete.

He was about to dismiss the surgery angle as mere coincidence when he reminded himself that Ann Danby's status had changed. She was no longer a wildcard: she was a contact, because she had contracted the disease from Victor Spicer. Spicer was the real wildcard in the Manchester pack: it was Spicer's medical records he should be looking at, and they were not yet available. The same applied to Frank McDougal. Steven contacted Sci-Med and asked for more details on Barclay's illness and also for McDougal's medical history. As for Spicer, he would go and see his wife, and find out for himself.

As he drove through the city, Steven was struck by how quiet it was. It was just after seven in the evening but it felt more like three in the morning. It was unusually dark. Many neon signs had been switched off because the premises they advertised were closed until further notice or FOR THE DURATION OF THE EMERGENCY, as the signs outside said. Pubs remained open at the licensee's discretion, as did off-licences, the authorities having decided that closing them would be tantamount to prohibition, a measure not noted for its success in the past. Buses still ran, but on a reduced service schedule, and the night service had been abandoned altogether.

On his way to Spicer's house, Steven came across three ambulances, blue lights flashing as they ferried patients across town, but there was no call for their sirens in the light traffic. Their silence added to the air of surrealism. Thinking about their destination made Steven wonder if Caroline would be working at St Jude's this evening. He resolved to drive down there after he had spoken to Matilda Spicer.

He was shocked at her appearance when she opened the door. She was no longer the confident political wife with the ready smile and charm to spare. He had been wrong to categorise her as a traditional, stoic Tory wife, for in her place stood a pale, haggard figure with a haunted look that suggested she hadn't slept properly for some time.

'You!' she exclaimed when she saw Steven. 'Just what the hell do *you* want?'

'I'm sorry. I hate to trouble you, but I need some more information about your husband, Mrs Spicer,' said Steven.

'Then why are you asking me?' she snapped. 'What the hell do I know about him? I seem to be the last person on earth to know what he gets up to.'

'I'm sorry. I know this can't be easy for you.'

'Easy for me!' she repeated. 'Can you even begin to imagine what all this is doing to my daughter and me? We've lost everything, absolutely everything. You appear on the scene and, abracadabra, our life disappears in a puff of smoke. I don't have a husband; Zoe no longer has a father; the charities I worked for don't want to know me; even the au pair has been taken away by the agency – apparently we're no longer a suitable placement for her.'

'I'm sorry,' repeated Steven. 'I assumed that friends and family would rally round at a time like this.'

'Oh, they are,' sneered Matilda. 'They're rallying round *him*. Victor's father more or less suggested that the whole thing was my fault. If I'd been a better wife, his precious son wouldn't have needed to look elsewhere – that's more or less how he put it.'

'Like father like son,' said Steven with distaste.

'Well, what did you want to ask me?'

'I need to know if your husband underwent surgery in the last year or so,' said Steven.

'Yes, he did,' replied Matilda, making an obvious effort to pull herself together. 'He had a heart operation last February.'

'Successful?'

'Unfortunately, yes.'

'Can I ask where the surgery was carried out?'

'He had it done in London.'

'Privately?'

Matilda named a well-known private hospital. 'We have insurance,' she added.

'Of course,' said Steven.

'Now, if there's nothing else, I really must be getting on . . . I have to prepare for Christmas,' she said with a look that challenged Steven to imagine what her Christmas was going to be like, and implied that it was all his fault.

Steven thanked her politely for her help and wished her well, although it sounded hollow in the circumstances. Matilda, who had shown no interest in why he had asked his questions, gave a half-smile tinged with sadness and regret and closed the door.

Steven heard the strains of 'Claire de lune' begin haltingly on the piano as he walked back to the car. He glanced back at the house and, through the branches of the half-decorated Christmas tree in the window, saw Zoe Spicer sitting on the edge of the piano stool, concentrating on her music while her mother, standing behind her, looked on.

The scene made him reflect on just how suddenly disaster

could strike. Matilda Spicer must have seen herself as comfortable, confident and secure. She might even have imagined herself as a government minister's wife in some future administration. Then suddenly, as she had said, abracadabra! None of it was there any more. The ball bounces, the cookie crumbles, shit happens and you're left with . . . zilch.

Three wildcards and three heart operations was the thought uppermost in Steven's mind as he drove back to his hotel. The coincidence had just got bigger, but on the downside it still seemed irrelevant when it came to understanding how these people got the virus. The fact that they had all undergone surgery – and successful surgery at that – was the *only* thing they had in common. As for the surgery itself, it had been carried out in different hospitals and in different parts of the country by different surgeons at different times. Taken at face value, this might suggest that people who had undergone surgery were more susceptible to infection, but that didn't help at all in establishing where the infection had come from. There had to be another linking factor.

As soon as he got back, Steven requested that the kitchen put together a variation on a picnic hamper which would supply dinner for two people, complete with a couple of bottles of decent wine. If Caroline didn't feel like going out to dinner – and it was odds on that she wouldn't after yet another ten-hour shift at St Jude's – dinner would come to her. He arranged to pick it up from the desk when he left just after ten, but in the meantime he went upstairs to see if any more information had come in from Sci-Med.

The first message contained the lab report on Victor Spicer's blood sample. It had contained a high level of antibodies to the new filovirus, indicating that he had recently been infected with the strain. Steven let out a grunt of satisfaction: it was good to see loose ends tied up, and now there was no doubt that Spicer had been the cause of the Manchester outbreak.

More information about Humphrey Barclay's medical condition had come. He had suffered from rheumatic fever as a child and this had resulted in a weak pulmonary heart valve in later years. His condition had worsened over the last two years, leading to the need for surgery, which had taken place in March this year. The operation was successful and, until he contracted the filovirus, Barclay had enjoyed better health than he had done for many years.

'Just like Sister Mary Xavier,' murmured Steven. 'You have successful heart surgery, you feel like a new person, and suddenly you're dead.' Matilda Spicer had not been specific about the type of surgery Victor had undergone, and Steven didn't feel like contacting her again in the circumstances. He did remember, however, the name of the hospital, so he asked Sci-Med to make contact and request details.

He was getting ready to leave for St Jude's when medical details on Frank McDougal came through. Steven scanned the screen with a frisson of anticipation and found what he was looking for. McDougal, too, had suffered from a heart problem. He had been diagnosed in December 1999 as suffering from age-associated degeneration of the aortic heart valve. Surgery had been performed to correct the fault in April this year and had been successful, so much so that McDougal had taken up hill-walking and had already bagged fourteen Munros (Scottish mountains over three thousand feet) during the summer.

'Jesus wept,' muttered Steven. He didn't pretend to understand what was going on, but the elation at making a connection between the wildcards was more than welcome and long overdue. Four wildcards, four heart problems, four operations, this was too much of a coincidence to be one at all.

Caroline looked more tired than ever when she emerged from the changing room with Kate Lineham. She was losing weight, thought Steven; hollows were appearing in her cheeks.

Kate was trying to persuade her to take the following day off. 'Do something else,' she advised. 'It doesn't matter what, just anything else for a change.'

'I'll be here. I haven't seen *you* taking the day off.'

'I'm more used to this sort of work than you.'

'No one is used to this sort of work,' retorted Caroline, holding her gaze for a long moment.

'You have a point,' conceded Kate, 'but there's no sense in making yourself ill.' She turned to Steven and said, 'I'm off. See that this one gets to bed early.'

Caroline had had to leave her car at home that morning because it had refused to start, so Steven drove her back. 'Rough day?' he asked, although the answer was plain in her face.

'The worst. You know, I'm beginning to wonder what the point is. We've had only three people show signs of recovery since I started down at St Jude's. All the rest have died. All we do is wipe up blood and vomit and urine and shit . . . all day, every day, over and over again . . . And then they die.'

Steven glanced at her out of the corner of his eye and saw that tears were running down her cheeks although she was not sobbing and her face was impassive.

'Kate's right. You need some time off,' he said gently.

'No way,' she said resolutely. 'Not until we get some more volunteer nurses down there.'

'Are you sure you're not doing this out of some misplaced sense of guilt?' said Steven as kindly as he could.

'Maybe at the beginning,' she agreed, without protest and to Steven's surprise, 'but not any more.'

'Then why?'

'You know, I think it's simply because I hope someone might do the same for me if I ever need it,' said Caroline. 'That's the best reason I've been able to come up with.'

'I think you do yourself an injustice,' said Steven. 'But I won't embarrass you by suggesting that you're an exceptional human being, I'll just feed you dinner.'

'You're serious?'

'I am.'

They completed the journey in silence. Caroline leaned her head on the headrest and closed her eyes.

*   *   *

The food the hotel had provided was plentiful if, of necessity, cold. Since both of them were hungry but not particularly interested in food, it didn't matter.

'You haven't said anything about your day,' said Caroline as they sat in front of the fire nursing the last of the first bottle of wine.

Steven told her what he had discovered.

'Heart surgery?' she exclaimed. 'What on earth can that have to do with the virus?'

'I know it's bizarre,' agreed Steven, 'but it's also a fact and I think it's too much of a coincidence to ignore.'

Caroline still looked doubtful. 'Now, if they had all had surgery in the same hospital at the same time, I might have to agree that there was something fishy but they didn't and even the timescale is all wrong. They had their surgery many months ago. The virus has an incubation time of around seven to ten days, so what exactly are you suggesting?'

'I don't know,' confessed Steven. 'I think I need to talk to a surgeon so I can get some feel for what's going on.'

'In the meantime, maybe we can open that other bottle of wine?'

'Water of Lethe coming up.'

After a while, Caroline slipped off her chair and sat on the carpet in front of the fire at Steven's feet. She rested her head on his knee. 'How long till Christmas?' she asked. 'I've lost track.'

'Ten days,' he said. The question made him think of Jenny. It seemed unlikely that he would be with her. He would have to speak to Sue and find out how she was going to take it.

'Where will you spend it?' asked Caroline, as if reading his mind.

'Here, I should think. You?'

'St Jude's,' she said quietly, 'piling up bodies for collection. Wonder how God will square that one.'

He stroked her hair gently and she made an appreciative sound. 'God, it seems such a long time since anyone did that,' she murmured.

The wine and the heat of the fire conspired to bring her eyelids together and it wasn't long before she fell fast asleep. Steven slid slowly sideways to stand up. He picked her up and took her upstairs to her bedroom, where he removed her shoes and loosened her clothing before putting her to bed and tucking the covers in around her. The central heating had switched itself off and the room was chilly.

Caroline stirred sleepily and without opening her eyes said, 'Are you putting me to bed, by any chance?'

'I promised Kate Lineham I would,' whispered Steven, and he clicked out the light.

He'd had too much to drink to consider driving back to the hotel, so he settled down on the couch in the living room. He awoke some four hours later with a crick in his neck. Rubbing it vigorously, he padded over to the window, opened a curtain, and cleared a patch in the condensation. He could see by the light from the street lamps that large flakes of snow were falling, laying a carpet of white over street and garden. He shivered and looked at his watch: it was 4 a.m. Not the best time of day to feel optimistic, but something about the way the snow was silently covering the city invited parallels with the virus and nurtured thoughts about the nature of good and evil.

'You must be cold,' said Caroline behind him. 'I didn't put out any blankets for you.'

Steven turned and saw her standing in the doorway. 'I'm fine,' he said. 'Couldn't you sleep?'

'Too many bad dreams. I need coffee. You?'

He nodded and closed the curtain again. Caroline made the coffee and they sat on the couch, hands wrapped round their mugs, staring at the fire, which Caroline had turned on full.

'I have such a bad feeling about the way things are going,' said Caroline.

'It's always darkest before the dawn.'

'Maybe there isn't going to be a dawn. Did you know that the suicide rate in the city has gone up by a factor of eight in the past week?'

'I didn't,' said Steven.

'They reckon it's guilt. Relatives of those going down with the disease feel helpless because they can't do anything to help – they can't even give their loved ones a proper funeral because of the restrictions.'

She shivered and Steven put his arm round her.

'Would you think me awfully forward if I suggested that we should go up to bed together?' she asked, still gazing at the fire.

'No,' replied Steven truthfully.

'Somehow I feel that time is not on our side,' she murmured.

FIFTEEN

'I thought I'd feel embarrassed, but I don't,' said Caroline as she dropped bread into the toaster.

'Good,' said Steven, wrapping his arms round her from behind and planting a kiss on the back of her neck. 'Me neither.'

'Must be that good old British wartime spirit you hear so much about,' she said thoughtfully. 'Normal rules of social engagement will be suspended for the duration of the hostilities.'

'My regiment marches at dawn,' said Steven.

'Only this time the war has come to us.'

He kissed her hair but didn't answer.

After breakfast he tried starting Caroline's car but found that it had a flat battery. Having failed to persuade her to take the day off, he insisted that she take his car to get to St Jude's. In the meantime, he would try to sort hers out.

'Will I see you later?' she asked.

'If you want to.'

'I'll see you later, then.'

A neighbour who had noticed Steven trying to start Caroline's car came out, still in his dressing gown, to volunteer the use of his battery charger. Steven was able to charge the dead unit and be mobile within half an hour. He stopped at a fast-fit service on the way over to the City General and had the battery checked. The technician declared it defunct – 'Won't hold a bloody charge, mate' – so Steven bought a new one and had it installed.

When he eventually reached the hospital he found George Byars alone in his office, sitting in shirtsleeves, juggling with columns of figures. 'It's been a while,' said Byars.

'I felt there was a danger of too many cooks,' said Steven. 'I've been trying to focus on my own job for a bit.'

'You weren't entirely successful if what I hear from St Jude's is correct.'

Steven shrugged and said, 'Some things you just can't walk away from.'

'I'm glad you think that way,' said Byars. 'I sometimes wonder about certain members of my profession.'

Steven decided not to push him on the subject. Instead, he asked, 'How are things at the sharp end?'

'Sharper than we'd like. I sometimes think I'm standing on the bridge of the *Titanic*, feeling the temperature fall. We've got an enormous problem with a shortage of nurses and another over accommodation for the victims. Three churches and two schools have been pressed into use so far, and all of them are just about full. The next step will be to close the city's secondary schools and bring them into the equation.'

'Why secondary schools?' asked Steven.

'Times have changed,' said Byars. 'It's the norm for both parents to go out to work these days. Suddenly dumping hundreds of young children back home would cause big social problems. Secondary-school kids are old enough to look after themselves till the folks come home.'

Steven nodded. 'What about the nursing volunteers who were supposed to come?' he asked.

'Slowed to a trickle.' Byars shrugged. 'Can't blame them. Watching people die without being able to do anything about it isn't exactly glamorous or uplifting. Apart from that, we've lost two nurses to the virus.'

'Two?' exclaimed Steven.

'It's not·common knowledge, like a lot of things in the city these days,' said Byars.

'Then you're managing to keep things out of the press?' asked Steven.

'Someone is,' corrected Byars. 'Don't ask me who, but I suspect government pressure's being brought to bear.'

'It certainly wouldn't be an appeal to the hacks' better nature,' said Steven.

'And you? Any progress?'

'Let's say I'm more optimistic than I was a few days ago, but there's still a lot to work out. That's really why I'm here. I need to talk to a cardiac surgeon – please don't ask why. Can you help?'

Byars picked up the phone and dialled an internal extension. After a short conversation he replaced the receiver, said, 'Our Mr Giles will be glad to give you all the help he can,' and told Steven how to get to the cardio-thoracic unit.

Steven smiled and thanked him. He'd come to like and respect Byars over the past few weeks, and was relieved that the crisis-management team had recognised his abilities and kept him on as crisis co-ordinator.

At the cardio unit, Steven was met by a formidable-looking woman who introduced herself as Martin Giles's secretary. 'He's expecting you,' she said brusquely. 'Go straight in.'

Steven's immediate impression was that Giles looked more like a heavyweight boxer than a surgeon but when he spoke it was as an educated, articulate man. 'How can I help?' he asked, hunching muscular shoulders as he folded his arms on his desk. What neck he had seemed to disappear, making his head look like a cannon-ball perched on a castle wall.

'I need to know something about modern heart surgery,' said Steven. 'What's on offer and what you do exactly.'

'Depends what the problem is,' said Giles. 'Anything from a couple of stitches in the right place to a complete heart–lung transplant.'

'Sorry to be so vague,' said Steven, 'but I've got no idea how common heart surgery is these days or how many people benefit from it.'

'Every cardiac unit in the country has a waiting list a mile long,' said Giles. 'Cardiac surgery has become commonplace.'

'Supposing a man is referred to you with a history of rheumatic fever in childhood, and this has led to current heart problems. Talk me through it.'

'That used to be very common,' said Giles. 'Rheumatic fever isn't as prevalent as it used to be but it often resulted in a bacter-aemia which in turn caused a build-up of bacteria on one or more of the heart valves with resultant stenosis. We would take a look at the problem with a range of options in mind. If the damage weren't too bad we might attempt a physical repair to the damaged tissue – we'd stitch the damaged portions together if at all possible. If a valve was irreparably damaged, however, we'd have to consider replacing it, either with a mechanical valve – a plastic one – or a tissue one should one be available.'

'Supposing the heart damage was age-related?' asked Steven, remembering Frank McDougal's medical records.

'The same options would apply. Age defects are usually associ-ated with the left side of the heart, the mitral and aortic valves, while infection usually affects the ones on the right, but either way we would repair or replace as appropriate, with repair being the preferred option.'

'And you say this is quite common?'

'I read recently in one of the journals that 225,000 heart-valve operations are performed every year in the developed world and 60,000 patients receive replacement valves.'

'How about post-op problems?'

'All surgery carries risks, of course, but heart-valve surgery has an excellent success rate. The vast majority of patients make a good recovery and generally feel like new people into the bargain.'

'And the ones who don't?' asked Steven.

'There's always a slight risk of stroke, bleeding, infection, kidney failure and, on occasion, heart attack and death; but they're the exceptions.'

'Heart-surgery patients haven't shown up as being susceptible to secondary illness in any way, have they?' asked Steven cautiously.

'Secondary illness?' queried Giles.

'Viral infections, that sort of thing.'

Giles said, 'Not in my experience, although it may be true of transplant patients if they're immuno-compromised because of the anti-rejection measures. I haven't noticed increased susceptibility in valve-surgery cases and I haven't heard that from anyone else in the business. We did have a major problem back in the eighties with mechanical failure of one make of replacement valve, the Björk-Shiley CCHV, which was prone to fracture, but that model was withdrawn way back in 1986, if my memory serves me right.'

'No, that's not the sort of thing I was thinking of.'

'Then I'm sorry, I can't help,' said Giles. 'Valve replacement is one of the most satisfying and rewarding surgeries we perform in terms of improving the quality of patients' lives.'

Steven nodded and got up to go. 'Thanks for seeing me at such short notice,' he said. 'I appreciate it.'

'Any time,' said Giles.

Steven smiled and said, 'I rather hoped you'd say that. I may have to call on you again.'

When he got back to his hotel, Steven called Sue in Dumfriesshire and told her that it was looking extremely unlikely that he would be able to be there for Christmas.

'I half expected it,' said Sue. 'It sounds as though things are getting worse down there. I've been warning Jenny that those poor people may need to hang on to her daddy for a little bit longer.'

'Thanks, Sue. How do you think she'll take it?'

'Your daughter is a remarkably mature young lady for her age. But if you aren't going to make it, I think you should tell her yourself.'

'Will do,' said Steven. He had scarcely put down the phone when it rang. It was the duty officer at Sci-Med. 'Dr Dunbar? Mr Macmillan would like you back in London at your earliest convenience' – that being a euphemism for 'now'.

Steven drove over to Caroline's house and left her car outside with a note in it saying that he'd had to go to London. He hailed a cab and asked to be taken to the airport. He was in London four hours after receiving the call and in John Macmillan's office at a quarter to five.

Macmillan smiled and said, 'I underestimated you: I'd allowed another couple of hours. I've called a meeting for seven. Perhaps you'd like to . . . ?'

Something about Macmillan's demeanour suggested that Steven shouldn't ask too many questions. He smiled and said that he'd be back for seven. He walked for a bit, enjoying the bustle of the early-evening crowds and the feel of Christmas in the air after the unnatural quiet of Manchester. He found a wine bar which was playing Christmas carols, and had a glass of Chardonnay. He'd have preferred a large gin but remaining alert for the meeting was a priority. Macmillan hadn't said that Steven would be asked to report on his progress, or lack of it, but it seemed likely.

Back at Sci-Med he found Macmillan alone.

'The meeting isn't here,' said Macmillan in response to his questioning look. 'It's in the Home Secretary's office.'

When they got there Steven was surprised to find two other cabinet ministers in the room besides the Home Secretary himself, who looked a worried man. In all there were eight people present. Steven nodded to each in turn as they were introduced.

'The truth is, we haven't been quite frank with you, Dunbar,' said Macmillan.

Steven remained impassive while he waited for Macmillan to continue, but his pulse rate rose.

'In the past it's always been Sci-Med's policy to pass on every scrap of relevant information to our people as soon as it became available. In this instance, however, we've been forced to hold something back.'

'Well, they say confession's good for the soul,' said Steven dryly.

'The decision wasn't taken lightly,' said Macmillan. 'It was taken at the very highest level and with the concurrence of the people present in this room. When Sister Mary Xavier caught the disease, a woman who had led a sheltered life in an enclosed order, it seemed to us that your search for a common linking factor could not possibly succeed. You don't have to be an epidemiologist to see that there simply couldn't be one. The implications of that conclusion were, of course, enormous: that our country is under attack from a lethal virus which can pop up anywhere and at any time, without the need for a continuous chain of infection.'

'So what was it that you didn't tell me?' asked Steven.

'We told you about Sister Mary but we didn't tell you about the others. There have actually been fourteen new wildcard cases across the UK. All without a linking factor.'

Steven blanched at the figure.

'Because of the medical authorities' vigilance these people were quickly isolated, but if this is the tip of an iceberg we are facing national disaster on an unprecedented scale,' said Macmillan.

'And the steps we must take are draconian,' said the Home Secretary. 'We are on the verge of declaring a national state of emergency, with all that implies.'

'Well, gentlemen, it seems to me that you've already made your minds up about the virus,' said Steven.

'We told you about Sister Mary because we thought you would investigate and reach the same conclusion before reporting back with your findings,' said Macmillan. 'That's why I brought you here tonight. You do agree, I take it, that there is unlikely to be a traceable source of this virus?'

'No, I don't,' said Steven, to the accompaniment of surprised looks around the room. 'In fact, I think there is one.'

'But the nun never left the convent.'

'She did,' said Steven. 'She had heart surgery at a local hospital nine months ago.'

'So she hasn't been outside the convent in nine months,' said a man from the British Medical Association testily. 'Same difference as far as a viral infection is concerned.'

'The other wildcards, at least the ones I was told about,' said Steven with a glance at Macmillan, 'had also had heart surgery recently.'

'And you think this is relevant?' asked the Home Secretary.

'I don't know exactly how at the moment, but yes, I do.'

The medical experts all travelled the road that Steven had travelled; they protested that there could be no logical connection between having heart surgery and falling victim to a deadly virus. Steven sat through it all patiently, nodding as people pointed out what he already knew about varying geographic locations, different hospitals and different surgeons, the operations having been performed at different times of the year and for different medical reasons.

'It's still a fact that all four had heart surgery,' said Steven when the protests had died down. 'And it's the only thing they had in common.'

'What d'you think, Macmillan?' the Home Secretary asked.

'In the circumstances, I think we should at least look at the medical history of the wildcards we didn't inform Dr Dunbar about,' said Macmillan.

'So we delay bringing in the new emergency measures?' asked the Home Secretary, looking to the others.

The meeting agreed with Macmillan, although with some reluctance since many still failed to see the relevance.

'I don't suppose anyone has done this already, by any chance?' asked the Home Secretary.

'As I understand it, the investigation of the patients' backgrounds was confined to a period of forty-two days, that being twice the conceivable incubation time for such a virus,' said the Health Secretary.

'Very well, then, I will recommend to the PM that we delay declaring a national state of emergency for . . . how long?'

'A week,' suggested the hardest sceptics. Suggestions of two weeks and one of a month were whittled down to ten days.

'What do you say, Dr Dunbar?' asked the Home Secretary. 'Can you come up with the source of this damned plague in ten days?'

'I can but try,' replied Steven.

'Anything you need, from secretarial assistance to an aircraft carrier, you only have to ask.'

Steven's first request when the meeting broke up was for food. He hadn't eaten since breakfast and he planned to work through the night, using Sci-Med's resources and computers to gather information about the undeclared wildcard cases. A small team of executive-grade civil servants was drafted in to help with fax and phone communications and by 9 p.m., when his Chinese take-away arrived, the phone lines were buzzing.

He ate at a computer desk while setting up a new database to accommodate information on the new patients as it arrived. Macmillan came in and caught him with his mouth full. He just wanted to know if Steven had everything he needed and, when Steven nodded, said that there wasn't much point in him hanging around. Steven agreed but sensed a reluctance in Macmillan to leave.

After an awkward pause, Macmillan cleared his throat and said, 'I owe you an apology about the missing information. When it became apparent that a state of emergency might be declared, it was unanimously agreed that no further details about the crisis should leave these four walls. We just couldn't risk it getting out and causing panic on the stock exchange and God knows where else.'

'I understand,' said Steven.

'Call me if there's any news.'

By midnight it was becoming clear that heart surgery was indeed the common factor. Nine of the fourteen wildcards had had heart surgery within the last year; information on the remaining five was still being sought. Steven called Caroline in Manchester to apologise for having had to rush away at such short notice and to tell her that he was finally making some progress, but there was no reply. He looked at his watch and hoped the reason was that she was fast asleep.

'So what do we conclude?' asked Macmillan when Steven phoned to tell him the news.

Steven took a deep breath and said, 'I think we have to conclude that it was the surgery itself that gave them the virus.'

'You mean they contracted a new filovirus as a post-operative infection?' asked Macmillan incredulously.

'Not in the conventional sense, but in a manner of speaking,' replied Steven. 'What we have to look for now is a common factor, something about the heart surgery that distinguishes these patients from the hundreds, if not thousands, of others who had heart surgery in the past year or so.'

By three in the morning Steven and the team had managed to obtain precise details of five of the operations, although they had had to deal with some pretty irascible people along the way at that time in the morning.

Steven rang Macmillan again as soon as he'd had time to appraise the information. He said, 'It looks as if the common factor is going to be a prosthetic heart valve. So far, five patients have a record of having had replacement valves fitted. No cases of surgical repair so far.'

'My God,' said Macmillan. 'Contaminated heart valves. Who would have believed it? You've done well.'

'We're not out of the woods yet,' said Steven. 'We still have to explain why there was a delay of many months before the infection took hold and how the valves came to be contaminated in the first place.'

'And with a virus that no one's ever come across before,' added Macmillan.

'Quite.'

'Well, I'll leave figuring that out in your capable hands,' said Macmillan. 'In the meantime, I'll wake the PM with the news.'

Steven asked his team to put out immediate requests for the type and make of heart valve used in the surgery. In the meantime, details on three more patients came in: they, too, had had surgery to replace a damaged valve.

'It's looking good, folks,' said Steven, accepting a mug of much-needed coffee from one of the civil servants. 'We could be talking a champagne breakfast here.'

Shortly before first light the first fax sheet came in with technical details of the valve used in replacement surgery. A human-tissue valve had been used in the operation on Humphrey Barclay. It had been a pretty nigh perfect immunological match for him and anti-rejection measures had not been necessary. Steven swore bitterly under his breath.

At six-thirty, feeling thoroughly depressed, he called Macmillan and told him, 'We've hit the wall. The first five results are in. They all had human-tissue valves fitted.'

'But how can that be?' asked Macmillan as if he were appealing to the gods for mercy.

'I don't know,' confessed Steven.

'One contaminated heart donor is a possibility, but there's no way all those people could have received heart valves from the same person,' said Macmillan.

'My maths tells me that too,' agreed Steven wearily. Tiredness was catching up with him.

'Get some sleep. We'll talk later.'

SIXTEEN

Steven took a cab home. The flat had been empty for some days and it was so cold that the air felt damp. He turned on the heating, then switched on the electric kettle and rubbed his arms while he waited for it to boil. It was just after seven-thirty. He would give Caroline a call before he tried to catch up on some sleep. There was still no answer. Steven tapped the receiver thoughtfully, wondering where she could be. As he sipped his coffee, huddled over the electric fire, curiosity became concern and then finally worry. He tried calling George Byars at the City General but he hadn't come in yet. He decided to wait and try again. His third call, at 8.45, was successful.

Steven told Byars he'd been having trouble contacting Caroline Anderson. 'Has she changed duty shifts, by any chance?' he asked.

The ensuing pause was more eloquent than any answer could have been. It spoke volumes and Steven felt his stomach turn over.

'I tried getting you at your hotel last night,' said Byars softly. 'Caroline's gone down with it.'

'Jesus, no,' murmured Steven.

'I'm sorry,' said Byars.

'Are they sure it's the virus?'

'There seems little doubt.'

'Where is she?'

'St Jude's. Sister Lineham insisted on nursing her personally.'

Steven put the phone down without saying any more, feeling as if absolutely everything was going against him and he was fighting a battle against insurmountable odds. At that moment he envied people who believed in God, any god, because they at least had someone to lean on, someone to turn to and ask for help in times of trouble. For his part, he felt the devastation of an utter loneliness verging on despair. There was no way he was going to be able to sleep now. Apart from anything else, he had to consider the possibility that he himself might go down with the virus because he and Caroline had slept together. The thought sent a chill down his spine. However, there was nothing at all he could do about it. It would be a case of wait and see – *qué será será*, or, as his grandmother had been fond of saying, 'What's coming for you will not go past you.' He had a second mug of coffee to raise his caffeine levels while he worked out the quickest way of getting to Manchester.

Remembering that the Home Secretary had assured him of 'every facility', he called Sci-Med and asked for a laptop computer equipped for mobile-phone-mediated download, as his own was still in Manchester. He also requested a car and driver immediately. This wasn't exactly in the spirit of the Home Secretary's offer but at least he'd be in Manchester by the time any shit hit the fan. Twenty minutes later a powerful Jaguar was outside his apartment block, its grey-suited driver waiting beside it.

Steven sat in the back and downloaded the latest information from Sci-Med as they sped up the motorway. Information on nine patients was now available, and all of them had received human-tissue valves. 'Shit,' he said out loud.

The driver looked at him in the mirror and asked, 'Problems?'

'You spend weeks working out a puzzle, then when you get the right answer it turns out to be impossible,' complained Steven.

'Maybe you only think it's impossible.'

'I *know* it's impossible,' said Steven.

'Have you eliminated all the other possibilities?'

'Yes.'

'Then whatever remains must be true, however improbable it seems. That's what Sherlock said,' said the driver.

'You're a Holmes fan?' asked Steven.

'He was a real detective,' said the driver, 'not like the sort you find on television these days, asking the public to do their job for them. I reckon old Sherlock could have shown these blokes a thing or two if he was around today. Lord Lucan would be in pokey before you could say, "Tea, please, Mrs Hudson."'

I'm sure he could show me a thing or two, thought Steven as he typed in a request for details of the donors of the tissue. He suspected that he was just going through the motions, but he didn't know what else to do. He'd probably finish up with just a list of dead people's names, but at least the paperwork would be complete.

As they entered the outskirts of Manchester, the driver asked him where exactly he wanted to go. Steven told him St Jude's, then helped with directions.

'Do you want me to wait?' asked the driver.

Steven said not.

'Good,' said the man. 'This place is giving me the creeps already.'

Steven appreciated what he meant: the streets around the city centre were eerily quiet. 'Turn left here.'

The driver drew up in front of St Jude's, just outside the police barrier, and said, 'Good luck with whatever you're doing, and remember what old Sherlock said about what you're left with being the truth.'

Steven smiled as he thanked him, but a lump had come into his throat when he saw his hired car still sitting where Caroline had parked it. After explaining to the nurses in the duty room who he was and why he was there, he changed into protective gear and entered the patient area. His heart sank: he found himself once again in a bloody nightmare. The only comfort was that the numbers had not gone up but even that was only because of the physical impossibility of cramming any more people in.

It took him a moment to work out which of the three hooded and visored orange-suited nurses was Kate Lineham, but he recognised her walk when she went over to a disposal bin to dump some blood-soaked swabs. He joined her, turning full-face so that she could see who he was.

She knew immediately why he was there. 'Over here,' she said, beckoning him to follow her. 'We made a little corner for one of our own.'

'Good,' said Steven.

She led him to the back of the nave to a corner behind one of the two main supporting stone pillars. Caroline lay on a camp bed along the back wall. Above her were a stained-glass window depicting the resurrection, and a board citing the names of those of the parish who had fallen in two world wars. Caroline's eyes were closed but she was moving her lips as if they were dry so Steven guessed that she wasn't sleeping. He knelt down beside her and laid his hand gently on her arm.

She turned her head to him and opened her eyes. Steven smiled at her through his visor. 'How are you doing?' he asked.

'Just fine,' she replied, as if giving a joke answer to a joke question. 'It's nice to see you.'

Steven patted her arm. 'I had to go to London,' he said. 'You probably didn't see the note I left in your car.'

She shook her head. 'No, I thought you'd done a runner.'

'I came back as soon as I heard. I'll be here if you need me – I plan to be with you every step of the way. You can beat this, I know you can.'

She smiled wanly and squeezed Steven's hand limply in lieu of a reply.

'Get some rest,' he said, smoothing her hair back from her forehead. 'I'll be back later.'

He found Kate Lineham again and asked, 'What do you think?'

She shrugged apologetically. 'Impossible to say. The statistics are against her, but if tender loving care can do it she's got it made.'

Steven nodded, grateful for an honest answer, then made for the exit and a shower. When he got outside his phone rang.

'Where the hell are you?' asked John Macmillan.

'Manchester.'

'May I ask why?' said Macmillan with barely suppressed irritation.

'There's more of the virus here than anywhere else,' replied

Steven. 'Apart from that, one of my friends has just gone down with it.'

'I'm sorry,' said Macmillan, the testiness disappearing from his voice. 'We know now that all eighteen wildcards received human-tissue valves, but getting the information on the donors is proving difficult. Organs and tissue are distributed through a central register in response to computerised requests from hospitals and clinics. The hospitals themselves aren't usually given personal details of the donors.'

'The names aren't going to make much difference, anyway,' confessed Steven, 'but I would like details of the register. Maybe someone could e-mail what you've got?'

'Of course. What are your plans in the meantime?'

'I need to talk to a heart surgeon again. There must be some-thing I'm missing in all this.'

Steven was desperately in need of sleep but he arranged to see Martin Giles again at the City General at two. He kept awake with constant cups of coffee and thought he was doing well until the surgeon greeted him with, 'God, you look rough.'

Steven made light of it and asked for more details about heart-valve replacement and how choices about the options were made.

'Basically, tissue valves are best,' said Giles, 'and human ones if you can get them, though only if they are a good match in terms of tissue type, of course. Ideally, we prefer repairing the patients' own valves using their own tissue. That way there are no problems with rejection and therefore no need to put them on immuno-suppression therapy, which almost always leads to problems. Mechanical valves, made of metal, plastic, carbon fibre or whatever, are okay but the flow through them isn't nearly as good as through a tissue valve because of restricted opening angles. The patients also usually have to be on anti-clotting agents for the rest of their lives. Age is also a factor. We'd give a tissue valve to a middle-aged patient, but probably fit a mechanical valve to an older one.'

'Can we just go back a bit there?' said Steven. 'You said that tissue valves are the best, human ones if possible.'

'Yes.'

'That implies that there's an alternative to human tissue?'

'Treated pig valves are also used.'

'Pig? What about foreign tissue rejection?' asked Steven.

'That's why I said "treated",' said Giles. 'They treat the pig valves with a chemical called gluteraldehyde to make them more acceptable. The valves themselves tend to be a bit weak and it's often necessary to give them an auxiliary scaffold – "stenting", they call it. They're not nearly as good as compatible human valves but they're used quite a lot, and with a pretty good success rate, all things considered – although there can be problems if, for instance, the patient's Jewish!'

Steven smiled. 'I take it tissue valves are screened for potential problems like AIDS, hepatitis, CJD, things like that.'

'Bet your life they are,' said Giles fervently. 'Litigation we can do without.'

Steven thanked him again for his help and drove back to his hotel. He lay down on his bed and slowly felt his limbs appear to double in weight as the prospect of sleep finally became a reality. His mind, however, was still troubled by conflicting arguments. Logic insisted that the replacement heart valves must be the cause of the outbreak, because they were the only common factor among the wildcard patients, but eighteen replacement valves could not possibly have come from one infected human heart. As he spiralled down into a deep sleep, the last image he had was of the driver saying, 'Maybe you only think it's impossible.'

Only four hours later he was jolted awake when a chamber-maid in the corridor dropped what sounded like a metal tray laden with the crockery from a royal banquet. He lay staring at the ceiling for a while before acknowledging that he was not going to be able to get back to sleep. He got up and showered, then ordered an omelette and a salad from room service. He turned on his laptop and downloaded his e-mail while he waited.

Skipping an apology for not yet having details of the donors' names, he read through the general details of how transplant organs and tissue were made available and how they were requested and allocated through a central register. It occurred to him that the register itself was a common link. All the replacement valves must have passed through it in terms of paperwork if not in substance. He asked Sci-Med to contact the operators of the register and request that they check their records for any factors common to the wildcard patients.

An hour and a half later he got his reply. There was another apology for still not having details of the donors but this one came with an explanation. The co-ordinating officer at the central register who was dealing with the request had been taken ill and sent home. Unfortunately, he had taken with him the computer disk with details of the donor files on it. People were trying to contact him urgently. With regard to Steven's request that the wild-cards be screened for common factors, one common factor had already appeared. The wildcard patients had all been found heart valves by the same co-ordinator, Greg Allan, and he, by a curious coincidence, was the man who had just gone sick.

'Well, well, well,' murmured Steven. 'Strikes me, I'd better take Mr Allan some grapes.'

He called Sci-Med and asked for Greg Allan's address as a matter of urgency. He was called back four minutes later by the duty officer, who said, 'I've got it but it won't do you much good. He doesn't seem to be there at the moment.'

'I thought he went home sick?'

'That's what his colleagues thought, and they all say he looked ill when he left. But when they tried to contact him about the disk they discovered he wasn't at home and his wife hadn't seen him since he left for work this morning.'

'Give me the address anyway,' said Steven and wrote it down; it was in Leeds. For once, luck was on his side. He was closer to Leeds here in Manchester than he would have been had he stayed in London. He could be at Allan's place in an hour; the question was, would Allan be there when he arrived? He told the duty officer of his plans and asked that Sci-Med contact the local police and ask them to put an immediate trace on Allan's car. 'Give them my mobile number and ask them to contact me the moment they find him.'

'Do you want him arrested?'

'No, just found. He knows something we don't about these heart valves, and I want him to tell me personally.'

Steven turned into Braidmoor Crescent in Leeds just after seven-thirty. There was a light in the window of Allan's bungalow, and he knocked on the door. A worried-looking woman in her mid-thirties answered. She put her hands to her mouth when she saw a stranger, and said, 'It's about Greg, isn't it? You've found him. What's happened? Where is he?'

He said apologetically that he couldn't answer her questions and that he was just another of the people who wanted to find her husband. He showed her his ID and asked if he could come in for a few minutes.

Her demeanour changed from alarm to worried bemusement as she showed Steven into the living room. 'What on earth is going on?' she asked. 'Where is Greg? First his colleagues tell me he's ill and he's supposed to be here, then they decide they need to speak to him urgently, then the police start asking about him and now you. Just what is all this about?'

Steven told her who he was and what his job entailed.

'But what has the virus outbreak got to do with Greg? He's an administrator: he deals with transplant requests, matching potential donors to recipients.'

'How long has he been doing that, Mrs Allan?'

'Six years, give or take. You still haven't answered my question.'

'Only because I can't,' confessed Steven. 'I don't know the answer yet, but your husband was the co-ordinator for eighteen heart-valve-replacement operations in which the recipients went on to develop the new virus.'

Mrs Allan's eyes opened wide and her face froze. 'But . . . that's outrageous,' she stammered. 'How can that possibly be?'

'I was rather hoping your husband might be able to help with that one,' said Steven. 'But he's not here.'

Mrs Allan started to come out of her shocked state, and he tried to guess what was going through her mind. She glanced briefly out of the window to where a new Ford Focus sat on the drive, and he guessed that it was hers. He had no idea what kind of wrongdoing, if any, Greg Allan was caught up in, but in his experience chicanery usually involved money. He wondered if there had recently been a change in the Allans' circumstances.

'What kind of car does your husband drive, Mrs Allan?' he asked innocently.

'A BMW. Why?'

Steven watched the thought process start again in Mrs Allan's eyes. 'Just in case he should drive into the street as I'm leaving,' he said pleasantly. 'New? Old?'

'New,' said she flatly. 'A silver 5-series.'

'Nice car,' said Steven. He sensed that she was on the brink of saying something, but his mobile rang and the moment was gone. He said, 'Excuse me,' and took the call. It was the local police.

'You requested a trace on Gregory Allan.'

'Yes, I did,' said Steven, cupping his hand tightly over the earpiece in an effort to contain the sound.

'I think you'd better get over here, to the woods at the east end of Gaylen Park,' said the policeman. 'The car's here and I think we've found him.'

Steven felt uncomfortable. The implication was that Allan was dead, and Steven was sitting less than six feet from the man's wife. He did his utmost to keep his face expressionless and said, 'Understood. I'm on my way.'

'News of Greg?' asked Mrs Allan.

'Not yet,' lied Steven. 'But I have to go.' He managed to avoid eye contact with her while he said goodbye: he felt that the news should not come from him.

Fifteen minutes later, Steven found several police vehicles parked beside Allan's silver BMW at the edge of the woods bordering a small park. There wasn't much activity among the officers, who were standing in a group, talking. He made himself known, and the inspector in charge said, 'We've been waiting for you to get here. We haven't touched anything.'

Steven guessed that Sci-Med had used full Home Office clout in making the request to the local police. 'Good,' he said. 'What have you got?'

The inspector led him through the trees and into a small clearing illuminated with police arc lights. 'I take it that's your man?' he said, pointing upwards. Steven saw a man hanging from the bare branches of a beech tree. 'Obviously decided to decorate a tree with himself this Christmas,' said the policeman.

Steven did not respond. Allan's face was purple and his distended tongue lolled out of his mouth, making him look like a hideous gargoyle on a medieval church. The fact that he'd hanged himself with a modern tow-rope, bright red with yellow bands at intervals, somehow detracted from the tragedy and lent substance to the policeman's awful allusion.

'Poor bastard,' said Steven.

'Can we bring him down now?'

Steven nodded. 'Sure.' He watched, grim-faced, as Allan was cut down and lowered to the ground, where the police forensic team were waiting to begin their work. They could have been about to begin a shift at a car-making plant: they were casual, at ease, relaxed; just another body, just another day. The police surgeon pronounced Allan officially dead and the inspector asked if Steven could confirm that the dead man was Gregory Allan.

''Fraid not,' said Steven. 'I've never met him.'

'Are we allowed to ask what he's done?' asked the inspector, squatting down with Steven beside the body.

'You can ask,' said Steven, almost mesmerised by Allan's face and wondering what had brought him to such a sad and sorry end, 'but right now I've no bloody idea. I wish to God I had.'

The contents of Allan's pockets were emptied out on to a ground sheet and one officer said, 'There's a note, sir.' The paper was obviously wet and the man held it by a corner as he passed it over.

The inspector put on gloves, took it gingerly and opened it with care. 'It's to his wife,' he said. 'It says, "I'm sorry" – obviously a man of few words. It's wet because he pissed over it when his sphincter went.'

'Any sign of a computer disk in his pockets?' asked Steven. Shaking heads said not. 'How about in the car?'

The inspector said, 'Take another look, will you, Edwards.'

Edwards, a tall red-haired constable wearing a white plastic 'noddy' suit two sizes too small for him, went over to the BMW and began searching it thoroughly. He returned as Allan's body was being zipped into its transport bag for transfer to the city mortuary. 'Down the side of the passenger seat,' he said. He handed the disk to the inspector who passed it on to Steven.

'Do you want me to sign for it?' asked Steven.

'Not with the friends you've got,' replied the inspector. 'Maybe you'd like it gift-wrapped?'

'This'll be just fine,' said Steven, slipping the disk into his pocket. 'Thanks for your help.'

SEVENTEEN

Capel Curig

Karen Doig and Ian Patterson left Capel Curig police station feeling thoroughly depressed. They had just been told by the inspector in charge that none of the local taxi firms had been called to the field station in recent weeks. How and why Amy and Peter had disappeared remained a mystery, and there was nothing more the police could do in the circumstances. They, like the Scottish police, had a policy of non-interference in domestic matters.

'I don't believe they walked down from the mountains,' said Karen with a shake of her head.

Patterson murmured his agreement.

'Apart from the fact that they weren't equipped to go walkabout in the Welsh mountains in winter – at least Peter wasn't.'

'Nor was Amy.'

'So why would they?' continued Karen. 'If they really wanted to run off into the sunset together, why not take the Land-Rover and leave it somewhere like the airport?'

'I know, it just doesn't make sense,' agreed Patterson.

'I still don't believe they've done it,' said Karen.

'So where are they?'

Karen stopped walking and looked at Patterson, her anger dissolving and despair taking its place. Her eyes filled with tears. 'I don't know,' she sobbed. 'I just don't know.'

Patterson put a comforting arm round her and they paused for a moment. 'Look, why don't we get a drink and decide where we go from here?' he suggested.

Karen dabbed her eyes with a tissue and nodded silently. They crossed the road and went into the hotel where they'd gone on their arrival. They'd chosen not to stay overnight there, opting instead for a bed-and-breakfast place along the road.

'Did you find it then?' asked the barman who'd given them directions to the field station.

Patterson said that they had and asked for two brandies.

The man, noticing that Karen was still wiping her eyes, backed off and delivered the brandy without further question. He went back to reading his paper behind the bar.

'I don't see that there's any more we can do,' said Patterson. 'If no one saw them and the police can't help . . .'

Karen took a deep breath to compose herself. 'I will not believe that Peter has left me, not until I see some proof,' she said. 'There must be someone in this bloody God-forsaken place who knows something. Excuse me—' and she leaped up and ran out of the room.

'Is she okay?' asked the barman, looking over his newspaper.

'She's upset,' replied Patterson. 'Her husband has disappeared without trace.'

'Like that, is it? I'm sorry.'

'No, I don't think it is "like that",' said Patterson. 'He and my wife were working at the field station we asked you about yesterday, but apparently none of the locals saw them and then suddenly they just disappeared completely. The Land-Rover they came down to Wales in was still at the field station when the fire broke out, and they didn't use any of the local taxis, so we can't work out how they even left the field station.'

'Maybe I can help there,' said the man.

'But you didn't see them, either,' said Patterson.

'No, but you aren't the only people to ask for directions to the station.'

Karen came back and sat down; she'd washed her face and re-applied her make-up.

'Go on,' said Patterson.

'Four people came in here about ten days ago asking for directions, two men and two women. I remember 'cos they were rude about the coffee, see.'

Karen, realising what the conversation was about, delved into her handbag and pulled out a photograph of her husband. She took it over to the barman. 'Was he one of the men?' she asked.

'No,' replied the barman, almost before he'd looked. 'They were Americans.'

'Americans,' repeated Patterson flatly. 'You mean tourists?'

'Shouldn't think so. The men were American, the women were Welsh, and local by the sound of them.'

'But you didn't know them?'

'Never seen them before or since.'

'But they asked about the field station?' said Karen.

'No doubt about it. I thought it a bit strange, like. None of them looked like boffins, if you know what I mean. They looked quite normal.'

'I suppose they didn't say why they were going to the field station?' asked Patterson hopefully.

''Fraid not.'

Karen asked if he could remember the exact date and he gave two possibilities. 'Either the Monday or the Tuesday, I'm not sure which.'

Karen turned to Patterson and said, 'That would be about ten days after Peter and Amy came here.'

Patterson agreed and added, 'And round about the time the two of them stopped phoning.'

Karen turned back to the barman and said, 'This really is important: can you remember anything else at all about those people?'

'Not really,' replied the man. 'They weren't the friendliest folk I've come across. They stayed for a meal, complained about the coffee and then buggered off. No bloody tip, either, as I remember.'

'How did they pay?' asked Karen; the man's comments had given her an idea.

He had to think for a moment. 'Credit card, I suppose,' he said. 'Ninety per cent of people do these days.'

'Then you should have a record of the transaction,' said Karen, her eyes bright with hope.

The man shrugged and said, 'I suppose. My wife deals with these things.'

'Would you ask her, please?' said Karen. 'It really is important.'

The man shuffled out of the bar and was gone for three or four minutes. When he came back he was arguing with a small grey-haired woman he called Megan. She was carrying a rectangular metal box, which she clutched to her bosom.

'Megan thinks you're from the Inland Revenue,' said the man. 'You're not, are you?' He gave an uncertain smile, revealing bad teeth.

'Definitely not,' said Karen.

'No way,' added Patterson.

The woman opened the box and tipped out a bundle of credit-card receipts on to the bar counter. Her husband put on a pair of black-framed glasses and started sifting through them, licking his fingers to assist their separation.

Karen felt as if she were watching a slow-motion replay of grass growing. She itched to snatch the forms and go through them herself, but she kept the impulse in check and made do with a glance at Patterson and a roll of her eyes heavenwards.

'This is the one,' announced the man. 'This is it.' He held the paper up closer to his glasses and read out with difficulty, 'American Express. J. Clyde Miller. Mean anything?'

Karen and Patterson shook their heads. 'May I see?' asked Karen. Her expression changed as she noticed something else. 'Look!' she said, handing the receipt over to Patterson. 'He was using a company credit card. Look at the company name.'

Patterson took the receipt. His eyes widened as he read out loud, 'Lehman International.'

'You've been a big help,' said Karen to the two people behind the bar.

'We can't thank you enough,' added Patterson.

'So you think you can trace these people?'

'They worked for the same company as my husband – at least, the one who paid the bill did. They must know something. You say the women were local?'

'Sounded like it.'

Karen looked at Patterson and said, 'Looks like we won't be going home just yet.'

'Might you be wanting some dinner, then?' asked Megan.

Karen smiled, thinking that the least she and Patterson could do was to eat at the hotel. 'I think we might,' she agreed.

Karen and Patterson made plans for the following day while they ate. 'I think we should call Paul Grossart in the morning and ask for the women's addresses,' said Karen.

'Grossart's not exactly been helpful so far,' said Patterson.

'You think he might refuse?'

'I think it's a possibility. I got the impression he wanted to wash his hands of Peter and Amy.'

'Jesus!' exclaimed the barman, who was reading his paper again. He called out something in Welsh and Megan appeared, drying her hands on a cloth. He showed her a story in the paper and they seemed to agree about something.

Karen and Patterson suddenly realised that the pair were staring at them. 'What is it?' Karen asked.

'It's her!' exclaimed the man, pointing to the paper as if he couldn't believe his eyes. 'This is one of the women who came here with the Americans.'

Karen and Patterson went over, and the barman showed them a picture of a middle-aged woman.

'She's in Caernarfon General,' said the man. 'They say she might be the first case in Wales of the Manchester virus.'

Manchester

Back in his hotel room, Steven slipped the disk into his laptop and felt a welcome buzz of excitement. Please God he was at last holding the key to the outbreak. The disk must be vitally important if Greg

201

Allan had chosen to end his life over it in a cold, dark wood a week before Christmas.

The disk contained a single Microsoft Word file with no title. Steven clicked it open and watched the first page come up under the header SNOWBALL 2000. Beneath it was a list of names in a vertical column, each aligned with the address of a hospital or clinic listed in a column to the right. His first impression was that the locations were pretty much spread over the entire UK. There was also a date assigned to each entry. Steven quickly scrolled to the bottom of the list to see what other information the document held, but there was nothing there. The list was all there was.

He recognised some of the names as those of wildcard patients so he felt confident that he had got hold of the right disk. In fact, when he examined the list in more detail, all eighteen wildcard patients were there but what he found puzzling was that there seemed to be no correlation between donors and recipients. If this was a record of the donors used in the supply of heart valves, as he supposed it to be, why weren't the donors matched up with their respective recipients? There was nothing to indicate who was what.

In all there were fifty-six names, an even number, so at least in theory they could be twenty-eight donors and twenty-eight recipients, but there was no way of telling. Steven felt a tide of bitter, hollow disappointment sweep over him. There was nothing here to help him establish what had caused the outbreak, and nothing to suggest why Greg Allan should have committed suicide when someone had routinely asked for details of donors. Steven logged off. He'd had enough of puzzles for the moment. He decided to go and see how Caroline was.

Kate Lineham had already come off duty and left for home by the time he got to St Jude's, so he had to explain all over again – this time to the night staff – who he was and why he was there.

'Dr Anderson's not too well, I'm afraid,' said one of the nurses. 'She had a bad afternoon, according to Kate, but recovered some ground later on and she's resting quietly at the moment. Kate left instructions that we should call her if there's any change.'

'Maybe I shouldn't disturb her?' asked Steven.

'No harm in sitting with her for a while, if you've a mind to,' said the nurse. 'It often helps to wake up and find a friendly face there.'

Steven agreed that was what he would do and got changed into protective gear before moving through the airlock into the nave. When he saw Caroline, he was shocked at the change in her appearance since earlier that day. Her skin had taken on a yellowish pallor and her lips were thin and cracked, though beads of sweat were trickling down either side of her nose.

He squatted down, rinsed out a sponge in the basin beside her and gently wiped the sweat away. Caroline stirred slightly, so he stopped for a few moments, shushing her with 'Sleep, my lady, sleep easy. Everything's going to be just fine.'

Caroline moved again, as if she were in discomfort.

'Think of sunshine . . . golden corn, white sails on blue water . . . the picnics we'll go on in the summer . . .'

One of the nurses came up behind him and laid a hand on his shoulder. 'Everything all right?' she whispered.

Steven nodded as he saw Caroline settle down again and heard her breathing become deep and regular. Once she was sleeping easily, his gaze drifted up to the memorial board above her bed and to the names of those who'd died in the 'bloody slaughter of war'. As he read through them, he couldn't help but think that they at least had had a tangible enemy, one they could see and fight against, unlike the poor souls in the church, who had been stricken by a colourless, odourless, invisible enemy. Its only function was to replicate itself and, in doing so, kill the body that harboured it. All things bright and beautiful, all creatures great and small . . .

Steven had been sitting with Caroline for about half an hour, holding her hand and soothing her, when she became restless again, as if in the throes of a bad dream. He tried shushing her through it, but this time to no avail. After a few more moments, he felt a convulsion ripple through her body and just managed to get a papier-mâché bowl up to her face in time to catch the bloody vomit that erupted from her mouth.

'Easy, my lady,' he soothed.

Caroline continued retching until there was nothing left in her stomach, her face reflecting her pain as the spasms racked her. When they at last stopped, her head flopped back on the pillow in exhaustion, blood trickling from her nose. He wiped it away and rinsed the sponge. Her eyes flickered open and recognition registered in them.

'It's you,' she said. 'God, I feel awful.'

'But you're winning,' said Steven with every ounce of conviction he could muster. 'Hang in there.'

She started to answer but another convulsion ripped through her and Steven held up the bowl again. Although her stomach muscles contracted so violently that her whole body heaved, she brought up only a trickle of bloodstained mucus.

'Jesus,' she complained, seeking relief from the pain of the spasms by wrapping her arms tightly round her stomach. Her nosebleed restarted with a vengeance and this time, when her eyes opened, Steven could see that conjunctival haemorrhages were turning the whites of her eyes red. He got up and waved his arm to attract the attention of one of the nurses. He asked her to stay with Caroline while he emptied the sick bowl and washed out the blood-soaked sponges at the sluice.

When he returned, the nurse said, 'I'd better call Kate.'

Steven knew the crisis had come. He sank to his knees beside Caroline again and did his best to make her as comfortable as possible with tender words and loving care. When she had a momentary respite from the spasms, she said haltingly, 'I remember telling you I hoped someone would be there to look after me if I ever needed them . . . I didn't realise it would be you.'

'I guess you drew the short straw,' said Steven.

Her attempt at a smile was cut short by another convulsion.

'I think I'm going to have to get some fluid into you, my lady,' murmured Steven, reaching for a saline pack. 'You've been losing too much.'

'Be . . . careful,' she cautioned. 'I'm not . . . too responsible for . . . my actions . . . right now.'

'Just try to relax.'

'You've no idea . . . how ridiculous that sounds,' said Caroline, grimacing with pain and drawing up her knees involuntarily.

A nurse appeared at Steven's shoulder and whispered, 'Kate's on her way. Can I do anything?'

Steven asked her to hold Caroline's arm steady while he inserted the needle. When it was secured in place he looked around for something to hang the saline reservoir from and settled on a corner of the memorial board. He pinned it next to the name of one Sergeant Morris Holmes who had died for King and Country at the battle of Ypres. He said, 'Just you hold that there for the time being, Morris.'

Steven's spirits rose as Caroline's spasms gradually became more infrequent and finally stopped, and she was able to relax into the margins between sleep and consciousness. But his optimism was short-lived: another wave of nausea overtook her and she started to retch all over again. When she at last settled again, she murmured, 'I think something just snapped inside me. I could feel it go.'

'What sort of feeling?' asked Steven.

'I think it was . . . my rubber band,' replied Caroline with a smile so distant that it froze Steven with its poignancy. It was the moment when he knew that she was drifting away from him.

'You're going to be just fine,' he said, although the words stuck in his throat and he had to swallow before he could say any more. 'You're over the worst now; the convulsions have finished and you're on the mend. You must rest and build up your strength.'

He was aware that Kate Lineham had arrived and was standing there with one of the other nurses. She chose, however, not to move into Caroline's line of sight or to say anything.

Caroline looked at Steven and he could read in her eyes that she was only minutes from death. He'd seen that look before in the eyes of fatally wounded soldiers. It was an almost serene acceptance of the inevitable. 'Oh, my lady,' he said, taking her hand. 'Hang in there. Please hang in there.'

'The joke, Steven.'

He looked at her questioningly.

'Tell me . . . the joke.'

Steven realised what she meant and slowly removed his hood and visor. He lay down beside her and put his cheek next to hers on the pillow. He kissed her hand and began, 'There was this little polar bear sitting on a rock, watching the ice floes drift by . . .'

As he delivered the punchline, Steven felt Caroline give his hand a tiny squeeze. He couldn't risk looking at her, because of the tears running down his face. All he could do was squeeze her hand back and remain there motionless, hating the entire world and its 'All things bright and beautiful' philosophy. Why didn't they understand what an awful place it was in reality? Not the fucking Disney theme park they kept pretending it was! Dog eat dog. Kill or be killed. Nature red in tooth and claw. Fucking nightmare!

The rolling tide of anger and grief that swept over Steven gradually abated, and he took a few deep breaths to try to get a grip on himself. Kate made the first move: she bent down and put her hand lightly on his shoulder. 'She's gone, Steven,' she said gently. 'Caroline's gone.'

He nodded and got up slowly. He replaced his hood and visor and acknowledged Kate's sympathy by taking her hands in his for a moment, before turning to head for the exit tunnel and the shower.

Back in his room, he managed to down the best part of a bottle of gin before sleep – or maybe it was unconsciousness – overtook him and excused him any more pain for one day. It was there waiting for him, however, when he awoke at ten the next morning with the maid wanting to do the room.

'Okay,' he said, his eyes closed against the light. 'But just leave the bathroom.' Suddenly fearing that the maid was going to use a vacuum cleaner, a sound he loathed even without a hangover – he felt sure that hell would be filled with the sound of vacuum cleaners – he opened one eye and saw that she was trailing an electric lead across the floor. This spurred him out of bed and sent him padding across the floor in his bare feet to seek refuge in the shower. He stayed there until he felt sure that the maid and her fearsome machine had gone, and then sent down for orange juice, coffee and aspirin. He got dressed while he waited.

Despite the distraction of a headache, he knew that this was going to be a crucial day for him. He wanted to grieve for Caroline – in fact, he wanted to wallow in grief, self-pity and sadness – but he couldn't afford to. He had gone through one personal hell when he'd lost Lisa and the world had ceased to have any point or meaning, and he recognised some of those signs and symptoms in himself at the moment. He couldn't let himself go down that road again, or he might end up in an institution staring at a blank wall. He would have to deal with Caroline's death by blocking it out of his mind as much as he could. Throwing himself into his work was going to help: he had to decide what to do about Greg Allan's list.

The hospitals probably wouldn't hand out the information he needed about the new names, so he asked Sci-Med for help. He hoped that once he had established who the donors were he might be able to see something they had in common.

The information when it came through left Steven speechless.

'You're absolutely sure about that?' he asked eventually. 'All of them?'

'Absolutely. They're all recipients. There are no donors at all on that list.'

'So what the hell were they given?' Steven wondered out loud.

'Heart valves,' replied the duty officer, sounding puzzled.

'Thanks, but that's not exactly what I meant,' said Steven. Then he suddenly saw the importance of what he'd just learned. 'Oh Christ!' he exclaimed. 'Is Mr Macmillan there?' As soon as he was patched through, he said, 'The list that Greg Allan had. They're all recipients.'

'I know,' said Macmillan. 'I've just been told.'

'But don't you see? Eighteen people on that list have already gone down with the virus,' said Steven. 'The remaining . . .' mental arithmetic was a challenge with this hangover . . . 'thirty-eight have still to go down with it. Don't you see? They're all potential wild-cards! They're people who had the same surgery as the others but haven't got the disease yet. We've got to isolate them. Once we've done that there won't be any more unexplained outbreaks popping up all over the place.'

'Yes, of course, I see what you mean,' said Macmillan. 'If you're right, it means HMG can forget about calling a state of emergency.'

'It certainly does. They can go back to worrying about fox hunting and the euro.'

'And maybe the cost of official cars for travel to Manchester,' countered Macmillan. 'How is your friend, by the way?'

'She died early this morning,' said Steven flatly.

'God, I'm sorry. That was thoughtless of me,' said Macmillan.

'You weren't to know,' said Steven.

There was a long pause; then Macmillan said, 'Change of subject. I don't suppose you've any idea about the relationship between the people on the list and the filovirus?'

'Not yet,' said Steven. 'But Greg Allan knew. I'm sure that's why he killed himself.'

'Pity he didn't think to tell us all about it before he did,' said Macmillan ruefully, and he rang off.

Steven went back to thinking about the fifty-six people on the list. They had all been given human heart valves, and that fact alone had exposed them to the ravages of a terrible infection, although not immediately. The delay was a stumbling block in itself. The other stumbling block was that, if fifty-six people had received human-tissue valves, there must have been at least fourteen donors, people who had, presumably, died in accidents all over the country and who had no connection at all with each other, and yet had all been carrying the same strain of a brand-new filovirus . . . That was – absolute bloody nonsense, he concluded. There was no other word for it.

EIGHTEEN

He was relieved to have put the constraints of so-called logic behind him. The real question he should be asking was: what was wrong with the heart valves those patients had been given? A few moments' consideration told him that there was only one way to find out for sure. He'd have to recover one of the transplanted valves from a wildcard victim and subject it to a whole range of tests.

This was going to be not only risky – a post mortem on a filovirus victim was a dangerous procedure – but difficult, because filovirus victims were cremated as soon as possible. He would have to move fast. He called Sci-Med back, asked them about the current condition of the wildcard patients, and told them why he wanted to know.

'All dead and burned except two,' said the duty officer.

'How come the exceptions?' Steven asked.

'One's a success story; it looks as if she might be one of the few who'll recover.'

Steven closed his eyes for a moment and wished it could have been Caroline. He forced the thought from his mind.

'The other one's the nun, Sister Mary Xavier. She wasn't cremated.'

'What?' exclaimed Steven.

'They came up with a special dispensation for her – apparently, her order has severe religious objections to cremation. Because of the special circumstances and because the convent's so isolated, the sisters were allowed to bury her in the grounds.'

'I didn't realise they made concessions over something like a filovirus,' said Steven acidly.

'A local decision in Hull,' said the duty man. 'I think they had to comply with strict conditions: sealed body bag, lead-lined coffin and all that. It's a possibility, don't you think?'

'A good one,' agreed Steven. He thanked the man for his help and rang off, already deep in thought. Requesting the exhumation of Sister Mary Xavier would be certain to meet with a lot of opposition on the grounds of insensitivity, but the only alternative was to wait until another wildcard case got ill and died. That could take another week or two, maybe even longer, and he needed to examine one of the heart valves as soon as possible. He decided to put in the request and get Sci-Med to fix the permissions and paperwork. He would deal with the flak as and when it came.

There was one other thing he'd have to get Sci-Med to set in motion: a thorough examination of Greg Allan's financial position at the time of his death. In particular, Steven wanted to know if any unaccounted-for sums of money had been paid into his account. If so, pressure must be put on Allan's wife, to find out how much she knew about her husband's alternative source of income.

By five in the evening, an exhumation order had been obtained, in the face of considerable opposition from the local council and senior representatives of the Roman Catholic Church, who saw it as sacrilege. The Church's opposition was heightened even more when they learned that, rather than risk moving Mary Xavier's body, the mobile containment facility used after the diagnosis of her illness would be put back and used for the post mortem and the recovery of her replacement heart valve. The only problem still unresolved was finding a pathologist willing to carry out the autopsy.

'It's proving difficult,' said Macmillan.

'All right, I'll do it myself,' said Steven.

'But you're not a pathologist.'

'I don't have to be,' said Steven. 'All that's required is for someone to open up her body and recover the mitral valve. I'm a doctor and I'm perfectly capable of doing that. In fact it might be unfair to ask anyone else to do it in the circumstances.'

'Well, if you're sure . . .' said Macmillan doubtfully.

'I take it Porton will be willing to carry out a full analysis of the valve?'

'No problem there. And the Swedish team will take responsibility for its safe transport.'

'Then it's settled,' said Steven. 'I'd better get up there.'

'When will you do it?'

'Tonight, if you can get the mobile unit back in position,' replied Steven.

'Will do,' said Macmillan. 'Oh, one other thing. The PM report on Greg Allan came in half an hour ago. Asphyxiation due to a ligature round his neck.'

'Not the best way to die,' said Steven. 'He must have got the jump wrong.'

'The police have talked to his wife. It wasn't a good time to do it, but their opinion is that she doesn't know anything about him being mixed up in anything illegal. She was aware of them having more money in the last year or so, but he told her that it was down to his shares performing well.'

'His must have been the only ones,' said Steven sourly.

'Quite.'

Steven decided to make one more call before he left for Hull. He rang Fred Cummings and asked if he could spare a few minutes to talk.

'Sure,' said Cummings. 'What can I do for you?'

'I'm sure we've spoken about this before, but I have to ask you again. Is there no conceivable way that a virus can lie dormant for a time before causing infection?'

'Not in the normal way of things,' replied Cummings. 'Viruses have to replicate in order to live. Take away their cellular host and they die.'

'How about inside a cellular host?' asked Steven.

'You mean, lie dormant within cells without replicating?'

'I suppose I do.'

'There's a state called lysogeny in bacteria,' said Cummings thoughtfully. 'Even bacteria have problems with viruses. Certain

bacterial viruses can enter the bacterial cell and interpolate themselves into their host's DNA. That way, when the bug's DNA
replicates normally the virus is replicated, too, but in a controlled
way, so no harm's done. Occasionally, when something out of the
ordinary happens to stimulate the virus, it goes into uncontrolled
replication and kills its host.'

'That's the sort of situation I've been looking for,' said Steven.
'What did you call it?'

'Lysogeny,' said Cummings. 'But it happens only in bacteria
and only with certain bacterial viruses.'

'Maybe we're about to learn something new,' said Steven.

'Come to think of it,' said Cummings, 'maybe a similar situation actually can exist in human beings.'

'Go on,' said Steven.

'I was thinking about the *Herpes simplex* virus,' said Cummings.
'You know, the bug that gives you cold sores. It seems to lie dormant
in the mucosa around your lips until something like sunlight
or stress triggers it off. No one has ever satisfactorily explained
that.'

'Food for thought,' said Steven.

Steven drove up to Hull, suspecting in his heart of hearts that he
had been too hasty in volunteering to carry out the pathology on
Mary Xavier. Not for the first time, he reminded himself – albeit
too late – that he wasn't the single man with no responsibilities
that he imagined himself to be when the bugle sounded. In reality,
he was a single parent with a daughter's welfare to consider. Jenny
needed a live father, not a dead hero, but here he was once again
courting danger and getting the buzz that he'd sought all his life.
He was on his way to carry out a procedure that even experienced
pathologists of many years' standing might baulk at. 'Oh, Jenny,
love,' he muttered to himself. 'You've got an idiot for a father.'

Pulling out now was not an option, though, so he'd do the next
best thing and think through the dangers ahead in order to try to
minimise them. In theory, it was simple; he just had to avoid

coming into contact with the reservoir of filovirus particles that was Mary Xavier's body. It was the minute size of the virus that constituted the real danger. The particles were invisible not only to the naked eye but to the 1000 × probing of an ordinary light microscope; it would take the power of an electron-beam microscope to determine their presence. Their sheer lack of physical substance meant that they were barely subject to the constraints of gravity and friction, and therefore had little or no positional stability. Millions of them could be carried on a droplet of moisture so light that it would remain airborne for hours. The slightest movement in the air could send clouds of them scattering off in all directions.

The only comfort Steven could find was in the fact that knowledge of the enemy was perhaps the most effective defence against it. He understood just how deadly a filovirus could be; there was no way that he would ever underestimate it. He would be wearing full protective gear with hood, visor and respirator, and have everything checked thoroughly beforehand for leaks. He would double-glove and, as an extra precaution, would use a chain-mail gauntlet on his left hand to give him protection against accidental cuts arising from a knife or scalpel slipping.

In his mind's eye, he went through the exact procedure he would use in the removal of Mary Xavier's heart. First, the central incision to open up the chest cavity, then the rib resection to give access to the heart, the freeing of the heart itself from associated tissues, and finally the removal of the organ itself. He would place it in a steel dish, and rinse it through with clean, sterile saline before dissecting out the mitral valve with fresh instruments. He would seal the valve inside an airtight container for transport to the lab at Porton, and the job would be done. Easy peasy. If only he could convince his stomach of that.

Steven had gone through the pathology in his mind several times by the time he reached the convent. Parked outside it were two police cars, a mechanical digger and two transporters associated with the Swedish mobile lab, which he could see had already been re-erected. He got out and walked over to the group of men standing by the vehicles.

'I'm Inspector Jordan,' said one of the policemen. 'Are you the pathologist?'

'Yes,' replied Steven. 'Everything ready?'

'The sisters have decided to show their disapproval by distancing themselves from the whole affair.'

'Understandable, I suppose,' said Steven. 'Will that affect anything?'

'Apart from no one getting a cup of tea, I don't think so,' said Jordan. He looked round the group. 'It's important we agree beforehand who does what, so I'll run through the plan of action. Mr Frost here from the council will operate the digger to excavate the grave and expose the casket. Dr Laarsen and his colleagues will then be responsible for its actual removal, but of course they'll have Mr Frost's help with the digger to lift it out, in view of the weight of the lead-lined casket. Dr Laarsen's people will oversee the transport of the casket to the mobile lab, where Mr Grieve from the undertakers who's an expert on the sealing of high-risk coffins will advise on the opening of the security lid. He will then retire and Dr Laarsen's people will remove the body. Dr Dunbar will then take over and carry out the post-mortem examination. When he has completed his work we'll go through the whole process in reverse. Everyone happy?'

'Happy' was perhaps the wrong word, thought Steven. In fact, it was definitely the wrong word; but he, like everyone else, nodded agreement.

'Right then, Mr Frost, if you please.'

The digger started up and diesel fumes filled the night air as the little yellow machine started to trundle slowly on twin metal tracks towards the graveyard at the back of the convent, where arc lights illuminated screens erected round Sister Mary Xavier's grave. One of Laarsen's people was detailed to provide Steven with protective gear, which he donned outside the mobile lab while the others trooped solemnly off behind the digger like members of a cathedral choir on their way to Mass.

Although there was no sign of the nuns, Steven felt the eyes of the Reverend Mother on him as he crossed the graveyard to join the others behind the screens. It might be his imagination, but he had a strong sense of her standing there in the darkness behind one of the upper convent windows, the dark birthmark on her face providing unwitting camouflage as she silently deplored and condemned that which he had instigated. It was almost a relief to step behind the screens and be shielded from view.

The digger bucked and scraped at the earth as Frost manipulated twin levers in the cab like a TV-series puppet, the spastic movement of its small shovel building up a growing pile of earth at the side of the trench. Nerves jangled as, with a sudden change in sound, the blade struck the coffin lid. The digger's work was done for the moment and its engine died away. Two of Laarsen's people lowered themselves into the grave to clear away the remaining earth by hand and to loop lifting cables under the casket.

As the minutes passed, Laarsen leaned over the grave to ask his men what the hold-up was. One of them reported that he was having difficulty getting the cable at his end far enough under the casket to make sure that it didn't slip.

'How far in is it?' asked Laarsen impatiently.

'Ten centimetres, not more,' replied the man.

'That'll do,' said Laarsen. 'Up you come.'

The two men clambered out of the grave and secured the top ends of the cables to the digger's shovel.

'As smoothly as you can please, Mr Frost,' said Inspector Jordan, but there was no way that the hydraulics of the small digger would permit completely smooth movement. There was a sharp intake of breath all round when the casket was jerked off the bottom of the grave. 'Steady, steady!' cautioned Jordan as it rose slowly from the grave. 'Let's have some help here.'

He put his hands on the lid of the casket to minimise the swing as it cleared the lip of the grave, and Laarsen's men stepped forward to provide stability at either end. 'It's clear,' said Jordan.

The digger driver took this as his cue to start swinging the casket round with a view to lowering it to the ground beside the grave. Suddenly a jerk in the hydraulics made the cable at the less-secured end slip free, and the casket slipped out of the loop and crashed down on the leg of the man at that end. The snap of bones sounded clearly above the noise of the machinery; as did the scream that followed.

There followed an anxious few minutes, which must have seemed like hours to the injured man, while the cable was once more looped under the casket by nervous helpers. Their fingers turned to thumbs in their haste and unease at having to use the small space between the base of the coffin and the ground, created by its resting on the man's broken limb. The cable was at last secured and the digger lifted the casket off the trapped leg. Steven tended to him and made him as comfortable as possible while they waited for the ambulance the inspector had called. He could not help but think that this was the last sort of thing any of them wanted at the start of an operation like this. It was going to put everyone on edge.

Laarsen was clearly upset and guilty about his error over the cable's security. Jordan felt bad about being ultimately responsible for the whole mishap. The digger driver felt guilty about his handling of the controls, and everyone else felt bad by association. There was a general surge of relief when the ambulance arrived and removed the accusing presence of the injured man.

The casket was secured to the digger's shovel and transported slowly over the ground at a height of only a few inches to the mobile lab, where it was manhandled with some difficulty into the facility. Steven decided not to involve himself in the opening of the casket and removal of the body. Instead, he used the time to walk up and down outside, calming himself and once again running through in his mind what he was going to do.

'All yours,' said Laarsen, emerging from the lab. 'We've put her on the table but we didn't take her out of the bag. Maybe you won't want to do that, either?'

'Maybe not,' agreed Steven. There was no need to have the

corpse totally exposed as if for full post-mortem examination. Exposing the chest area should be sufficient, and the less handling of a filovirus-infected body the better. Steven did up the seals on his suit and lowered his hood and visor. Laarsen himself checked him over thoroughly, giving his approval with a tap on the shoulder.

Steven entered the lab through the plastic-walled airlock and sealed himself inside. He was suddenly very aware of the silence. The digger's engine had stopped and even the generator for the lights could not be heard in the inner compartment. Mary Xavier's body lay in its sealed bag on the examination table.

Steven removed the seal over the zip and started to undo it. It stuck after the first inch and refused to budge. He cursed as he struggled with it, thinking that this might have been an ill-fated venture from the outset. He recognised the danger of such a negative train of thought and took a moment to compose himself before looking around for some mechanical assistance. He found a pair of Spencer Wells forceps and slipped them through the loop on the zip so that he could apply strong downward pressure with both hands. He managed to move the zip down a few more inches but it was a struggle; and so it continued until it was at last fully open. Inside his helmet his breathing sounded as though he was running a marathon.

Steven checked his gloves and cuffs yet again, making sure no cuts had arisen during the struggle with the zip, then donned the chain-mail gauntlet before opening the bag to expose the body. The weather had been cold so decomposition was minimal but the blue/grey skin was distended around the chest area, which started alarm bells ringing in his head. It was almost certainly due to an accumulation of body gases which had failed to dissipate. They would escape when he made the first incision, bringing with them a cloud of filovirus particles.

'Shit,' he murmured, wondering what to do. He could feel the pulse beating in his temples as he sought inspiration. He removed the chain-mail gauntlet and looked through the equipment cupboards. What he found there sparked off an idea of how to divert the gases. He rigged up a two-way plastic syringe to a length of clear plastic tubing, one end of which he immersed in a beaker full of Virkon disinfectant. He fitted a large-bore needle to the barrel of the syringe and checked all the joints. The plan was to insert the needle into Mary Xavier's chest cavity and release the gas. It would flow through the tubing into the disinfectant, which would kill the virus but allow the gas to bubble to the surface.

There was a moment when Steven experienced for the first time in his life what he thought afterwards must have been stage fright. He found himself unable to do anything but stand there motionless for a few moments. He was imagining what would happen if the condition of Sister Mary's skin turned out to be so bad that the needle had the same effect as on an inflated balloon.

The seconds passed until, calling on every reserve of courage he could muster, he pushed the needle into the grey skin. To his enormous relief, the puncture site held its integrity and the disinfectant in the beaker started to bubble violently as the escaping gas passed through it. For an awful moment he thought the beaker might up-end and spill over, allowing the gas to escape directly into the atmosphere, but, as he stared at the shuddering beaker, the flow lessened and eventually the bubbles stopped coming.

He removed the needle, put the chain-mail gauntlet back on and selected a suitable knife for the first incision. He murmured an apology to Sister Mary as he opened her up, and got on with the business of removing her heart without further incident. When he had dissected out the mitral valve and it was safely stored in the high-security container, he sewed up the chest incision with large stitches and sluiced disinfectant liberally over the area before re-zipping the bag. He had just as much trouble with the zip as before and was sweating with the effort before the seal was complete and he could wipe down the outside of the bag with yet more disinfectant. He placed all the instruments and equipment he had used in steel security containers for autoclave sterilisation later, and proceeded to sluice down the entire lab.

One of Laarsen's men was waiting for him when he emerged

from the lab, and he stood still while the man sprayed his suit with disinfectant. When he'd finished, Steven removed his hood and visor and took deep breaths of the night air. It didn't matter that it was cold and damp. It tasted oh so sweet.

'How did it go?' asked Laarsen.

'I got it,' said Steven.

'Can we put her back?' asked Jordon.

Steven nodded and gave a simple, 'Yes.' He didn't feel communicative. He was no longer running on adrenalin and all he could think about was writing to Jenny. He wanted to tell her that he was thinking about her and that he hoped she would have a lovely Christmas.

NINETEEN

It was four in the morning when Steven got back to Manchester, but he sat down and wrote to his daughter straight away, telling her how much he missed her and how sorry he was that he couldn't be there on Christmas Day. He would, however, phone her and was looking forward to hearing all her news about what Santa had brought her and the other two children. When his job was finished, he promised, he would spend lots more time with her and, come the summer, they would do lots of lovely things together. With Robin and Mary, they would build the biggest sandcastle anyone had ever seen on their favourite beach at Sandyhills and surround it with a moat that they could all paddle in.

His eyelids were becoming increasingly heavy but he forced himself to stay awake long enough to check for messages from Sci-Med on his laptop. There was one, saying that two new wildcard cases had been reported, one in Preston and the other in Exeter. Both names were on Greg Allan's list and the authorities had been well prepared. John Macmillan sent his congratulations. Files on the two new patients were appended. Steven did not bother opening them. He just lay down, closed his eyes and fell into a deep sleep.

The 'Do Not Disturb' sign that he'd hung on the door did its job and he slept straight through until eleven-thirty next morning. He felt better than he had done for many days and lay still for a while, thinking about Sci-Med's last message and, in particular, John Macmillan's congratulations. He had been keeping so busy – mainly to blot out things that he couldn't afford to dwell on – that he had not been giving himself credit for having done the most important thing in any outbreak: identifying the source. He might not yet understand why the people on Allan's list were the source, but that was academic when viewed against the fact that the outbreak was now under control. Wildcards were no longer wildcards. The authorities knew exactly who these people were and where they lived, and would be prepared and ready for new cases of the disease, which would be isolated before they infected anyone else. Steven got up and had a leisurely shower before dressing and starting to think about food. He was going to have a day off, he decided: he deserved it.

He didn't want to take breakfast or lunch in the hotel, so he decided to walk for a while and eat where the fancy took him. The sky was clear and blue and, although the temperature was close to freezing, it was perfect weather for walking. He walked for close on an hour before deciding to have lunch in a pub which looked as if it might have a bit of character. Before going in he bought himself a newspaper to read while he waited for his meal.

He found, as he sipped a pint of Guinness, that the newspaper seemed to share his good mood. The number of new cases in the Manchester area had been dropping over the past few days and, although the public were urged to remain vigilant, there was a cautious hope that the worst was over. Health boards in other areas had been very successful in isolating new cases where and when they occurred, and a government statement had announced that the source of the outbreak had been identified and steps taken to eliminate it, although no details had been released. Steven smiled at the last bit.

His meal arrived and he remarked to the waitress that the place was very quiet; he was the only one having lunch, although two old regulars by the look of them were seated on stools at the bar.

'Been like this for weeks,' she said. 'Worst Christmas season we've ever had.'

Steven nodded sympathetically. 'Looks like it's over, though,' he said, gesturing to the newspaper.

'About bloody time. If it hadn't been for that stupid bitch of a doctor letting all those kids from the disco roam around all over the place at the beginning, this would all have been over ages ago. I mean, I ask you . . .'

Steven felt as if he'd been kicked in the stomach. Thankfully, his momentary surge of anger was almost instantly overwhelmed by a realisation that, whatever he said, this woman and countless other people would go on believing that the Manchester outbreak had been caused by Caroline's mistake. This was what Spicer had done to her, and there wasn't a damn thing he could do about it. His only comfort lay in the knowledge that Spicer himself would be going to prison for a long time. He wished him a particularly unpleasant time. In the meantime, his good mood had evaporated and taken his appetite with it. He put a ten-pound note under his untouched plate and left.

It took another couple of hours of aimless walking for Steven to calm down and realise that he was by now very hungry. He wasn't exactly spoiled for choice when it came to eating-places in the area, but he came across a small teashop, where he made do with toast and cheese and no conversation.

Steven spoke to Macmillan in the early evening and was informed that Mary Xavier's mitral valve had reached Porton safely. Work had already begun on analysing it, but he shouldn't expect quick results. The material would have to be handled under category BL4 conditions, and safe meant slow.

'Why don't you take a couple of days off?' suggested Macmillan. 'We'll call you on your mobile if anything breaks. Go up to Scotland and see your daughter.'

'Not possible,' said Steven. 'I've been exposed to the virus. I can't take the risk.'

'Of course not,' said Macmillan contritely. 'That was stupid of me.'

'But I think I will take a couple of days off. I'm sure I'll find something to do.'

'Good,' said Macmillan. 'On a different subject, I had a letter from the PM this morning. He sends his thanks, as do the others. Having to call a state of emergency would have been no joke.'

'Suppose not,' agreed Steven.

He had a drink downstairs in the bar while he thought about what to do the following day. Getting out of Manchester seemed a very good idea. He needed to be away from it all, even if for just a few hours, somewhere away from people, somewhere where he could see the sky and breathe fresh air. It occurred to him that he wasn't that far from the Lake District. It was ages since he'd been back to that part of the country where he'd been brought up. He could drive up there first thing and have a day out, walking in the hills. The more he thought about it, the more he warmed to the idea. When he was a boy, being out in the Cumbrian mountains had always helped him get things in perspective. That was exactly what he needed right now, a sense of perspective, a sense of proportion.

Steven ordered another drink and moved away from the bar to sit down in a quiet corner and think about things in general. On the positive side, he had identified the source of the outbreak and had been thanked by the Prime Minister for doing it. His disdain for politicians could not entirely extinguish a feeling of satisfaction over this, but on the down side he was still a long way from explaining it and the unknown was always a cause for worry.

Caroline's death had left an ache inside him that he couldn't yet bear to face up to. He had been successful in pushing it to the back of his mind until the waitress had brought home the awful truth. Not only had Caroline lost her life to the virus, but she was going to be blamed wrongly by many for the outbreak. Victor Spicer had ruined her career and indirectly caused her death, and had also ensured that even history would vilify her. The realisation made Steven very angry. Caroline's only crime had been to use common sense instead of following procedure like a mindless automaton.

It was no comfort to think that was the direction the whole country was going in. Somewhere along the line, common sense had been replaced by political correctness. The meek, in the form of the stupid and ill-informed, were now inheriting the earth a little earlier than planned. When he thought about the job Caroline and the others had done down at St Jude's, Steven started to feel guilty. It was true that the outbreak was slackening but it wasn't over. Caroline had gone, but Kate and the other nurses would still be doing their best for the sick while he sat there sipping gin and tonic. He now knew what he must do for the remainder of the evening.

Kate was drinking coffee from a chipped mug with a teddy bear on it when Steven arrived at St Jude's. She gave him an uneasy grin when he walked in and said, 'Hello.'

'Hi, how are you?' Kate asked with plain meaning.

'Fine. How are things?'

'Much better now that we know the source of the outbreak's been identified. Well done.'

The other nurses in the room added their congratulations.

'I'm perfectly well aware of who the real heroes are in this affair,' said Steven. 'And they're heroines, not heroes. Frankly, I don't know how you all do it, day in, day out.'

'It's 'cos we're too stupid to know any better, sir,' said one of the nurses in a burlesque country-bumpkin accent.

'No, Mavis,' said the other in the same accent. 'As I see it, shit-shovelling's an art and we're sort of artists, like—'

'Cut it out, you two,' said Kate.

All three nurses broke into laughter and Steven joined them.

'Well, this unworthy man has come to offer his unworthy services for the evening if you can use them,' said Steven.

'We never turn down an extra shovel,' said Kate.

He was pleased to find that the church was only three-quarters full, proof that the newspaper story had substance. Kate indicated where he should start work and he set about doing his bit, working his way along the line of patients, ensuring that they were clean and comfortable. But when he came to the second to last patient in the line, a shiver of horror ran down his spine: it was Trudi, the Spicers' au pair.

He looked long and hard at her, hoping he was mistaken but

knowing in his heart that he wasn't. She was only semi-conscious, her hair was lank and she had lost a lot of weight, but she was the girl who had opened the door to him on his first visit to Spicer. He thought back to the look on Spicer's face, when Steven had warned him about the possibility of having given the virus to his wife. Now it made sense. Spicer had shown no relief when he said he and his wife hadn't made love, and this was why. He'd been having a fling with Trudi and knew he'd put her at risk. Maybe this was also the real reason why he'd dropped Ann Danby: he'd simply moved on.

'Bastard!' Steven whispered under his breath. 'Slimy little bastard.'

At the end of their shift, Kate and Steven left the building together. Kate remarked that he seemed preoccupied and asked why. He told her about Trudi and got the reaction he expected: 'The little shit!'

'About sums him up,' said Steven.

'You know, I hold him personally responsible for what happened to Caroline,' said Kate quietly. 'She just wouldn't take any proper rest and, whatever she said, it was because that man blamed her for the spread of the outbreak. She felt driven to atone for something that wasn't her fault.'

Steven nodded his agreement.

'The word is they've reduced the charges against him,' said Kate.

'*What?*' exclaimed Steven, unwilling to believe his ears.

'There's a rumour going round that they're reducing it to manslaughter.'

'It was murder,' he insisted.

'Maybe not when you're an MP with a powerful daddy and friends in high places.'

Steven had a restless night but when he awoke to see the sun shining in through the windows he decided to follow his original plan and drive up to Cumbria to have his day out on the hills in crisp, clear conditions. The mountains, as he knew they would, made him feel very small, and thoughts of the timescale involved in their formation made his own lifetime seem like a mere breath in the cosmos. He was as unimportant as a single grain of sand on the face of the earth, and that was exactly the feeling he wanted. It always brought with it absolution.

In all, he walked for five hours, pausing only once, high above Windermere, to sit on a rock and eat the sandwiches that he'd bought earlier. He didn't rest for long, though, because he felt his body cooling rapidly and his fingers becoming numb in the sub-zero temperatures. Darkness was already falling by the time he got back to the car, and his calf and thigh muscles were telling him that they'd had a hard day.

On impulse, he decided to make a detour on the way back and drive through Glenridding, the village where he had been brought up. He drove slowly through it but didn't stop. His folks were long dead and there was no one there he wanted to see again. Ullswater, however, on whose shore the village sat, was unchanged, and he took comfort from that as he followed its north shore. The place triggered memories of a happy childhood and the friends he'd known when the summer days went on for ever.

Although his day out had helped him relax, Steven's thoughts turned to what Kate had said about the charges against Spicer being reduced. Despite his best efforts, her words played on his mind all the way back to Manchester. The man had stabbed Pelota with a kitchen knife in his own restaurant, and had admitted doing it. How could the Crown Prosecution Service possibly consider a reduced charge?

Steven tried hard to cling to his anger, but it was all too easy to see how clever lawyers might present Spicer's case. Pelota had been blackmailing him, and that would be the key to the defence. No one would contest that fact, so there would be no argument about it in court and certainly not much sympathy for Pelota by the time defence counsel had laboured the point. Spicer's lawyer would maintain that his client had decided to do the right thing and go to the police. He would say that he had gone first to the

Magnolia to tell Pelota just that, and Pelota, no longer able to wield the threat of exposure, had threatened him with a knife. A struggle had ensued, and during it Pelota had been accidentally stabbed. Ye gods, Spicer might even get off with a light sentence instead of the life term Steven had been counting on. He might even come out of it on a wave of public sympathy!

Recurring thoughts of Spicer and his role in Caroline's death haunted Steven all evening, so much so that he came to a decision about what he would do with his second day off. It might not be the most sensible thing in the world, but he would try to see Spicer in prison. Spicer was the only man who could put right the wrong done to Caroline's reputation. There was also a chance that the little shit might not know what he'd done to Trudi. He should know about that. He definitely should.

Tiredness was catching up as Steven logged on to his computer before bed and found that the first result had come in from Porton. The lab had carried out a tissue-compatibility test on the mitral valve taken from Mary Xavier and found it was a very good match – almost perfect, in fact.

'Nice to know,' murmured Steven.

'Spicer might want his lawyer present,' warned the prison governor when Steven made his request.

'It's completely unofficial,' said Steven. 'There's no question of interviewing him under police caution, so there's no chance of him incriminating himself any further. I just want a chat.'

'A chat,' repeated the governor with a knowing smile. 'He may well refuse to see you, in that case,' he said.

'He may. But there'd be no harm in letting him think there might be some official basis for the request . . . ?'

The governor's smile broadened. He said, 'All right, we'll play it your way and give it a try, but if he asks for a lawyer he gets one. Understood?'

'Understood.'

Leaning over the desk, the governor said, 'There's actually a very good chance he won't. Our Mr Spicer has been experiencing a resurgence of self-confidence, shall we say, ever since the charges were reduced.'

'Then it's true?'

'Oh yes,' said the governor. 'It's what happens when your pals in high places retain the services of the best silk in the country and the local Crown prosecutor starts spending a lot of time in the lavatory.'

'And they tell me we don't have plea bargaining in this country,' said Steven.

'Like we don't have a class system,' said the governor, picking up his phone.

Before long a return phone call informed them that Spicer was waiting in the interview room. 'I'll take you down,' said the governor.

Despite the prison clothes, Spicer looked both smart and smug, thought Steven as he was shown into the room. 'Nice of you to see me,' he said.

'Just call me curious,' replied Spicer, wearing the self-satisfied grin Steven had come to loathe.

'I hear you got the charges reduced,' said Steven.

'I had every confidence in British justice, and it hasn't let me down.'.

'You murdered Anthony Pelota to keep him quiet, and, what's more, you're responsible for the deaths of well over a hundred people in this city.'

Spicer's grin faded. 'Let's get something straight,' he hissed, leaning across the bare table that separated them. 'There's no way I could have known I had that damned virus, and you know it. My medical history's confidential, and if any suggestion of this reaches the papers I'll hold you personally responsible and sue your arse off.'

'You also destroyed the reputation of Dr Caroline Anderson to score cheap political points,' continued Steven.

Spicer relaxed back into his chair. 'So that's why you're here,' he said with a knowing grin. 'She sent you here to try and salvage her career.'

'She's dead,' said Steven. 'She died nursing victims of the virus.'

Spicer looked questioningly at him, as if trying to see an angle that wasn't immediately apparent. 'And you had a soft spot for her, right?'

'I think I loved her,' said Steven matter-of-factly.

Spicer swallowed. 'Why are you here?' he asked, clearly unsettled.

'I want you to put the record straight on Caroline.'

'She meant that much, huh?' said Spicer, his expression showing that he thought he might have the upper hand. 'Well, no deal. She made a wrong decision. She should have sent out a call for all those kids at the disco.'

'That wouldn't have made the slightest difference. As it was, she used her common sense and prevented panic. She was a good and dedicated doctor. She deserves to be remembered as such.'

'No deal, Dunbar. I have my own career to think of.'

Steven's open incredulity brought a smile to Spicer's face. He said, 'All right, I had an affair, I admit it. I'm not the first and won't be the last. Then some wop tried to blackmail me and accidentally got himself killed trying to stop me going to the police. No one's going to lose much sleep over that. It's not inconceivable that I might be forgiven in time. There's even a rumour going around that my barrister's sponsored by Kleenex because of the number of jurors he's reduced to tears.'

Steven didn't smile. He felt his loathing for Spicer become an actual taste in his mouth. 'Trudi is in St Jude's,' he said. 'She's gone down with the virus.'

Spicer went silent and still. 'So?' he said eventually; but his bravado was diminished by the hoarseness of his voice.

'We both know how she got it.'

'Even if what you're suggesting is true – and I don't accept that for a moment – there's nothing you can do. Like I said, my medical history is confidential, and there's no way I could have known at the time.'

Steven looked at Spicer as if he were a stain on the floor but said nothing. Spicer was psyched into leaning across the table and saying, 'Nothing you can do, Dunbar.'

'It's true I can't reveal your medical record, or do anything to stop a smartarse lawyer minimising your crime, but I'm not entirely without influence.'

'What's that supposed to mean?'

'It would be naïve of you to believe that no one else knows about your involvement in the outbreak, or that rumours won't start.'

'So what? They won't be able to make it public any more than you can.'

'It's my guess that you're still going to go to prison – not for as long as I'd hoped, I grant you, but you're still going down.'

'So? I'll catch up on my reading.'

'That's where my influence comes in.'

'Just what are you getting at?' asked Spicer uneasily.

It was Steven's turn to lean over the table. 'Just this. Either you admit publicly that you falsely accused Caroline of incompetence and clear her name, or I'll put the fix in over where and how you spend your sentence. And believe me, you little shit, I'll see to it that your arse becomes a bigger attraction than Blackpool Pleasure Beach.'

Spicer turned pale. He tried to splutter a response but nothing came out.

'Your call,' said Steven. He got up and knocked on the door. The warder opened it at once, and Steven was gone before Spicer could say any more.

Steven needed a drink. He headed for the nearest pub and downed a large gin. He was annoyed with himself for letting Spicer get to him again; he'd come dangerously close to hitting the man, and he knew it. He was about to order another drink when his mobile phone rang, attracting derisory looks from the other customers.

He went outside, and Macmillan said, 'There's been another wildcard case.'

Warning bells went off in Steven's head: why was Macmillan phoning him personally? 'Where?' he asked.

'North Wales.'

'And?' Steven had a nasty feeling there was bad news to come.

'She's not on the list.'

Steven closed his eyes and mouthed the words 'Oh fuck!' Aloud, he said, 'Oh dear.'

'Oh dear indeed,' said Macmillan. 'You do realise what this means?'

'We're not out of the woods yet.'

'That's one way of putting it, although the PM used a different expression when I told him fifteen minutes ago. He's reconvening the national emergency committee.'

'Makes sense,' said Steven, his voice heavy with resignation. 'Any ideas at all?'

'I suppose there could have been more than one list,' suggested Steven weakly.

'Then why wasn't it on the disk? There was plenty of room.'

'Don't know, but it's worth checking out.'

'I'll have Greg Allan's colleagues go through his stuff with a fine-tooth comb,' said Macmillan. 'Just in case there is another disk.'

'You're absolutely sure this woman's not on the list?' said Steven. 'I mean she might have changed her surname if she got married recently.'

'She's been married for twenty years. And, what's even more important, she's never had heart surgery in her life.'

Steven felt the weight of the world descend on his shoulders. 'I see. Send me the details, will you?'

'On their way,' said Macmillan gruffly, and he hung up.

When Steven got back to his hotel, the information on the new case was waiting for him when he connected his laptop. The sick woman was Maureen Williams, aged forty-four, a retired nurse who lived with her lorry-driver husband in the village of Port Dinorwic on the Menai Strait. She was currently in isolation in Caernarfon General Hospital and local Public Health officials were keeping a close eye on her neighbours and relatives.

The file made depressing reading. Steven couldn't find one solitary thing to connect Maureen Williams to any of the other cases. She had never been involved with anyone connected to any of the outbreaks, and she didn't have a heart problem. 'So how the hell did she get it?' he exclaimed out loud. 'Jesus Christ! Give me a break here.'

He sat down on the bed and stared at the floor, taking deep breaths and trying to get a grip on his emotions. For two pins he'd pen a letter of resignation and piss off into the sunset . . . but the thought didn't last. If there was any resigning to be done he'd do it at the end of an assignment, not in the middle, and certainly not at square one, which was where he seemed to be back once again. He got up and started pacing round the room.

Despite the new evidence, he still could not and would not accept that any virus could appear out of thin air and infect at will. There had to be a connection. It was just that he couldn't see it. 'Yet!' he spat out the word defiantly. Almost unconsciously, he started throwing things in a bag. He was going to North Wales.

TWENTY

It was late when Steven arrived in Caernarfon. He'd driven non-stop and felt the need to stretch his legs, so he parked down by the waterfront and walked from the harbour round the walls of Caernarfon Castle where they stood guard over the Menai Strait. He paused halfway round, leaned on the railings and looked down at the cold, dark water lapping on the shingle. The sound of a foghorn somewhere on Anglesey added to the gloom surrounding him. He shivered, rubbed his arms and returned to the car to drive up to Caernarfon General.

At that time of night only junior medical staff were on duty, so Steven spoke to the young houseman in charge of the special unit where Maureen Williams was in isolation.

'There's not really much I can tell you,' said the doctor, 'apart from the fact that she's very ill.'

'I take it no line of contact has been established in the past twenty-four hours?' said Steven.

'None at all. It's a complete mystery how she got it. She hasn't been out of Wales in the past year, and Y Felinheli isn't exactly a crossroads for the international jet set.'

'Ee Felin what?'

'Sorry, it's the Welsh name for Port Dinorwic. That's where she lives.'

'Is she conscious at all?'

'Some of the time.'

'Does she know what's wrong with her?'

'Not from us, but we told her husband, of course, and the papers have somehow got hold of it, so it's no big secret.'

'How did her husband take it?'

'Oddly,' said the houseman, tapping his pen thoughtfully against his front teeth. 'I was there when my boss told him, and he said something very strange. He said, "The bastards. They knew all along."'

'Knew what?'

'We asked him, of course, but we couldn't get any more out of him. He just clammed up.'

'Interesting,' said Steven, encouraged by the likelihood that Williams knew something about his wife's illness. 'Got an address for him?'

The doctor checked the files and wrote it down for Steven.

'Any other relatives on the scene?' asked Steven.

'There was a woman who called up three times a day when Mrs Williams was first admitted. She was a friend, not a relative; Mair Jones, her name was. She seemed very concerned, but then she rang to say that she just wanted to leave a message. She said to tell Mrs Williams she was going away for a holiday, just in case.'

'In case of what?'

'I've no idea. She said Mrs Williams would understand.'

Steven nodded. He was glad he'd come to Wales. He'd learned a couple of things he could pick away at. He got up to go, saying he would probably be back in the morning. 'Where will I find a hotel at this time of night?' he asked.

'In North Wales?' exclaimed the houseman, feigning shock. 'Where all doors are bolted against the devil before midnight? You could try the Station, but I wouldn't bet my buns on it.'

Once outside, Steven stood for a few moments, thinking about what he'd been told and wondering whether or not to wait until morning before pressing on with his enquiry. If Mr Williams knew something – anything at all – he must talk to him, and the sooner the better. That unguarded comment about the bastards knowing all along demanded explanation.

Steven glanced at his watch; it was a quarter past one in the morning; but if he was still up and working on a bitterly cold night, he could see no reason why Mr Williams should be allowed to slumber on undisturbed. He would go to see him.

Steven checked his road map and was pleased to see that Port Dinorwic was no more than a fifteen-minute drive from Caernarfon. He hoped it wouldn't turn out to be a large place, because there would be no one about at that time of night to ask for directions.

The more he thought about it, the better he felt about going to see Williams at this ungodly hour. Police forces all over the world knew the effectiveness of the middle-of-the-night knock on the door. It was usually a sight more productive than a call at any other time. People were disorientated when their sleep was disturbed, and so were much less likely to lie successfully.

To his relief, Port Dinorwic was manageably small. It clung to a steep hillside, and tumbled down through a series of steps and winding lanes to a harbour and marina. Steven parked on the main street and started his search by walking down a steep, cobbled lane, careful of his footing on the frosty stones and thinking of *Under Milk Wood*. A small town, starless and bible-black . . .

At the bottom of the lane, Steven walked towards the harbour, looking at the names of the other streets leading down to it. The third one along was the one he was looking for and number 12, Williams's house, was four doors up. There was no bell so he gave three loud raps with the heavy knocker and waited. A fourth knock was necessary to get a response.

'All right, all right, I'm coming. Who are you and what the hell d'you want at this hour?'

'The Sci-Med Inspectorate,' said Steven, sounding as official as possible.

'The what?'

'Just open the door, please.'

The door opened and a thin, wiry, ginger-haired man, with a plaid dressing gown wrapped unevenly round him, stood there, rubbing his eyes. 'Who did you say you were?'

Steven showed his ID and said, 'I have to ask you some questions.'

'What about?'

'About how your wife contracted the filovirus infection,' said Steven, stepping inside before Williams could block the way.

'How the hell should I know?' asked Williams, getting his wits back and closing the door. 'I'm a lorry driver not a bloody doctor.' He led the way into a small, cluttered living room and cleared piles of newspapers and magazines off the armchairs.

'Because of what you said when you were told about your wife's condition. You said, "The bastards. They knew all along." What did you mean by that? What did the bastards know, Mr Williams?'

Williams was flustered. He knelt down to light the gas fire, and took his time over it. 'Did I?' he answered eventually. 'I was upset. I'm not sure what I said.'

Steven stared hard at Williams, his dark eyes accusing him of lying.

'Who did you say you worked for?' asked Williams.

'I'm an investigator with the Sci-Med Inspectorate,' said Steven.

'What kind of investigator's that, then?'

Steven pulled out the gun from the holster under his arm. He didn't point it at Williams but let it rest in the palm of his hand. 'One with a gun,' he replied.

Williams's eyes opened like organ stops. 'Jesus!' he exclaimed.

'The UK's a hair's breadth away from having to declare a national emergency, and all because we can't find out where the virus is coming from. You know more about it than you're letting on, and that's making me angry, Mr Williams. Tell me what you know.'

The threat had the desired effect. Williams, who couldn't take his eyes off the gun, said, 'All right, for Christ's sake. Put that thing away. I'll tell you.'

Williams had to clear his throat and regain his composure before he could begin. Steven waited patiently.

'Two Americans,' said Williams. 'They recruited Maureen and another woman.'

'To do what?'

'It was a nursing job, looking after two very sick people, they said.'

'Why them? Your wife has retired from nursing, hasn't she?'

'They needed a particular kind of nurse. Maureen and the other woman had both trained as fever nurses, and apparently fever nurses are like gold dust these days. They said it was very important.'

'Were the nurses told what was wrong with these people?' asked Steven.

'Not exactly, just that they should take every precaution in dealing with them.'

'But why would anyone in their right mind take on such a job?' asked Steven.

Williams looked at the floor and said almost inaudibly, 'Three thousand pounds each, that's why.'

It was Steven's turn to be surprised. He let out a low whistle. 'And part of the deal was that they didn't say anything about it?'

Williams nodded.

'Who were these Americans?'

'I don't know.'

'How did they pay?'

'Cash in advance.'

'Where were the patients?'

'Somewhere up in the hills behind Capel Curig. They weren't supposed to tell anyone, but Maureen told me that much.'

Steven looked silently at Williams for a moment, and the man put his hands to his eyes and began to sob. 'I'm going to lose her,' he said. 'I never thought for one minute that anything like this would happen. We were going to use the money to visit Malcolm and his wife in Australia. It's ten years since we last saw them.'

'There's still hope,' said Steven softly. He had got what he wanted, so there was no need to play the hard man any more and he felt for the man. There was every chance that the welcome addition of cash to the Williams household was going to pay for his wife's funeral. 'Did Maureen say anything at all about the patients she nursed?' he asked.

Williams shook his head. 'She told me not to ask.'

'This other woman. Was her name Mair Jones, by any chance?' asked Steven.

Williams nodded. 'That's her. She went off to Majorca. I think she was scared she was going to get the virus, too. She wanted to have a last fling in the sun in case it happened.'

Just in case, thought Steven.

'Cup of tea?' asked Williams.

'Please.'

When he returned to his car Steven called the duty man at Sci-Med and told him about Mair Jones. He wanted her found in Majorca and brought back to the UK as soon as possible.

'On what grounds?'

'She has vital information about the virus epidemic. Pull out all the stops and get her back here under any pretext you like – get Special Branch to go out there and kidnap her, if necessary.'

'Would you like to have a word with Mr Macmillan?'

'He's there?' exclaimed Steven, automatically looking at his watch and seeing that it was after two-thirty.

'Been here all night.'

Macmillan came on the line. 'Dunbar, where are you?'

'I'm in Wales. You're up late.'

'There was a long meeting of the national emergency committee. We couldn't agree, so we're still holding off.'

'Good,' said Steven. 'Maureen Williams isn't a wildcard, she's a contact.'

'You know how she got it?' exclaimed Macmillan.

'Just that she got it from someone else. It's all a bit complicated at the moment.' He told Macmillan what he'd learned and about the need to find Mair Jones.

'I think the Home Secretary's still in the building,' said Macmillan. 'I'll have a word and impress on him the importance of finding her.'

'Good.'

'What will you do in the meantime?'

'Go back to the hospital in the morning and see if Mrs Williams regains consciousness.'

Steven opted to drive into Bangor rather than return to Caernarfon. He thought his chances of finding a hotel open in the early hours of the morning might be better in a bigger place, and so it proved. There was no chance of getting anything to eat, but at least he found a bed for what remained of the night and a bathroom with hot running water. There was an electric kettle in the room, with sachets of tea, coffee, sugar and whitener and, thankfully, a few biscuits. He had a warm bath, then dined on instant coffee and digestive biscuits. Luckily he was so tired that he fell asleep quickly, putting his hunger on hold until the morning.

The consultant in charge of the special unit at Caernarfon General, Dr Charles Runcie, had been made aware of Steven's interest in the case. He smiled and offered his hand. 'I don't think I can tell you any more than my houseman, Roger Morton, did last night,' he said.

'But I can tell *you* something,' said Steven. He told Runcie of his success in establishing that Maureen Williams was no wildcard case.

'A nursing job!' exclaimed Runcie. 'So what in God's name happened to her patients?'

'That's what we have to find out,' said Steven. 'They're trying to trace Mair Jones at the moment. I don't suppose she ever came here in person?'

The consultant shook his head and said, 'I think not. There would have been no point. We would only have given out information to relatives.'

'What are the chances of getting any information out of Mrs Williams?'

'Slim,' replied Runcie. 'Frankly, I don't think she's going to last beyond—'

There was a commotion outside, then the door burst open and they saw a harassed-looking woman trying to restrain another woman.

'I'm sorry, Dr Runcie, but this woman insists on seeing Mrs Williams. She seems to think she knows something about her husband's disappearance.'

'I'm afraid Mrs Williams cannot receive visitors because of her condition,' said Runcie calmly. He got up from his chair. 'Mrs . . . ?'

'Doig, Karen Doig. I'm sorry to burst in like this, but there seemed to be no other way. We've been trying to see Mrs Williams for the past two days, and I'm at my wits' end – we're both at our wits' end,' she added. She gestured at a man who, looking slightly embarrassed, was hovering in the background. 'This is Ian Patterson. His wife, Amy, and my husband, Peter, have disappeared from a company field station near Capel Curig where they were working, and Mrs Williams knows something about it.'

Runcie looked at Steven and said, 'I'm sorry, the world seems to have gone mad this morning.'

Steven's bemused detachment had changed when he heard Capel Curig being mentioned. He ignored Runcie's apology and asked, 'What kind of field station?'

It was Runcie's turn to look bemused. He turned to his secretary, who was smoothing herself down, and said, 'Claire, do you think you could bring us all some coffee?'

'Peter and Amy both work for a company called Lehman Genomics, just outside Edinburgh,' explained Karen. 'They were sent down to the company's field station here in Wales, and now both of them have disappeared. The company claims that they ran off together, but we won't accept that until we have more than Lehman's word for it. We came to find out for ourselves.'

'Where does Mrs Williams come into it?' asked Steven.

'She was one of a party of four people who stopped in Capel Curig about twelve days ago and asked for directions to the field station. There were two American men and two local women – one was Mrs Williams. We've been able to establish that at least one of the men worked for Lehman, but the company denied all knowledge of this when we phoned them earlier.'

Steven was beginning to feel that his luck had turned. 'Mrs Doig,' he said, 'you don't realise it but you've done your country a great service by coming here this morning.'

Karen was not the only one to look puzzled, but Steven was already on the phone to Sci-Med. 'I need to know everything about Lehman Genomics' was his request.

Runcie asked to be excused, but said Steven was welcome to use his office for as long as necessary. Steven questioned Karen and Ian Patterson closely for the next thirty minutes, trying to establish whether there was a connection between the company and the virus outbreak. He didn't say as much, but it was clear that Peter Doig and Amy Patterson were the two patients Maureen Williams and Mair Jones had been recruited to nurse.

'Have you no idea at all what Peter and Amy were working on?' asked Steven.

'They weren't allowed to say,' replied Patterson. 'Secrecy is important to research companies like Lehman.'

'What kind of scientist is your wife?'

'She's an immunologist.'

'Not a virologist?'

'No.'

'And Peter?' asked Steven, turning to Karen.

'He's a medical lab technician by training. He worked at the Royal Infirmary in Edinburgh from the time he graduated, but he got fed up with the low pay. The job with Lehman came up about nine months ago.'

Steven nodded. 'I take it he didn't say what he was working on, either?'

''Fraid not, although he did have a name for it. He called it the Snowball project. Maybe it was a pet name he made up. I'm not sure.'

'Thank you,' said Steven with heartfelt sincerity. He had the link he was looking for. The disk with the heart valve recipients' names on it had been headed 'SNOWBALL 2000'. He said, 'Could I ask you folks to show me the way to this field station?'

'It burned down,' said Patterson.

'The night before we got here,' added Karen. 'But there was no one inside at the time, although the company Land-Rover that Peter and Amy had used was still parked there.'

'But they had gone?' said Steven.

'Yes, but we're not sure how. The police checked the local taxi firms for us but with no joy.'

Steven felt a hollowness creep into his stomach. He didn't like what he was hearing, but he tried his best not to show it. 'I think I'd like to take a look at the place anyway,' he said.

'That's how we felt,' said Karen.

'Did the police have any idea what caused the fire?' Steven asked.

'They didn't say,' replied Patterson. 'But they obviously kept some pretty inflammable chemicals there. There was only a burned-out shell left.'

Steven's hollow feeling got worse. 'There's no point in us all going,' he said. 'Why don't we arrange to meet later—'

'Wait a minute,' interrupted Karen. 'You haven't told us what you know about this. Who are you exactly, and what's going on?'

'You're quite right and I'm sorry,' conceded Steven. 'If you'll just bear with me for the moment, I promise I'll tell you as much as I can later on.'

Reluctantly, Karen and Patterson agreed, but only after getting a firm undertaking from Steven that he would meet them again that evening. They then gave him directions to the field station.

Steven called Sci-Med as soon as he got to his car, and asked if there was any information available about Lehman Genomics yet.

'Reputable biotech company, American parent company, shares rose thirty per cent last year, several products licensed and doing well in the marketplace, strong research group believed to be working on transplant organs from animal sources, UK arm fronted by Paul Grossart, a former senior lecturer in biochemistry at the University of Leicester. Any use?'

'Transplant organs from animal sources,' repeated Steven slowly. 'Any more information on that?'

'There's a rumour going around that they pulled the plug on a major animal project recently.'

'I'll bet they did,' murmured Steven. 'It was called the Snowball project. Any more from Porton about Sister Mary's heart valve?'

'No. What more do you want? They say there was nothing wrong with it. It was in good working order and a perfect immunological match for her.'

'Ask them to carry out a DNA sequence on it,' said Steven. 'As fast as they possibly can.'

'What are they looking for?'

'Let them tell us that,' said Steven.

'Okay, you're calling the shots. Anything else?'

'Not right now.'

'Word is that Special Branch have located Mair Jones in Majorca. She should be back in the UK by this evening.'

TWENTY-ONE

Steven followed the directions he'd been given and three hours later he found himself high on a Welsh hillside, collar up, shoulders hunched against a bitter wind, looking at the charred remains of the field station. The bad feeling he'd been harbouring was made worse by the sight of the twisted metal frame of the Land-Rover. Unlike Karen Doig and Ian Patterson, who saw its presence as a puzzle, he feared it was stating the obvious: that Peter Doig and Amy Patterson had never left. They – or more correctly their bodies – were still here.

The police had found no human remains, but he suspected that that was exactly what they had been set up to find. Finding nothing suspicious, they would have no further interest in the building, which would be left as a ruin but still be owned by Lehman, who would leave it untouched in perpetuity. Steven examined the stone-flagged floor, which had largely been cleared of debris during the initial search, but ash and carbon dust had filled all the cracks so that it was impossible to tell if any of the flagstones had been disturbed before the fire. He looked around outside and found a metal bar he could use as a lever. He started in the centre of the first of the ground-floor rooms, but by the time he'd raised four of the heavy stones he'd decided that this was no job for one man on his own. He called in the local police for assistance.

Two hours went by before one of the officers doing the digging called out that he'd found something. He held up a human femur like a fish he'd just caught. The talking stopped and for a moment the only sound was that of the wind blowing through the ruins. 'There's more,' said the officer almost apologetically.

Steven took little pleasure in having his worst fears realised. As he'd suspected, the burned-out building had been obscuring the site of an earlier cremation.

'Almost the perfect murder,' said the inspector in charge of the operation, who was clearly embarrassed that the police had overlooked this possible reason why the Land-Rover was still there.

'No,' said Steven, without taking his eyes off the bones being removed gingerly from the trench and laid on a tarpaulin beside the rim. 'It was natural causes.'

'What? How can you possibly say that?'

'These are the remains of two scientists who were sent here to work. I think they fell ill with the same virus that's been affecting Manchester – don't ask me how. They were given expert nursing care, but they died. Their employers sought to cover up their deaths by cremating them and burying their remains beneath the floor, before setting fire to the building itself.'

'Bloody hell, you've got that all worked out,' said the inspector. 'Dare I ask what the reason was?'

'Tomorrow,' replied Steven sadly. 'Ask me that tomorrow.'

He drove back to Caernarfon with a heavy heart: he would have to break the news to Karen Doig and Ian Patterson. He had arranged to meet them at a hotel near the castle, but didn't want to tell them in a public place, so he called Charles Runcie at Caernarfon General and asked if he could provide more suitable surroundings.

'My office?' suggested Runcie.

'Perfect,' agreed Steven. 'I'd like you to be there too, if that's all right?'

'Whatever you think,' replied Runcie.

Telling the pair was as awful as Steven had imagined. The look that came into Karen's eyes when he told her that Peter was dead was something that would remain with him for a long time. After that she collapsed into tears and Runcie did his best to comfort her. Ian Patterson seemed to take the news about his wife more stoically. He sat very still in his chair, looking wordlessly at the floor, but then Steven saw tears start to fall, and he felt a lump come to his own throat.

Even in her pain, Karen was thinking. 'How can you be sure,' she asked, 'if there was only . . . bones and ash?'

'I know,' agreed Steven. 'It will take DNA profiling to be absolutely certain, but all the circumstances point to it being Peter and Amy.'

'I don't understand any of this. How could they possibly get the virus? And why would anyone want to keep it a secret and cover it up?'

'I think Lehman Genomics can tell us that,' replied Steven softly. 'In fact, I think they can tell us how everyone got the virus.'

'That bastard, Paul Grossart!' exploded Karen. 'He knew all along what had happened to them! And he let us go on thinking . . .'

'In the long run he'll answer for it,' said Steven. 'I promise.'

Karen and Ian were persuaded to stay overnight in Caernarfon and drive back to Scotland the following day. Their original instinct had been to leave for home immediately, but Runcie persuaded them that neither was in a fit state to undertake a long drive; they should wait until morning. Besides, the police would probably need a word with them before they left.

Steven had turned his phone off while he spoke to Karen and Ian. As soon as he switched it back on, Sci-Med rang to tell him that Mair Jones was due in on a flight from Palma to Manchester Airport at ten-thirty that evening. Did he want to speak to her? After the day he'd had, Steven thought that was probably the last thing he wanted to do. Her importance in the affair had diminished since the appearance of Karen Doig and Ian Patterson on the scene but, because so many people had gone to so much trouble, he said that he would be at the airport. He took the opportunity to check that Sci-Med had passed on his request about the heart valve to Porton.

'The analysis is already under way. They'd actually decided to do some sequencing on the valve before you asked so you'll get the result sooner than expected. They say they'll run a homology search on it as soon as they have enough sequence data to feed into the computer.'

'That's exactly what I was going to ask them to do,' said Steven.

The flight from Majorca was only a few minutes late. Mair Jones, a small woman with sharp eyes and jet-black dyed hair, was escorted to the interview room, while the police took care of retrieving her baggage.

'Well, I've certainly had my fifteen minutes of fame,' she said in a strong Welsh accent. 'Who are you when you're at home?'

Steven told her, and showed his ID. 'How are you feeling?' he asked.

'Pissed off,' she replied, missing the point of the question. 'Wouldn't you be if two British policemen turned up at your hotel in the early hours and suggested you accompany them home without giving any reason?'

'You've no idea what this is about?' asked Steven, disbelief showing in his voice.

'I suppose it's something to do with poor Maureen and the job we did?'

Steven nodded and said, 'Yesterday, we had no idea how Maureen Williams contracted the virus, but then I spoke to her husband and he told me about the nursing assignment and your involvement. Maureen was in no position to tell us what we needed to know. That left you.'

'Poor Mo,' said Mair. 'I suppose I panicked and ran off to the sunshine in case I was going to get it too.'

'You could have taken it with you,' Steven pointed out.

Mair Jones held up her hands and said, 'All right, I know, I know, but I just had to get away. What happens now?'

'I need to ask you some questions.'

'What do you want to know?'

'Who your patients were, what happened to them, and who paid you to look after them in the first place.'

'We were paid in cash up front,' said Mair, confirming what Williams had said. 'Our patients were a man and a woman in their early thirties, Peter and Amy – we weren't told their surnames, just that they had been diagnosed as having an extremely rare but very contagious viral infection. They were already pretty ill by the time we arrived at Capel Curig.'

'What happened to them?'

Mair sighed and looked down at her feet. 'They died,' she said softly. 'Mo and I did our best, but all to no avail, I'm afraid.'

'Then what?'

'What d'you mean?'

'What happened to them?'

'Their bodies, you mean?' exclaimed Mair, as if it were an improper question. 'I really don't know. Our job was over, so we were driven back to Bangor, and that was the end of it as far as we were concerned.'

Steven said, 'Peter's wife and Amy's husband turned up this morning, so I was able to piece together quite a lot of what has been going on. They'd come to Wales to look for them.'

'Oh my God,' said Mair. 'We had no idea. I suppose we assumed that they were married to each other. One of the Americans told us they were scientists who had infected themselves through their research work. We weren't allowed to ask questions.'

'Peter had a baby daughter,' said Steven.

'Poor love,' murmured Mair. 'We just never thought – not that there was much we could have done, mind you.' After a few moments of silent contemplation, she asked, 'Are you arresting me?'

Steven shook his head and said, 'No. Private nursing's not a crime, even though you and your friend may have been mixed up in something criminal.'

'Does that mean I can go?'

'Subject to surveillance by the Public Health people,' said Steven.

'I don't have to give the money back?'

'No, you earned it.'

Mair smiled ruefully. 'Considering what's happened to Mo,' she said, 'I think maybe I did.'

Steven decided to stay overnight in Manchester, because he suspected that he would be heading north in the morning to tackle Lehman Genomics and fit the last remaining piece into the puzzle. The Snowball project was the key to the whole outbreak, and the introduction of a new virus into the public domain had been part of it. There was just one more piece of information he needed before going to Lehman, and that was the report from Porton. He had a bet with himself that it was going to explain how so many human heart valves could have been contaminated with the same virus. He would hold off going north until he knew but, whatever the details, Lehman was going to be hounded out of business for what it had done, and Paul Grossart, as head of the company, was going to go to prison for a long time. With a bit of luck, the evidence would sustain a murder charge.

Steven was shaving when his mobile rang. His heart leaped: it might be the Porton result.

Instead, Charles Runcie asked, 'You haven't heard from Karen Doig at all, have you?'

'No. What's happened?'

'Ian Patterson has just phoned me. Apparently, she disappeared from their hotel some time during the night and she's taken his car.'

Steven closed his eyes and groaned, 'Hell's teeth, that's all we need.'

'I'm sorry?'

'It's my bet she's gone north,' said Steven. 'She wants to get to Paul Grossart before the police do.'

'Good God, I never thought of that.'

'No reason why you should, Doctor.'

'What will you do?'

'I'll catch a plane up there and hope I get to Grossart first. I don't suppose Patterson had any idea when she left?'

'Don't think so. He just said she wasn't there when he went down for breakfast and his car was gone.'

Steven called Sci-Med and told them what was going on.

'Do you want us to contact the Edinburgh police?'

'No,' said Steven after a moment's thought. He didn't want Grossart spooked by the police turning up on his doorstep. 'Is Macmillan there?'

Steven heard the duty man briefing Macmillan before he took up the phone.

'Nothing in from Porton yet?' asked Steven when Macmillan came on the line.

'Not yet. I gather you have a problem?'

Steven told him about Karen Doig's disappearance.

'You think this is significant?' asked Macmillan.

'She's an angry lady and she holds Grossart responsible for the death of her husband.'

'So she might be thinking of doing something silly?'

'Hard to say,' said Steven. 'The fact is that she came to Wales and did pretty well in finding the field station and establishing the connection with Maureen Williams. That alone says that she's a pretty determined and capable woman.'

'Damn, this could be messy,' said Macmillan. 'Are you sure you don't want us to warn the local police?'

'No. I'm going to try getting up there before her. I want to see Grossart and hear what he has to say before the police get to him.'

'You'll be lucky.'

'Why do you say that?' asked Steven.

'It's Christmas Eve.'

'Shit. I'd lost track. I'd better go. Could you e-mail me the file on Lehman and Paul Grossart? I'll download it en route.'

'Will do. Good luck.'

*　　*　　*

Steven had to use his ID and all the extra clout the Home Secretary had promised him in order to secure a seat on the plane up to Edinburgh. He was sipping orange juice when, twenty minutes into the journey, he was called to the flight deck. The captain handed him a handset and said, 'It's for you. A1 priority.'

'Dunbar,' said Steven.

'It's Clive Phelps here at Porton Down. We've done some DNA sequencing on the heart valve and it's really amazing. All the immunological tests suggested that it was human and a perfect match for the patient, but it turns out the damned tissue isn't human at all. The DNA says it came from a pig.'

'Thank you,' said Steven, silently congratulating himself on having won his bet. 'Thank you very much indeed.'

'Good news?' asked the captain.

'My cup overflows,' replied Steven with a smile. He returned to his seat, confident that the last piece of the puzzle was now in place. It was no secret that biotech companies had been experimenting with pigs with a view to using them for human transplant purposes. The big prize in this line of research was to breed a strain with a genetically altered immune system so that human beings would not reject the acquired organs. It looked as if Lehman had succeeded where others had failed. But at what a cost. Talk about the road to hell being paved with good intentions.

Steven thought he'd better check at the Lehman laboratories first. Although it was Christmas Eve there was a chance that a guilty conscience might be keeping Grossart at his desk, so he had a taxi take him to the Science Park on the south side of the city. There was only one car in the car park, a six-year-old Ford Escort with chequered tape on the back bumper, and it belonged to the security guard.

'There's nobody here, mate. It's Christmas Eve.'

'I thought Mr Grossart might be in,' said Steven.

'That bloke needs the rest more than anyone, if you ask me,' replied the guard. 'He's been looking like a basket case for weeks now.'

'Thanks,' said Steven. 'I'll try to catch him at home.'

Steven gave the taxi driver Grossart's home address and asked, 'Is it near here?'

'Ravelston Gardens? Other side of the bloody city,' grumbled the driver, who'd maintained a sullen silence since the airport.

'Then we'd best get moving,' said Steven.

As they turned into Ravelston Gardens some thirty minutes later, Steven saw a green Toyota Land Cruiser some thirty metres ahead and told the driver to stop. 'Okay, this'll do,' he said. 'How much?'

'Thirty quid on the meter,' replied the driver, turning to offer a smile that was meant to encourage the tip.

'Here's forty,' said Steven. 'Buy yourself a personality for Christmas.' He got out, leaving the driver unsure of whether to feel pleased or insulted.

There were probably thousands of green Land Cruisers in the country, and probably several in a well-heeled area like this, but something told Steven that this was Ian Patterson's and that Karen Doig had beaten him to it. When he got nearer and saw in the window the wildlife stickers he remembered from the car park at Caernarfon General, he was sure. This was a complication he could have done without.

From across the street he took a quick look at the house, hoping to glimpse someone through one of the front windows. He wanted to get a feel for what was going on, but one window was net-curtained and the other had a large Christmas tree in it. His main problem was that he wasn't sure about Karen Doig's mental state and why she had come to Grossart's house. If she was there to take an awful revenge, he didn't want to spook her into action by startling her.

He walked slowly past, noting that there was a garage entrance at one side, shielded from the house by a tall hedge. It should be possible to get round to the back without being seen, and he decided that that was probably the safest option. He checked that there was no one coming up behind him, then crossed the road and started walking back. Another quick glance over his shoulder and, with the coast still clear, he slipped into the garage entrance and up past the hedge, pausing for a moment before moving in a crouching run along the side of the house to the rear corner.

He lay down and snaked his way round the corner, fearing that there might be someone in the back garden, but there wasn't. In the back wall there was a window that he could easily pass under without showing himself, and then there was the back door, which he hoped would afford him access to the inside. He lay still for a few moments under the window, listening for sounds from within, but all was quiet, worryingly quiet: the sound of angry voices would have been reassuring.

The back door was a modern double-glazed one, so Steven would be able to see inside, but only at an angle unless he left the shelter of the wall and exposed himself to all the back windows. He watched, listened and waited for a full minute before deciding that the odds against someone standing silently where he couldn't see them were suitably remote. He reached up and applied gentle pressure to the door handle. To his relief, the door was unlocked and opened smoothly. He slipped inside and closed it behind him. At once he became aware of a strong smell of petrol.

The feeling that there was something dreadfully wrong pushed Steven's pulse rate higher as he moved towards the door to the hall. Grossart was a family man and this was Christmas Eve. The silence was all wrong . . . and that smell . . . A floorboard creaked as he stepped on it and he froze. He was about to continue when the silence was broken by Karen Doig's voice saying, 'So you've finally come round, have you?'

Steven thought for a moment that she was talking to him, but then realised that the sound had come from the front room to his left. He moved cautiously to the door. It was ajar, and he saw a man he presumed to be Paul Grossart lying on the floor in front of the Christmas tree. His hands were tied behind him and there was dried blood on his forehead. From what Karen had said, Steven deduced that Grossart was just regaining consciousness after a blow to his head. His clothes looked soaked, presumably with petrol from a red plastic container lying at his feet.

'I wanted you to be conscious,' continued Karen. 'I wanted you to understand why I'm doing this. Was my Peter conscious when you burned him?'

'No, no,' gasped Grossart. 'He died of the virus – they both did. You have my word. Everything possible was done for them, right to the end.'

'Your word!' sneered Karen. 'What do you imagine your word's worth, you bastard? You made me believe my husband had run off with another woman and all the time you knew . . . you knew, you little shit!'

'No, no, please no, you don't understand. It just all got out of hand . . . I never meant any of this to happen.'

'I'll bet you didn't, now that you're ten seconds away from hell.'

Steven heard the metallic rasp of a cigarette lighter being lit. He burst into the room, shouting, 'No, Karen! Don't do it!'

Karen was startled and dropped the lighter, but she picked it up again before Steven had a chance to get to her. 'Get back,' she warned.

'You're not thinking straight, Karen,' said Steven. 'You've lost Peter and you're sick with grief, but you've still got your daughter and she needs you. You mustn't do this. Let the law deal with him.'

'I want him to burn like he burned my Peter,' said Karen through gritted teeth. 'I want his children to be without their father on Christmas Day, just like Kelly will be.'

'It won't make you feel better,' said Steven. 'Revenge is never sweet. It'll taste like poison and you'll end up regretting it for the rest of your life.'

She looked at him for the first time and he saw doubt creep into her eyes.

'Give me the lighter,' he said softly.

'Get back,' she said again, with new determination.

'Look,' stammered Grossart from the floor. 'I never meant any of this to happen. God knows I didn't.'

Steven saw Karen's thumb move to the lighter wheel. 'At least hear him out, Karen,' he said. The thumb relaxed.

'We succeeded in breeding a strain of pigs with a genetically altered immune system which made them perfect donors for human transplants,' said Grossart.

'The Snowball project?' said Steven.

'Yes. All the lab tests suggested that we were on to a winner, so we took a shortcut through all the red tape. We reached an agreement with one of the co-ordinators at the transplant register.'

'You mean you bribed him to slip your heart valves through as matching human ones,' said Steven contemptuously.

'If you like,' said Grossart. 'Christ, we'd done every test we could think of on them. They seemed perfectly safe.'

'But they weren't,' said Steven.

'No,' agreed Grossart. 'One of our American virologists found a viral DNA sequence in the genome of our pigs and it was damn nearly identical to Ebola. It wasn't doing the pigs any harm, but there was a chance that it might suddenly become active inside a human being. We pulled the plug on the whole thing, but it was too late for the patients who'd already been given the valves.'

'And Peter and Amy?' asked Karen.

'They both worked on the project. A routine blood test showed that they were developing antibodies to the new virus, suggesting that they had been infected by it. We decided to send them away for a bit, to see if anything came of it – the trip to the field station in Wales. Unfortunately, they both went down with the virus. As soon as they reported feeling unwell, two of our American people, who had been standing by, went into action to make sure that they got proper nursing care and everything they needed . . . but they both died. I'm sorry.'

'Sorry!' exclaimed Karen. 'You didn't even let me say goodbye to him.'

Grossart shook his head. 'It would have been too dangerous,' he said. 'One of the nurses was infected, too.'

'And she's very ill,' said Steven.

Grossart shook his head again and said, 'When things started to go wrong it was as if the whole affair took on a life of its own. There seemed to be nothing we could do to make things better.'

Steven disagreed strongly but he bit his tongue in case he provoked Karen into throwing the lighter.

'I'm desperately sorry about Peter. He was a good bloke – everyone liked him,' continued Grossart.

The kind words seemed to bring Karen to an emotional threshold. Her anger evaporated in an instant, to be replaced by overwhelming sorrow and grief. She dropped the lighter, covered her face with her hands and started to sob. Steven took her in his arms. When she had recovered sufficiently, he said, 'Go on home, Karen. Kelly needs you. Start rebuilding your life.'

She nodded silently and left without looking again at Grossart.

Steven freed Grossart's hands but he continued to sit on the floor for a few moments, rubbing his wrists. 'You do believe me, don't you?' he said. 'There really was nothing we could do once the genie got out the bottle. We never meant to harm anyone – in fact, quite the reverse: we're in the business of saving lives, not taking them. It was just one of those . . . unfortunate things.'

Steven's eyes were dark with anger. 'No,' he said flatly. 'I don't believe you. There was a whole lot you could have done in order to save lives, but that would have meant being punished for your greed and dishonesty, so you kept quiet. Lots of people died need-lessly because we didn't know where the wildcards were coming from. You could have told us but you didn't.'

Grossart looked like a rabbit caught in headlights.

'You knew what was happening out there. You knew people were going to die, and you let it happen. That knowledge makes it malice aforethought. You and your greedy bastard colleagues are going to be charged with murder.'

'You don't understand,' said Grossart as he got to his feet.

'Clean yourself up while I call the police,' said Steven. 'Where are your wife and family?'

'They're at June's mother's. I had to tell her what had been going on.'

'And she didn't understand, either,' said Steven sourly. 'Get cleaned up.'

As Steven went over to the phone, Grossart got unsteadily to his feet. As he did, he lost his balance and fell backwards into the Christmas tree. He clutched at the branches but succeeded only in tearing at the wiring for the lights and pulling the tree over. Steven turned when he heard the crash and started towards Grossart to help him up. The cable Grossart was holding parted with the strain, and a spark from the shorting electrics caused the petrol vapour surrounding Grossart to explode into flame.

Steven staggered backwards and shielded his eyes as the wall of heat hit him. When he could bear to look again he found he was looking at Paul Grossart's funeral pyre. He called the Fire Brigade and tried dousing the flames as best he could with an extinguisher he found in the kitchen. He managed to localise the fire to the bay-window area, but then the extinguisher ran out and he changed to using basins of water from the kitchen after disconnecting the electricity.

Although Grossart's death was an accident, there would be awkward questions about how his clothes had come to be soaked in petrol, and the answers might well put Karen Doig in prison. Steven decided not to let that happen. Leaving the smouldering pyre to take its course for a moment, he went out to the garden shed and there found, as he hoped, several bits of garden machinery powered by petrol engines. He selected a heavy-duty chainsaw, brought it back into the house and laid it on the kitchen table, along with the red petrol can. He would leave the authorities to draw their own conclusions.

* * *

Steven called Macmillan to fill him in on what had happened.

'You did well,' said Macmillan gravely. 'Pity about Grossart – I'd have preferred crucifixion for him. But there will be the others.'

'Will there?' asked Steven. The question was loaded with silent reference to past cover-ups by politicians in the so-called public interest.

'I promise,' said Macmillan. 'There will be no backing-off. Sci-Med will go for broke over this. You have my word.'

'Even if Uncle Sam doesn't like it?'

'Even if,' Macmillan assured him.

'Good.'

'And Steven?'

'Yes?'

'Merry Christmas.'

As he rang off, Steven wondered where he was going to spend Christmas. He couldn't be with Jenny, because it would be another ten days or so before he could be absolutely sure he hadn't picked up the virus, so he might as well stay in Edinburgh.

Finding a place to stay on Christmas Eve was not easy. It took him an hour and a half before he found a hotel which agreed to give him a room on condition that he would not want dinner that night or the following one. Steven settled for a place to lay his head, and went out for some take-away food. He returned to his room with a bottle of gin and some tonic, just in case the hotel bar had been taken over by a private party. He also picked up a handful of daily newspapers in the lobby to catch up on what had been happening in the world.

On page two of *The Times*, an article headed 'Disgraced MP Puts Record Straight' reported that William Victor Spicer, currently awaiting trial for the manslaughter of a man who had been black-mailing him, had admitted that he had deliberately misrepresented the contribution made by Dr Caroline Anderson, the Public Health chief at the time, to the handling of the Manchester outbreak. He now recognised that Dr Anderson's management of the crisis had been beyond reproach and that she had, in fact, sacrificed her own life in fighting the infection on behalf of the inhabitants of the city. He wished to apologise to her friends and family for the distress he had caused.

Steven smiled for the first time in many days. He rested his head on the back of the chair and looked up at the featureless ceiling. 'Bless you, Caroline,' he murmured. 'Merry Christmas, love.'

POSTSCRIPT

Downing Street, London

'The US ambassador, sir.'

'Thank you, Ellen. Come in, Charles. A happy New Year to you.'

'And to you, Prime Minister,' replied Charles Greely, the tall, distinguished-looking ambassador to the Court of St James. His immaculate light-grey suit highlighted smooth, tanned features.

'You went home for Christmas?' asked the PM.

'I did, sir. The call of California in late December was just too strong to ignore.'

'I understand you wish to discuss the requests we made to your government over the Lehman affair,' said the PM, waving Greely to a chair.

The American sat down, his body language betraying a certain unease. 'Yes indeed, Prime Minister,' he began. He paused to clear his throat unnecessarily. 'I spoke at length over the holidays to the President and his advisers, and believe me, sir, I left them in no doubt as to the strength of the British government's feelings over this matter.'

'And?'

'Well, sir, the President fully realises just how serious this outbreak was, and in no way wishes to diminish what happened, but he wonders, sir . . . if you might see your way to viewing it more as a private-sector matter, where a few greedy individuals were responsible for the mayhem that ensued. It is of course perfectly reasonable that you would wish to see those individuals punished – and punished severely – but as for US citizens standing trial here in the UK for . . . manslaughter, I think was the charge you had in mind?'

The PM nodded.

'The President wondered, sir, if you might reconsider in view of the negative publicity involved to both our governments?'

The PM looked long and hard at Greely before asking, 'And our other requests?'

Greely looked uncomfortable again. 'Well, sir,' he said hesitantly, 'the President would wish to point out that withdrawal of all FDA licences from Lehman in the US would destroy the company. He perfectly understands that revocation of their British licences is well within your rights, and the winding-up of their UK operation is only to be expected, but he respectfully requests that you reconsider your position over Lehman in the US.'

'You mean there's big money involved?'

'With respect, sir, I don't think it's just a question of money. There are other factors.'

'What other factors?' asked the PM coldly.

'Lehman is one of the biggest biotech organisations in the US and therefore the world, sir. We are talking of several thousand jobs across the globe disappearing if Lehman International goes down. The research potential of such an organisation, considering the millions of dollars of venture capital tied up in its future, is probably inestimable. It would be a severe blow to medical science in general, sir, if its labs were to close.'

The PM looked at Greely in silence for a moment digesting what he had heard, then leaned forward in his seat and said, 'Mr Ambassador, this company has treated my country – as several pharmaceutical companies have been known to treat Third World countries – as a laboratory for its experiments. It used citizens of the United Kingdom as experimental animals to further its own greedy ends.'

Greely swallowed but did not respond.

'I understand that there is a saying among scientists that if something can be done it will be done, whatever legislation may say to the contrary. Well, I accept that, but I want the message to go out loud and clear that, if you do do it, this is what will happen to you.'

Greely nodded.

'Please convey my thoughts to the President and give him my regards. Tell him I want all Lehman's licences revoked; I want what assets they have left used as compensation for the families who suffered, and I want Vance and Klein to stand trial here in England. Do I make myself perfectly clear?'

Greely swallowed again before saying, 'Indeed, sir.' He got to his feet slowly. 'Sir, in view of the difference of opinion between our two governments over this matter, which I am sure we can work through, given time and the special harmony we've always enjoyed, is there any possible area of compromise I might be able to highlight to the President?'

'None,' snapped the PM.

Greely was taken aback. This was not the language of diplomacy. 'Such a firm stance, sir, does beg the question—'

'You're wondering about the "or else" clause,' said the PM. 'You may tell the President that this matter is of paramount importance to Her Majesty's government. In fact, it's at least as important as the proposed US global missile defence system is to him.'

Greely seemed to stop breathing for a moment, then he gave a slight nod of understanding and withdrew.

Six hours later the PM smiled at an incoming message. He phoned John Macmillan at Sci-Med. 'They've agreed,' he said. 'I'm tearing up your resignation.'